The Newcomer

As Peter Blessing took his leave, Winifred raised her dance card and fanned herself, but stopped suddenly when she realized it was not at all appropriate to fan oneself after the departure of a fabulously handsome man. She flipped her dance card open to see what he had written, then gasped. He had claimed her as partner for the last cotillion before supper, which meant she would have to eat with him as well!

Winifred cursed him for a rake as she watched him move gracefully through the crowd, bending over young ladies' hands and complimenting them. There was no need for this, of course, since every young woman seemed to melt whenever he cast those glorious eyes of his upon her. She was grateful that she was not the only one who had made a complete cake of herself.

Blessing
in
Disguise

Jenna Mindel

A SIGNET BOOK

SIGNET
Published by New American Library, a division of
Penguin Putnam Inc., 375 Hudson Street,
New York, New York 10014, U.S.A.
Penguin Books Ltd, 27 Wrights Lane,
London W8 5TZ, England
Penguin Books Australia Ltd, Ringwood,
Victoria, Australia
Penguin Books Canada Ltd, 10 Alcorn Avenue,
Toronto, Ontario, Canada M4V 3B2
Penguin Books (N.Z.) Ltd, 182–190 Wairau Road,
Auckland 10, New Zealand

Penguin Books Ltd, Registered Offices:
Harmondsworth, Middlesex, England

First published by Signet, an imprint of New American Library,
a division of Penguin Putnam Inc.

First Printing, July 2001
10 9 8 7 6 5 4 3 2 1

 REGISTERED TRADEMARK—MARCA REGISTRADA

Printed in the United States of America

PUBLISHER'S NOTE
This is a work of fiction. Names, characters, places, and incidents either are
the product of the author's imagination or are used fictitiously, and any
resemblance to actual persons, living or dead, business establishments, events,
or locales is entirely coincidental.

To my favorite person, my husband, Steve—
Thank you for the gift of unfettered time!
Let's hang this higher than my fish.

Prologue

February 1813

"John, I am in a bit of a pickle." Peter Blessing forced his hands to remain casually at his sides. When his elder brother by seven years looked up at him, he hurried to add, "As always, I shall repay you, with interest."

"How much this time?" John frowned with disapproval.

Peter swallowed. He ran a finger inside his cravat to loosen it. He knew John had the blunt, plenty of it. What he asked for was merely a loan.

"Peter, how much?"

Words gathered in Peter's throat and stuck there. He dreaded to see disappointment lurking in his brother's eyes again. The slump of his broad shoulders told Peter that he, too, wearied of this all too often request.

Peter sighed as he scanned the interior of John's study in the family estate at Surrey. It reminded him of mellow autumn warmth with the gleam of cherry-paneled walls and rust brocade drapes. The room bespoke of everything John was and Peter was not—steadfast, reliable, and made for work. There was nothing Peter could do but be the scapegrace he had always been. He met his brother's gaze squarely and answered, "Ten thousand."

Silence.

Peter shifted from one foot to the other. He would not sit down until there was some sort agreement between them.

John sat behind his huge mahogany desk shaking his head. "Where did I go wrong?" he asked in a voice barely above a whisper.

"Beg your pardon?"

"Did I fail you in some way?"

Peter thought he could feel no worse than he did now. He had expected his brother to shout at him, curse him for losing so much. Never did he expect John to blame himself.

"What are you talking about? I lost. I thought I had won, and yet with one trick, I lost. My odds run superior most of the time. But, I have to take the bad with the good. Next time I shall end with eight thousand ahead. That is the way of it." Peter cursed himself silently for rambling, but he still could not believe he had actually lost so much.

"No. There cannot be a next time, not for me, at least. You seem to be losing more oft than not this past year and still you play too deep." John rose from behind the desk and walked over to stand in front of him.

"I've had a bad streak is all. My game will turn, it always does."

"But what if it does not? You cannot keep coming to me for such sums."

"I see," Peter said, taking a step back.

"I do not think you do. What is wrong with you? Are you so keen on self-destruction? Never before have you played for such high stakes." John's voice rose.

"I know what I am doing. I have a head for this, you know that." Peter looked down and ran his finger along the corner of the desk. Even with a stack of papers and John's writing quills strewn about, the top of the desk shone like a still lake. He looked up into his brother's eyes. "Well, what is it going to be?"

John stood directly in front of him and placed his hand on Peter's shoulder. "I will not give you the money. It is time the dissipation stopped. I can no longer be a part of it. I care about you too much."

Peter shrank away from John's touch. His anger rose like smoke from a cheroot. "I am not you. I can never be like you. This is what I do and if you've no stomach for it, then I'll go elsewhere!" Peter saw the hurt flash in his brother's eyes before he turned away.

"Look, John." He reached out his hand in amends. "I

am not the settling-down type. I ain't good at it. Numbers and playing the odds, that is what I do best, and the only way for me to make a decent living is by gambling."

"You have never given yourself a chance to do otherwise, how can you be so certain?"

Peter shrugged his shoulders. He did not like speaking of such things. To be like his brother was only grasping at a dream. The kind of dream that haunted him in the wee hours after a night spent carousing. It was easier to gamble for his living. Besides, he could think of no good reason to try and change his ways. None at all.

"There is a lot more to you, little brother, than a devil-may-care smile and a fancy turn of the card. I just hope it will not take too long for you to finally figure that out for yourself."

"I am what I am, John," Peter said as he turned to leave. "There's no use in changing now."

His brother's frown deepened and Peter did not waste time saying good-bye. He walked stiffly out of his brother's study, pulling at his cravat. Lord, the bloody thing would smother him.

Striding through the hall, Peter looked around at the home where he had been raised. Their father would have been so proud of John, had he lived to see how well the baronetcy prospered.

What would his father think of him, Peter Blessing—rake and gambler? Peter chuckled bitterly under his breath. He had turned out exactly as his father had predicted.

He could almost hear his father's voice softening after he had scolded him for landing in a coil. *"Peter, you'll be a good for nothing if you don't watch out, son. You have a stubborn streak and a mind for mischief."* Peter had proved his papa right far too often. But it was much easier to fall into scrape after scrape than try to be a good boy like his brother and end up failing anyway. He had failed enough to finally quit trying.

Grabbing his hat and gloves and coat from John's butler, Peter stumbled down the stairs into the weak sunshine of early February. He adjusted his beaver to the roguish angle he preferred and looked over the large circular drive where he had left his horse tethered. Where was he going to get ten thousand pounds?

He had some funds stockpiled, but not nearly enough. There was the small estate he had inherited from his mother's side. It could easily fetch upwards of twenty thousand pounds. No! It made him sick inside whenever he contemplated selling it. That place was all wrapped up in silly dreams he dared not contemplate in the light of day. Plus, he could not help but think it would betray the memory of his mother to sell Trenton Manor. There had to be another way.

Peter let his eyes narrow to a squint as he focused on the bare fountain. He muttered softly and kicked at a pebble in the path. This time he had to take drastic measures. The last thing he wanted, he knew he now must pursue. He had to find himself a rich virgin and find a way to marry her.

Chapter One

"John, come on man, stop dawdling." Peter Blessing gave his brother a nudge. Carriages lined the drive of the Sefton estate in a string of stamping horses and impatient coachmen. He was glad that he'd been able to talk his brother into walking the few blocks from John's London townhouse.

"Are you sure about this?"

"It is what has to be done." Peter swallowed his irritation. If his brother had coughed up the blunt, he would not need to go to a society function to hunt for a rich wife.

"Yes, but under these circumstances, do not expect me to be happy about it." His brother straightened his dark gray waistcoat with a snap.

"What else do you suggest that I do? It shan't be that bad. This sort of thing is done all the time, don't ya know," Peter said.

They paused at the front steps of the huge home belonging to the Countess of Sefton. Candlelight twinkled from the windows of rooms already filled with guests and strains of laughter floated in the air. John looked hesitant and Peter guessed that one of two things bothered his brother.

The first could be that John did not agree with his decision to marry for money. Perhaps he felt a tad guilty for securing an invitation for his little rake of a brother. The second might be that John was just plain nervous. It had been eight years since John had attended a society gathering. Eight years ago Anne, his wife, had died.

Regardless of the reason, Peter wished to lighten his brother's dark mood. "Cheer up, old man. Perhaps you will find yourself a lady too." He slapped John on the back, but his brother did not look pleased with his show of bravado. Peter wished he could quell his own anxiety. He had come this far, there could be no backing out nor room for failure.

The two men soon stood in the anteroom and handed their hats and gloves to a servant. As they approached the landing of the main stairs that overlooked the ballroom, Peter tugged at his cravat. While he waited patiently for the butler to announce them, he scanned the large ballroom filled with glimmering beeswax candles and crystal chandeliers. Virginal white gowns were positively everywhere. " 'Tis an ocean of modesty, eh?" he whispered toward John.

That earned him a slight smile.

Peter tugged at the starched linen about his throat again. He suddenly felt like he would smother. "There's not enough bloody air in this place."

"We can always leave," John said.

"No." Peter continued to look about. He experienced the odd sensation of being watched. He supposed it was natural for those present to stare at him. This was, no doubt, the last place anyone of his acquaintance would expect to find him. As his gaze took in the pristinely dressed ladies and dark-jacketed gentlemen, he saw her.

A young woman stood taller than most of the men near her. She leaned next to the refreshment table with a cup held dangerously crooked. She was by no means a beauty but the sheer awkwardness of her stance and the steadiness of her stare made him smile and wink at her in return.

He wished he was close enough to see just how dark was the blush that must be covering her cheeks. She nearly dropped her cup, then she turned to set it down. He let his gaze linger over her form. She was slender and wore the kind of plain dress that most women he knew would run away from screaming. But the simplicity of the pearl-white silk gave this statuesque young woman an air of almost goddess-like elegance. The clinging material afforded him a lovely eyeful as it molded to her shapely backside when she bent down.

Peter heard his name announced and looked away. As he expected, his and his brother's presence created a small stir. Although John was more mature in years than most, he was still highly regarded as a prime catch on the marriage mart. Many had given up hope of ever seeing him return to such come-outs. His attendance at the Season's opening ball was big news indeed.

Peter knew that every eligible young miss of means had been invited. He had gotten this information from his mistress, who was a regular mingler in society's nonsense. She had promised to meet him here and guide him through introductions to the *right* ladies. He doubted it would pose too much of a problem since very few people knew of their relationship.

Then again, he would no doubt be considered undesirable in the extreme, with neither money nor a title. He supposed his reputation as something of a hand at cards would not help his chances either. He had only his good looks and impeccable family name to recommend him. They had reached the bottom of the stairs when his mistress, a vision in deep cranberry, approached them.

"Peter, you truly were serious! I cannot believe you are here." Lady Dunstan strolled up next to him with a swish of her skirts.

"Hello, Liz. You look ravishing." Peter placed a kiss upon her outstretched hand. He turned to his brother and said, "You remember Lady Dunstan."

"Yes, of course." John bowed.

"He came in order to get me in," Peter explained.

"I could have done that for you, Pet."

Peter flashed her a look of warning. He figured that John already knew of his involvement with the beautiful Elizabeth Dunstan, but he did not want her flaunting their relationship in his face.

With a pretty pout on her full red lips, she asked, "Do you want to meet all the maids awaiting a match?"

" 'Course I do."

She brushed a speck of dust off of his sleeve. Peter

noticed that this gesture of familiarity caused·his brother discomfort.

"If you will both excuse me, I see an old friend," John announced. "Lady Dunstan, Peter." He bowed and left.

Seemingly unfazed by John's obvious disapproval of her, Liz wrapped her hand around the inside of Peter's elbow and asked, "Are you ready?"

"As ready as I shall ever be."

"Then let us go and meet your future bride."

Peter could not quite hide his distaste for the word *bride* and he grimaced.

" 'Tis not the end of the world, Peter. People do this sort of thing every day. Your life need not change overmuch."

Peter's own words were spoken back to him, to his utter annoyance. And therein lay his fear. Although many people married, very few kept their lives the same as before. His life was about to be irrevocably changed, and not necessarily for the better. Somewhere deep inside, he fervently hoped for the better.

He let out the breath he had been holding and nodded to his mistress. He knew he must sacrifice his freedom in order to settle his vowels. His creditor had been more than generous to agree to accept payment by the end of the Season. He had less than three months to woo and win a rich lady to wed. The interest he paid was high, so the sooner he got the thing done, the better. Peter Blessing was a gentleman, after all, and one who always made good on his debts.

Winifred Augusta Preston fingered a leaf of the potted palm and wished for the hundredth time that she was anywhere else but London during the Season. She looked at her sister, Melanie, who stood with a small court of swains about her, each vying for her attention. Winifred did not understand why her sister could not have chosen someone to wed in Bath last spring. If she had, then it would have saved Winifred all sorts of headaches!

Reluctantly, she berated herself for her meanness. Melanie was picky and, worse yet, she longed for a love match.

She said that she had never felt drawn to the men in Bath. At least that is how she had explained it to Winifred on the million-mile journey to this godforsaken city.

Their father had been no help at all. He had taken it into his head that Melanie's failure in Bath was somehow Winifred's fault for not accompanying her sister. And so here she was a year later, dragged to London to play companion. Winifred often wondered if this trip was more likely punishment for her behavior last autumn.

"Well, Miss Winifred, why are you hiding behind a fern?"

She jumped with a startled gasp. One of the dragon aunts she had been named after came up behind her. "Aunt Augusta!" She breathed in deeply. "I did not hear you."

"Of course not, I was quiet. You did not answer my question. You are supposed to be helping Melanie."

"It appears to me that she does not need any help."

"Well then go and stand beside her. Perhaps you may meet a nice boy. Your papa brought you both to London, you may as well get some use of the Season." Her aunt drew up her formidable bosom and let it sag when she let out a large breath. She was nearing fifty, but she had not a strand of gray in her dark auburn hair.

"Oh no, not me. Only Melanie wants to find a husband. I want nothing to do with one of those. I am merely present for moral support since Melanie does not know anyone in town."

Aunt Augusta eyed her suspiciously. "What of her friends from the seminary for young ladies? Surely some of them have come to town for the Season."

"Probably already married and enjoying the miseries of their state," Winifred answered.

"Come now, Winnie, you cannot truly believe marriage to be such a horrible thing. Look at your parents, they were a love match."

"True, but you and Aunt Winifred never wanted my mama to marry Father. Besides, neither of you have married, and not from lacking in offers from what I have been told." Winifred leaned close to her aunt. "So tell me, Aunt, what is the real reason you never married?"

"You are a saucy young lady and that is none of your business."

"As it is *my* business to remain completely unattached. I want to travel, and husbands and babies only get in the way." She suddenly noticed Melanie looking at her with frightened eyes. A young man leaned too close for her sister's comfort. "Excuse me. Now 'tis time for me to come away from the plant."

Winifred walked with purpose in her step across the marble floor. It was so far a terribly dull party given by a friend of the two dragons. The least she could do was protect her sister, who was too kind-hearted to say *boo* to any man who made her uneasy. It was still early. She supposed that something could yet happen to liven up the evening.

She edged her way through the young men surrounding her sister. Some were fresh-faced puppies just down from university while others were older, more jaded-looking men of town. She found them all disgusting.

"Excuse me," Winifred said as she elbowed the blond man with hair too short away from crowding her sister. "Mel, would you like to take a turn with me to fetch some lemonade?"

"Yes, thank you." Melanie's cheeks were flushed a soft shade of pink and her blue eyes sparkled with agitation. She had never looked better.

"So, who was that man nearly drooling on you?" Winifred asked as they stepped away.

"Mr. Frederick Roth, I think," Melanie whispered. "He is a silly fortune hunter to be sure. Not a feather to fly with."

"How do you know?"

"It is the way they go about everything, so desperate and clinging." Melanie pushed back a stray golden curl from her forehead. "Where have you been all evening? I finally spotted you with Aunt Augusta."

"Oh, I have been here and there."

"You are bored to tears, Winnie, admit it."

"I do admit it, willingly."

"If you would just stay by me, I could introduce you to some young men."

"And be even more thoroughly bored?" Winifred asked.

"But you might meet someone you liked, someone Papa would approve of."

She snickered with contempt in response. She knew she was nothing fair to look upon. Melanie had thick gold hair and was beautiful and just the right height. Winifred was too tall, too thin, with too many freckles and blond hair that was more red with a tendency to frizz too much.

She could not put herself through such torture as to meet a man only to see his interest turn toward her older sister. Worse yet, she could hardly trust any of these society gentlemen's motives for paying her attention. London was merely a larger place of users and despoilers.

When they finally reached the refreshment table, Winifred raised her glass in mock salute to all the young puppies watching her sister with soulful eyes. They were a bunch of dripping wet clodpoles to her. She doubted very highly that she would ever find someone she liked. Or, more the point, someone who genuinely cared for her in return.

She looked around the room and stopped in mid-sip of her lemonade when she saw two late arrivals standing at the top of the stairs.

"Lord John Blessing and Mr. Peter Blessing," the aged butler announced in a loud if rather thin voice.

The names blurred through her ears as a hush settled upon the guests. Never had she seen a more handsome man. Unable to help herself, she stared openly at him. His golden hair lay in waves about his perfectly chiseled face. His looks were classic and devastating. Suddenly, he caught her staring and, with a devilishly crooked grin, winked at her.

Her stomach did a strange dance and she worried that

the slightly tepid lemonade she was drinking threatened to come back up. She set her cup down with a bobble, then bent over to pick up her napkin.

"Winifred?" Melanie asked.

"What?"

"What were you staring at and why are you so red in the face?"

She straightened and flipped her napkin onto the refreshment table. "Those two men who just arrived. The whole room seemed to quiet, did you not notice?" She refused to give the reason for her sudden blush.

"No. Where are they now?"

Winifred searched the crowd, but they must have moved away from the stairs. Then she spotted the golden Adonis standing close to a beautiful woman. She was the type of creature he belonged with since she was every bit as stunning as he. Where he was golden and sunshine, she had dark tresses with lips as red as roses and creamy white skin. "He is over there with the dark-haired lady in the deep red gown." Winifred pointed discreetly. "Do you see, by the middle column?"

"My, they are a handsome couple. But I thought you said you saw two men," Melanie said.

"The older gentleman must have gone somewhere."

"They seem very much in love, do you not think?" Melanie asked.

"Who?"

"The couple." Melanie shook her head in admonishment.

Winifred watched as the woman with the Adonis pulled his arm possessively, and wondered if love had anything to do with the pair. Was he her husband? The hostess looked surprised to see him, so he could not be. Relief filled her and she cursed herself as a fool to even think a man such as he would take notice of her.

But then, he already had.

She flushed when she remembered how he had winked at her.

She continued to spy as the dazzling couple made a round of what looked like introductions. Could they be intended? They did seem to be on intimate terms. They lingered with each person until finally the dark beauty pulled the Adonis toward Aunt Augusta. Her aunt's eyebrows nearly disappeared under her turban, so high did she raise them. She obviously did not approve of the pair, and Winifred wondered why.

"Winnie." Melanie pulled at her elbow. "Come, let us meet the handsome couple talking to Aunt."

Winifred hesitated. She was not certain her admiring gaze could be controlled. She would feel like an absolute idiot should he detect her ogling him again.

"Winnie, come on," Melanie urged.

"What is your hurry?"

"I simply want to meet them and find out where to purchase such a striking gown. Do quit stalling."

Winifred followed her sister, hating the idea of being introduced standing next to Melanie. Her sister's loveliness was bound to capture the Adonis's attention. She might as well fade into the background this minute. She chided herself for even thinking that she wanted to capture his attention. The idea was ridiculous, she cared not a whit what he thought of her.

Melanie rushed her along until they were finally standing before the small group consisting of their aunt, the couple, and a matron who was also bringing out a relative. Her sister coughed demurely hoping to get an introduction. Aunt Augusta's annoyed gaze scorched Winifred as if she should know better than approach them.

Winifred rolled her eyes.

"Ah, Lady Dunstan, I do not believe you have met my nieces," Aunt Augusta began.

"Why no, I have not." The dark beauty smiled with a most practiced expression.

"Lady Dunstan, may I present to you the Misses Melanie and Winifred Preston," their aunt said.

Winifred bowed slightly.

"How do you do." Melanie reached out to offer her hand.

The dark beauty hesitated before she shook Melanie's fingers. "And this, Misses Melanie and Winifred Preston,

is my dear friend, Mr. Peter Blessing." The timbre of
Lady Dunstan's voice deepened slightly when she said
the word *dear*. A strong unbidden dislike for the woman
rose in Winifred's throat, making it hard to swallow.

There was something wrong here. Aunt Augusta
clearly looked unhappy that this man was being introduced to them. But she could not openly cut him since
he was welcomed by the hostess. Aunt Augusta looked
even more flustered when the matron cornered her for
a conversation. Her aunt tried in vain to keep her attention on Melanie and Mr. Blessing.

"How do you do, ladies." Mr. Blessing bowed deeply.

He looked Melanie over from head to toe with such a
quick assessing manner, Winifred almost thought she had
mistaken it. For herself, she received the briefest of nods.

"Miss Melanie, I do hope I may beg a dance."

"I am sorry, Mr. Blessing, but my card is already full.
Another time perhaps?"

"I shall be honored." He turned toward her. "And
you, Miss Winifred, your card must also be full."

She felt a tightening in her midsection. His eyes were
the softest brown with tiny flecks of gold in them. They
had a melting quality and Winifred thought she would
end up as a puddle at his feet.

Her brain told her to fib and tell him she did not
dance, but her mouth somehow managed to deliver, "Oh
no, of course, my card is quite empty."

What a disastrous response! How could she inform him
that her card was pathetically untouched. It did not matter that when men looked about to approach her, she
had turned her back on them and examined the plants.
She thought she saw the corners of his mouth twitch.

"Please make me the luckiest of men and let me be
your first," Mr. Blessing murmured.

His gaze seemed to caress her as he spoke and she
suddenly felt overly warm. When she did not hand him
her card, since she could barely move from the sound of
his seductive voice, he bent forward to retrieve the card
that dangled at her wrist.

His fingertips brushed her bare arm just above the

inside of her elbow. She froze as he deliberately let his fingers slide slowly down the soft part of her arm to her wrist. She thought at any moment her knees would buckle and she would fall to the floor in a heap. But she stood as stone, daring not to breathe as he raised her hand by the string of her dance card.

Mr. Blessing did not bother to unwind it from her flesh. He quickly scribbled his name in two places. Then, of all the guineas in London, he placed a lingering kiss upon her knuckles.

"Time will be an eternity until then," he whispered.

Winifred closed her mouth. It had fallen open when he had kissed her hand. Quickly, she looked around her to see if anyone had noticed their exchange. No one appeared to have taken note except for Lady Dunstan, and she did not look pleased.

Winifred stole a glance at Mr. Blessing, who again winked at her.

Dear Heaven! Winifred knew then that he was up to no good. As he and Lady Dunstan took their leave, Winifred raised her dance card and fanned herself. She stopped suddenly and realized it was not at all appropriate to fan oneself after the departure of a fabulously handsome man. She flipped her card open and gasped. Of course, he had claimed her as partner for the last cotillion before supper. Which meant she would have to eat with him as well!

She cursed him for a rake as she watched him move gracefully through the crowd, bending over young ladies' hands and obviously gushing his compliments to them. There was no need for him to do so, as every young woman seemed to melt whenever he cast those glorious eyes of his upon them. She was grateful that she was not the only one who had made a complete cake of herself.

Yes, Mr. Peter Blessing was definitely a rake. She hoped, for her own sake, that he did not care much for cake!

Chapter Two

"Peter, what do you think you are doing?" Lady Dunstan hissed.

"What do you mean?" He leisurely poured himself a cup of lemonade and took a slow sip. The stuff was weak.

"That, whatever you call the nonsense you performed for the Preston girl."

"I was just having a bit of fun."

"Why not simply announce to the entire *ton*, that you are looking for a rich wife."

"I don't know how to do this sort of thing." Peter shrugged his shoulders.

"That much is obvious."

He watched his mistress look around the room.

"Do you want my help or not?" she asked quietly.

" 'Course I do."

"Meet everyone first before you single one out like that. Your chances are far better with less money, I think. Even though 'tis said the Preston fortune came from dealings in trade. Besides, she is not even pretty."

Peter did not bother to answer but continued to sip his watery lemonade thoughtfully. It was true, Winifred Preston was not pretty by society's standards, but she had a freshness that appealed to him. She looked like she belonged out of doors with blue skies and puffy white clouds. He forced such fanciful thoughts away and wondered what had come over him to tease her so.

Perhaps it was her immediate reaction to him that had goaded him on. He knew when a woman wanted him, he had seen it enough times to know. He guessed that Miss Winifred Preston hardly knew what to do with her attraction for him. She looked as innocent as the sunrise. She was no doxy, nor was she Liz. He could not snap his fingers and expect satisfaction. No, she was a gently bred young miss, and a rich one at that. To pay court to such an innocent, he would have to play his cards right and play them carefully.

The Misses Preston were the richest maids on the market and he wanted one of them, either one would do. It would probably be wiser to woo the elder and prettier Miss Preston. She seemed docile and would likely be an easy maid to pay one's addresses to.

He wondered if he should keep Miss Winifred as a trump card, to be played only if needed. For some reason, Peter expected that playing with Winifred Preston would prove far too entertaining. He dared not risk an emotional entanglement, not now, when his debt and word as a gentleman was at stake. He needed to keep a cool head and proceed with utmost caution. Success was the only outcome he would accept.

Lady Dunstan nudged his arm and he dutifully followed her as she introduced him to more maids than he would remember in the morning. He scratched his name in as many dance cards as were left open to him under the watchful eyes of mamas and sponsors.

He made a mental note of each young lady, pairing the color of their hair or dress with the dance he had reserved. It was not very different from memorizing the last cards played at the table.

He was feeling very confident indeed when the dancing started and he whisked the first young miss onto the ballroom floor. Applying himself at his most charming, Peter left a none-too-steady young lady with stars in her eyes to her mother's care.

On and on he went, dancing with one marriageable maid after another. He returned each of them with all the bowing and scraping required of a young gallant. He played his role well but could not have been more thoroughly bored. Any one of the misses he had danced with was valuable enough in dowry to correct his current situation of pockets to let, but none seemed to strike his interest like the Preston heiresses had. He would discuss each lady with Lady Dunstan later, then focus his attentions accordingly. He could not afford to waste time with a chit if he had no chance of garnering acceptance of an offer of marriage.

Peter stood alone for a moment when his attention was caught by the opening of the door to the room designated for cards. Smoke seeped from a poorly lit oil lamp. He could see it on the stand just beyond the tables. The smoke beckoned him with teasingly long wisps, like fingers. How perfect it would be to pay off his current debt with new winnings. But he owed too much and could not risk losing more. It was tempting to forgo this farce of bride searching and enter the predictable world of cards. His fingers positively itched to embrace a deck of cards. It took all of his willpower to keep from dismissing the rest of the evening's plans and entering that room.

The musical strains of a country dance started and he remembered that he had promised this dance to Miss Winifred. He pulled on his cravat and scanned the room. He found her standing against the wall conversing with her sister. A branch of candles shone from behind her, casting an ethereal glow about her head which made her reddish-gold hair appear as if she had a halo. Not at all a good sign, he thought.

A smart-looking gentleman approached Miss Preston and the two joined the couples already gathered in the set. Winifred checked her dance card, then looked around with an irritated air. He caught her gaze when he finally approached her.

"You, sir, are late," Winifred stated. "The dance is already in progress."

She was a study of indignation. All she needed was a balance of scales or some such nonsense and she would represent justice, or rather the lack of it.

"I humbly beg your pardon." Peter bowed, but not before capturing her hand in the process to place a kiss upon her knuckles. As he straightened, he wrapped Miss Winifred's hand around the inside crook of his elbow. "Perhaps we can stroll about the room."

She did not look pleased with him. He knew it was the fact that he had not removed his hand from covering hers as it rested upon his arm. "Too crowded?" Peter asked innocently. "Ah, then I suggest we take our turn on the balcony. It should prove to be a much more intimate setting."

"Precisely why we shan't head that way, Mr. Blessing." She gave his fingers a severe pinch, which forced him to pull his hand from hers.

It was all he could do to keep from laughing aloud at her tactics. She obviously had summed him up. "Nicely done, Miss Winifred. I give you the advantage of that round."

"Are we playing a game, Mr. Blessing?" She cast large eyes of the brightest blue at him with a most provoking expression of sarcasm. "If so, please deal me out. I should not like to play. I have had my fill of games."

"Ah, but do not be such a poor sport. The fun of any game is all in how it is played."

"But what are the rules? One must know the rules beforehand, in order to decide whether it is worth playing, whether it is worth the risk."

Oh, she was a clever one. She wanted to know what he was up to. Well, he would give her tit for tat. He leaned close to her then, so close that the curls of her hair tickled his cheek. "Rules, my wise Athena, are meant to be broken," he whispered next to her ear. He was rewarded when she shivered slightly. He had hit his mark as he knew he would.

Winifred forced herself to remain calm, but her insides refused to obey and her stomach continued to flip about. Mr. Blessing was the kind of man that every young girl's governess warned her to keep away from. And he was dangerous in the extreme for arousing wanton physical reactions that if indulged could lead to trouble. By all that was holy, he had singled her out, and there could only be one reason for it.

They walked in silence around a group of maids huddled together and Winifred could not help but feel a sense of satisfaction at having the most handsome man in the room on her arm. The thrill of his attentions was enough to make her knees buckle, but it was a pale feeling of victory. She had to be realistic. She knew what he wanted. The only interest he could possibly have in her was her money.

Knowing that, she figured she should try to handle him as best she could without acting like the complete fool she'd been when they first met. If she let her attraction for him get the best of her, 'twould spell her disaster.

But, she was not some silly moon-faced gel like the ones he had danced with earlier in the evening. She had brains. Brains enough to know better than to *play* anything with Mr. Blessing. She was made of sterner stuff than most young ladies and she would not be taken in with sweet words and whispers. She had, after all, painfully learned that lesson not too long ago.

"Mr. Blessing," she began as they rounded the corner of the room, "there are always consequences to the breaking of rules."

"Exactly so," he said with a mischievous smile. They passed an acquaintance of his and he nodded toward them.

Taken aback, she turned to look him straight in the eye, which was easy for her as she stood as tall as he. "I disagree with your response of pleasure for the consequences. Ladies rarely fair well in such situations."

"Such a bold reaction, my fair Athena. Have you experience with such 'situations'?"

Yes, she did in fact have experience with such a situation. Fortunately, she had escaped with her virtue in tact, if not her heart. If only he knew the pain and humiliation ladies suffered, but she was in no mood to enlighten him. "Now you are the one speaking out of turn, sir," Winifred said. "Whether I have or not is most definitely none of your business."

"Touché, my dear."

Winifred ignored Mr. Blessing's boyishly crooked grin that displayed a dazzling set of white teeth. "I see the dance has ended. I must get back to my sister, and you sir, I am sure, must not keep your next partner waiting."

They continued their promenade in silence and Winifred soon found herself next to Melanie. Mr. Blessing paused to briefly take her hand and kiss the air as was proper. She hoped that she had effectively put him in his place.

"Until our next dance then, Miss Winifred," Mr. Blessing said. He bowed briefly toward Melanie and said, "Miss Preston, your servant." Then he took his leave.

"My goodness," Melanie sighed. "He is too handsome by half."

"Yes," Winifred whispered. Her hand tingled even though, this time, his lips had not touched her skin.

"He certainly favors you, my dear," Melanie stated with a smile.

"Mel, you did not have any dances left, remember? And there I was with my card entirely empty. What else could he have done?"

Winifred walked away from her sister feeling raw and hating herself for experiencing such envy. It was not Melanie's fault that she was the pretty one. Nor was it Melanie's fault when boys passed Winifred over to flirt with her. Melanie had never encouraged them. If anything, she was quite the best of sisters. No doubt had Mr. Blessing been able to reserve a dance with Melanie, she would have been the one he chose to annoy with his forward attentions.

Winifred stood alone as she watched her sister dance another set. Melanie did not look like she enjoyed the attention she received. Actually, she looked tired.

"Winifred!" Aunt Augusta came up behind her.

Again she jumped. "Are you ever going to approach me in a way so as not to startle me?"

"Sorry, my dear, but I haven't the time for correct approaches when I turn to see you in the clutches of that man!" Aunt Augusta tried to catch her breath and her bosom heaved.

"What man is that, pray tell?"

"Oh, do not play coy with me, miss. You know very well that Peter Blessing is a no-good wastrel who spends more time on his arse with cards in his hands than using the noodle God gave him."

"The noodle?"

"His brains, child, brains. The man has them, I have heard said, but does not exercise them nearly enough."

"So as a stupid man, you feel he is beneath me?"

"Heaven's no, 'tis not his lack of intelligence that worries me. 'Tis his lack of morals that makes him unfit for your company, my dear."

Winifred was not surprised to hear her aunt's concern. Had he not spoken to her in a most inappropriate manner? But surely her aunt overreacted. Mr. Blessing was a gentleman, after all, and he appeared to know many who attended this evening's ball. "What has he done, aunt, that is so immoral?"

"For starters, 'tis well known that he makes his living from gambling. And Lady Dunstan and he—well just you never mind," her aunt said in a huff. "I tell you, he is immoral."

Winifred found little satisfaction in the confirmation that Lady Dunstan was his mistress. The gall of the man, to be introduced to young maids on the arm of his own mistress! And just what would make him seek such introductions?

"Aunt, why do you think he is here? Everyone seemed surprised to see him."

"Of course they are, he never goes near decent functions. My guess is that he is on the lookout for a plump young miss. And I am not speaking of her figure."

Money! Winifred had guessed correctly regarding his motives. The cur was only seeking a rich wife. No doubt to line his reserves for card playing. Or perhaps he was looking to retire from his jaded way of life?

Well, he would come up empty-handed where the Prestons were concerned. Winifred had a sinking feeling that with this man, Melanie was no match. He was neither clinging nor desperate, as Mel had described typical fortune hunters, and she feared that Melanie could be easily charmed by him.

But not Winifred Augusta Preston! She was determined to give Mr. Blessing a solid distaste for her. And, she would do a fine job of keeping him away from her sister too. She would watch him like a hawk, if she had to, and make him regret their meeting. Winifred rubbed her hands together with glee. She figured that her chance had come to exact a little repayment for the ill-treatment she had received from the male population in the past. Yes, and a man such as Mr. Blessing, she decided, was the perfect type to pay dearly.

Melanie made her way through a throng of young ladies to the room set aside for their comfort and privacy. She had a small tear in the hem of her gown and she feared that if she did not correct it, she would tread upon it and trip. She sat down with a weary sigh and looked for thread and a needle. It was only the beginning of the Season and already she was tired of it. Why could she not simply meet the man of her dreams and be done with it?

She longed to be married with a house of her own to run and children to care for. It was a simple wish, a dream that she had cherished since she was a small child. She was not adventurous like Winifred, who often acted more the tomboy than could possibly be good for her.

Melanie was glad that she had talked their father into forcing Winifred to come to London. She was convinced that Winifred needed to find a love match. She needed confidence and she needed healing from the heartbreak of last autumn. Not all men were cads, as Winifred professed, even though many of the boys at home had grown up Winifred's friends. But the good ones tended to treat her simply as one of them. They could not see that Winifred was turning into an appealingly elegant woman. The ones that had noticed Winifred's late blooming were not worth their salt. And one in particular had already proved that quite nastily.

Melanie wondered if perhaps this Peter Blessing could be the kind of man Winifred needed. He certainly acted like he was interested in her sister. It was obvious that Winifred found him appealing. He was an extremely handsome man, and perhaps if Winifred could capture such a man's attention, then she would no longer think of herself as unattractive.

Melanie tied a knot and bit off the thread. There, that should hold until she could have it properly fixed by her abigail. She left the room with her head down concentrating on her repaired hem, and she bumped into a gentleman. Her head connected with a solid bit of chest encased in a somber black waistcoat.

"Oh my." Melanie backed up hurriedly. "I beg your pardon, sir."

"No apology needed. I was in rather a hurry to leave and was not watching where I was going."

"Leave? But the party has just begun." Melanie looked into a pair of velvety brown eyes steeped with such pain that her heart went out to him. Impulsively she reached out and touched his sleeve. "Is there something amiss? You appear troubled."

The expression changed to a guarded veil of indignation. He was a perfect stranger and she had overstepped the bounds of politeness with her inquiry. "I humbly beg your pardon a second time," she murmured. "I did not mean to pry."

He looked at her and smiled slightly, but the shadow of grief remained. "No. Again, the fault is mine. I am definitely out of sorts, and my presence here can only be burdensome."

"Sometimes it helps to talk about it." He was obviously hurting and she could not in good conscience not try to be of help.

He hesitated, as if considering her invitation, and Melanie noticed how fine-looking he was. A bit slight of build, but judging from the hardness of his chest when she ran into it, he was not at all weak. His hair was a dark blond that was liberally streaked with gray near his temples. It gave him a distinguished air.

"I am sure you have a point, miss, but I cannot bore you and keep you away from the dancing."

"I am considered an excellent listener, sir. If I may tell you the truth, I have already become bored with the dancing. I would be most grateful for a quiet break from it."

"I see," he said.

"And so we can both benefit."

"Yes, I suppose we can."

He looked unsure of himself, so Melanie boldly took him by the hand. "Here, come with me and we can have a comfortable coze." His hand felt warm and strong. Melanie wondered what in Heaven's name she was doing, leading a man she had never met to a bench on the opened terrace. But he followed her quietly and she knew she was doing the right thing. The poor man needed help.

When they were seated, he pulled his hand from hers and started, "I do not usually allow young ladies to lead me out onto balconies." His cheeks were slightly flushed.

Goodness, he was embarrassed, Melanie thought. "Nor do I make a habit of leading gentlemen out onto them," she stammered. "I am not ever so bold, but you look like you have lost your last friend and I cannot ignore someone in need."

She was a fetching little lady and he knew he was crazy to be sitting here with her. She was so young and sweet. She kept dropping her lashes shyly, not at all aware of how alluring it was. He looked around quickly and felt comfortable that they were not secluded. They could easily converse privately, but there were many couples and groups lingering about the terrace. There was nothing improper about the spot where she had placed them.

She waited expectantly, and John wondered if he should not make up some other reason for his doldrums. But he felt an incredible need to talk about it, finally. After years of bottled-up grief, this golden slip of a girl had tugged on the cork.

"I have not attended a society function in years, eight years in fact," he found himself saying. He looked at her and she waited patiently, her hands held comfortably in her lap. She nodded encouragingly. "Since my wife died."

"I am so very sorry." She reached out and grabbed hold of his hand again.

"And so I have stayed away from anything that would remind me of her."

"And tonight, you are reminded of your dear wife?"

"Yes, and it nearly got the better of me," John said. He did not realize that he was stroking the young lady's hand with his thumb. "Like a coward, I tried to run away. But I suppose it is past time for me to face her memory."

"I am sure that she would want you to move on past your grief."

"Yes, she would. She was a delightfully giving creature." John smiled. It felt good to discuss his wife. He had never felt comfortable speaking about her to Peter. He could not bear to rouse his younger brother's guilt.

When Anne had died from a fever, Peter was twenty. For some insane reason, Peter blamed himself for calling Anne out into the rain. She had had the beginnings of an infection which rapidly progressed to a raging fever. Whenever John had brought up the subject of his wife, Peter would not speak of it. So, he had stopped. The rain had nothing to do with his wife's infection, the doctor had said, but Peter would not be convinced.

"How did you meet?" she asked.

"At a ball similar to this one," John answered. "She was the Season's reigning toast and I could not believe that she had set her cap for me. I am a very dull fellow, you see."

"She sounds like she was a very smart lady, indeed."

He smiled at the compliment and the golden girl next to him blushed. She was a shy bird and so very different from the lively chatterbox that was his Anne. "Well, my dear, I cannot in good conscience keep you any longer from your dance partners."

When she suddenly became alarmed and put a delicate hand to her opened mouth, he knew that she had just remembered a partner that she must be promised to. "There, see, I have made you miss a dance," John said.

"Oh, my, I forgot about Mr. Roth." She breathed deeply, then added, "I will have to apologize, but in truth, I am grateful to have missed him."

She looked so remorseful at her admission, that he

chuckled. "I must take my leave, but I thank you for your kindness."

She jumped up from the bench as he rose, before he could even extend his hand to give her aid. "You are most welcome, and I do wish that you would reconsider leaving. Perhaps it is time for you to enjoy yourself," she said, then looked apologetic. "Forgive me, I have no right to tell you what to do."

He lifted her chin, which had dropped low, with his fingertip. "Do not worry. I am sure you quite have the right of it. But I have some business to attend to at my club."

"Of course," she said.

"Thank you, Miss—I cannot believe I have been so remiss in not introducing myself. I am Lord John Blessing, and you, my dear?"

"Miss Melanie Preston." She bowed, then added, "Blessing? Are you Mr. Peter Blessing's brother, my lord?"

He experienced an odd disappointment at the excitement shining from her eyes. So, she had met Peter. Somehow he found himself dissatisfied with the possibility that his brother might try to woo Miss Melanie Preston. "Yes."

"How wonderful." She smiled.

"Yes." He looked at his boots a moment, then added, "Miss Preston, I must bid you good evening and I thank you for listening."

"Has it helped to talk about it, my lord?"

He gazed down at her upturned face and her blue eyes that were changing to a decidedly green color, and agreed, it had helped immensely. "Yes, thank you."

"You are most welcome, Lord Blessing."

Chapter Three

Winifred sat next to the rest of the wallflowers and their companions while they watched the dancers. She could not describe how she felt. Her gaze followed Peter Blessing as he turned one maid after another out onto the ballroom floor. He was so full of his own consequence that she often snorted with contempt for him, which gained her a look of censure from the elder ladies around her.

But deep inside, she could not keep the excitement from creeping along her spine as each dance ended and she knew the supper dance drew ever nearer. And try as she might, she could not douse the thrill of anticipation she experienced waiting for Mr. Blessing to lead her onto the floor. Finally, the object of her thoughts appeared in the flesh and Peter Blessing bowed before her.

"Our dance, I believe, Miss Winifred."

She took his hand as he led her forward to join the set forming for a cotillion.

"Did you miss me?" he whispered close to her ear.

"No, sir, I did not." Winifred curtsied, then turned to do likewise to the gentleman at her right. The music started and the dance began.

"Well, I missed you," Peter said as they passed one another.

"Sshhh. Do not be absurd," she hissed. They turned and faced each other.

"And what have you been doing, my proud Athena, while we were apart?"

He knew what she had been doing. Did he not seek her out among the flowers lounging along the sides of the room? She, like all the other young ladies with no dance partners, merely watched. Winifred had had a delightful conversation with Lady Drohmes, an infamous bluestocking whose wits, some said, wandered. But on the whole, Winifred had watched and wished that she was one of the pretty young ladies twirling upon the arms of a genuinely gallant young man.

She looked at Mr. Blessing. "I watched you dance with every eligible maid on the market." She remembered her plan and added, "But, I stand corrected, you danced with only those dripping large dowries."

She smiled with satisfaction when she saw that her intended barb hit home. His surprise at her sarcasm was quickly covered, and he smiled in return.

"My dear Miss Winifred, do you make a habit of knowing folks only by their financial situation?"

"Of course not." She felt her defenses rise.

"There are many ladies of means present and I assure you that is not my consideration for seeking them out. Why some of the richest women sat near to you and did you see me dancing my attendance upon them?"

He was a shameless liar! "Then you must also consider their beauty, for every maid you chose was beyond fair."

"Exactly so," he said. "And it is the reason I chose you for the supper dance. You are by far the fairest of them all."

Winifred snorted. "Now that is a Banbury tale if ever I have heard one. You tell a pretty lie, Mr. Blessing, pretty indeed."

The music changed, and they broke away from each other to turn and weave with the dancers in their set. She would not let him get the better of her. She peeked a glance at him, but he caught her and winked. Warmth flooded her cheeks, to her utter shame. She had to do something to disturb his calm charm. There must be a way to chase him off.

The dance came to an end, and supper was announced. Mr. Blessing held out his arm for Winifred but she hesitated slightly.

"I won't bite," he said.

"This time, perhaps, but eventually all dogs do."

He chuckled, then leaned close to her. "Trust me,

Athena, when I do bare my teeth and take a bite, you will enjoy it," he murmured.

She sucked in her breath. His meaning was clear and it took very little imagination for her to visualize him acting upon his promise. Suddenly, she felt his finger tracing a path along her neck, just under her ear, all the way to her shoulder.

"And this," he said, "would be the first place I should like to nibble."

A shiver passed through her. She looked up into his eyes and stared at him. He stared back at her and she could have sworn that something in his eyes softened. It took but a moment to realize they had stopped walking.

Clearing his throat, he said, "We had best find the supper room, Athena, you look hungry."

Whatever magic spell he had cast, his teasing broke it completely and she was more than relieved. "Yes, I am hungry, Mr. Blessing. You had best take care to keep your hands to yourself else when I bare my teeth, I am liable to bite them off."

"Touché, my dove. Nicely said."

They walked down the hall to the room reserved for supper. Tables laden with tempting treats were scattered everywhere. She looked up to read the time and the clock chimed midnight. The bewitching hour, she thought. She hoped she could quickly give Mr. Blessing such a complete dislike of her that he would go away and throw his charm at someone else.

They managed to weave through the standing crowd and he left her near an opened window while he went to the nearest food table. She turned to look out over the gardens which gleamed under the full moon's light. The cool breeze caused her bare arms to turn to gooseflesh, but she did not care. It felt good. Unfortunately, she always managed to become overheated in Mr. Blessing's presence.

When he returned, he carried two plates filled with turkey, ham, fruit, and bread. She had to admit, she was indeed hungry.

"Oh great goddess," he said with mock fear, "I have

brought you offerings of worship. Please do not scorch me dead with your flashing blue eyes."

She laughed at him then.

"Are you cold?" He reached across to close the window.

"Yes, but the fresh air feels good," Winifred said as she held out her hand to stop him. She took a piece of ham with buttered bread and swallowed the thing in no time. "Tell me, Mr. Blessing, do you live in London year-round?"

"I do."

"Do you never long for the clean air of the country?"

"Seldom, very seldom. But every year I join my friend Lord Sheldrake at his estate in Gloucestershire during the summer," he answered.

"I see." She took a piece of turkey from the plate. "The Cotswolds are quite lovely."

"They are. And you, Miss Winifred, you seem very fond of country life."

"I am. I love it, actually, and have little desire to live elsewhere. After I have traveled my fill, of course." Winifred reached for the last piece of food on the plate. She noticed Mr. Blessing's surprise at her healthy appetite, and an idea formed.

"Mr. Blessing, I wonder, would you mind returning for more refreshments?"

"Would you like punch?" he asked.

Winifred smiled. "I would like more of everything, if you please." She almost burst out laughing at his incredulous expression. She hoped he would feel more than embarrassed, returning to the tables. She watched him go, feeling quite proud of herself, for the truth of the matter was that she truly wanted more to eat.

When Mr. Blessing returned, she felt like the joke had been turned back at her. He had a plate stacked at least six inches high with meat and cheese and bread. She looked around to see if anyone noticed the ridiculous amount of food he had on the plate. Of course, they had.

In fact, Miss Whent, one of the silly chits Mr. Blessing had danced with earlier, leaned over and whispered into her supper partner's ear. The two looked at her and tittered and laughed. She glanced at Mr. Blessing, who merely smiled at her and offered the overly loaded plate.

"Your sacrifices, my goddess," he said.

"Thank you, but, I am afraid that you have forgotten the punch," Winifred said, her mind working furiously.

Mr. Blessing bowed slightly before turning, the plate still in his hands.

Winifred acted without thinking. It was almost as if she were a child again, being dared by the boys at home. She slipped out her foot, as quick as you please, as Mr. Blessing stepped away. He tottered slightly and lost his grip upon the plate, which flew forward to crash upon the floor. Mr. Blessing remained upright. He managed to give her a furiously angry look, before pulling his charming self back together.

Servants rushed to his aid, people stared, and Winifred thought she had won. But Mr. Blessing proceeded to bow with a flourish and announce to all that for his next performance he would make the mess disappear. Which it did, when the footman promptly took the damaged plate of food away. Winifred could not help but giggle, as Mr. Blessing continued to bow. His audience actually clapped their approval and even asked for an encore.

"Oh, well done," Winifred said grudgingly when he returned his attention to her.

"No thanks to you, you minx." The expression in his eyes was no longer angry, but amused. "Come, I believe you owe me, Miss Winifred."

"Owe you, sir?"

"You have played foul, and by any game's rules, you shall have to pay a penalty."

"Mr. Blessing, I do not think . . ."

"You surely did *not* think, my dear," he interrupted. "I shall exact a fair punishment because of it. The only honorable thing for you to do is oblige me."

Winifred swallowed her nervousness and asked as calmly as she could, "And what shall this penalty be?"

"I am thinking, Athena, I am thinking. But one thing

is for certain, there will be no more refreshments for you
this evening."

He took her arm to escort her out of the supper room.
What had she done? Such a childish thing to do, and
now, she needs must pay for her prank. "Mr. Blessing,
where are we going?"

"I shall require you to walk with me, Athena, in the
moonlight, around the fountain at the very least."

"But Mr. Blessing, surely that cannot be proper." But
in truth, what was not proper was the feel of his arm
cradled against her own. The havoc his nearness wreaked
on her senses was positively indecent.

"Nonsense, there are many couples strolling about, so
there can be no harm. See there, the terrace doors have
been opened and many are already outside."

She scanned the crowded hall. He was correct in that
many couples had strolled through the opened doors to
the gardens. "Very well. Is that the penalty then?" She
could survive a mere walk with him.

"Only the first part, I am afraid."

Her eyes widened. "And the second part?"

"You must go riding with me."

"Riding?" She did not like the idea of spending any
more time in his company. But the temptation to ride
was overwhelming.

"You do ride, Miss Winifred? You are, after all, a
lover of the country," he said.

"Yes, of course." She felt her defenses weaken.
"When do you wish to ride, Mr. Blessing?" she asked
with a defeated sigh. Better to get the penalty done and
paid in full.

"A time and place of my choosing."

His smile was crooked and boyish and her insides
turned to butter. What was she doing? Did she possibly
think she was any match for the man who stood before
her? His practiced charm and seductive smiles were far
beyond her realm of retaliation. She thought herself thoroughly sunk.

"Very well, Mr. Blessing," she agreed. "I suppose I

do owe you that much, but do make it soon so that I may have my penalty paid."

Mr. Blessing ordered a servant to fetch her wrap.

"There," he said as he arranged the shawl around her shoulders. "That should keep you warm. If not, I am only too happy to place my arms about you."

"You are quite the forward man, Mr. Blessing," Winifred scolded. "I promise you will regret it very much, should you decide to act in an inappropriate manner."

"I shall behave."

"Promise me." She looked him directly in the eyes, which were a marvelous shade of brown. "Your word as a gentleman."

"You do not play fair, Athena."

" 'Tis not me, Mr. Blessing, but you who does not play fair. I shall have your word, sir, else I shall not walk with you, penalty or no." Winifred did not know whom she mistrusted more, Mr. Blessing or herself.

He bowed. "You have my word."

They exited through the terrace doors into the moonlight. Torches along the path burned brightly in the cool April night air. Couples strolled about, never veering far from the main path.

"Are you enjoying your visit to London?" he asked.

"*Enjoy* is too strong a word for me, I am merely tolerating my stay here." She clasped her hands firmly in front of her, hoping he would get her silent message that she did not wish to take his arm.

"Do you not like London?" he asked.

"No, I do not believe I do. It is a dirty city, Mr. Blessing, filled with shallow people who care little for humankind other than what can be gained from them." She looked pointedly at him.

"So cynical, Athena. Surely you did not come to this conclusion since you arrived here."

"No, Mr. Blessing. I speak from experience."

"Not very pretty words from such lovely lips. I must inform you that there are good people to be found, even in London. Take my brother John, for example, there is not a shallow or deceitful bone in his body."

"I notice that you did not include yourself as one of the *good people*."

"Of course not. I am, as you have so astutely recognized, a scoundrel."

She laughed and reluctantly accepted that her low opinion of Mr. Blessing had suffered a positive turn. At least he did not pretend to be all chivalrous honor as David Stanton had. "Yes, which is exactly why I shall not pursue our acquaintance any further after we have taken the ride I owe you."

"You mortally wound me, Athena." Mr. Blessing dramatically threw one hand across his chest and the other across his brow. Then he suddenly looked at her with very serious eyes. "What can I do to change your mind?"

"Nothing, Mr. Blessing. Not a single thing." A sense of regret filled her as she thought how enjoyable Mr. Blessing's company could be.

They walked in silence until they came to the fountain in the center of the gardens. Couples sat on benches placed around the deep and large structure as its water sprayed and bubbled. She dipped her fingers into the darkened pool, mesmerized by the ripples she made with her hand. She leaned against the stone base fully aware that Mr. Blessing stood beside her, watching her silently. She wondered what he was thinking. No doubt he wished she were prettier. Too bad her fortune was the only thing that held his attraction. Peter Blessing was decidedly different from any other gentleman she had ever met.

"Is the water cold?" Mr. Blessing asked quietly.

"Yes."

"Here, give me your hand."

Against her better judgment, she did as he asked.

His gaze found hers. "Your fingers are ice."

Slowly he rubbed her cold wet hand between his own. She stood as still as she could, trying to gain control of her breathing. He kneaded her palm gently and fire raced from her skin where he touched it to her heart. It was maddening, this physical response he stirred in her. Why could she not be a proper lady and feel nothing? Her head grew light and she grasped the edge of the fountain with her other hand to steady herself. With every ounce of willpower she could muster, she finally pulled away from him.

"Thank you, sir. I believe my fingers have quite thawed."

"My pleasure," he murmured, and stepped closer.

Winifred instinctively stepped back, but the fountain was in her way. "Shall we return to the ballroom, Mr. Blessing? I do not wish to make you late for your next dance partner." Winifred's voice sounded loud and shrill to her ears. But she did not like the look Mr. Blessing gave her. His eyes had darkened and he wore that lopsided, boyish grin that made her mind weak.

"I have no other partners, Miss Winifred. I saved you for last." He stepped closer to her, so close that she could detect the clean scent of his cologne. "The best for last."

He was shameful! Her heart beat wildly, and her insides had completely lost control and she trembled. Winifred breathed deeply, rallying all her strength to break out of the spell Mr. Blessing was casting. Then she heard a voice from behind them. A familiar voice that sounded distressed. Melanie!

She turned quickly and spotted her sister, trying to persuade a large gentleman to turn left, back toward the party. He tried to coax her to turn right and walk further into the garden. Winifred grabbed Mr. Blessing's hand and pulled him along. "Come, my sister needs our help."

Mr. Blessing followed.

"Please, my lord, we must return to the ballroom. My aunts wish to leave and I believe my sister is not out here," Melanie said.

"I tell you, I saw her. I think we should check the bushes to be sure." The large man pointed toward a row of trees.

"And what would Winnie possibly be doing in the bushes? I say, she is not here, now let us please go back." Melanie's voice was tense.

"Is there a problem, Miss Preston?" Mr. Blessing asked when they were upon them.

"Winifred!" Melanie exclaimed. "Where have you been? Aunt Augusta and Aunt Winifred wish to leave."

Guilt seared Winifred's midsection. She had left Melanie without her support. Her sister had been forced to seek her out with a man who obviously made her nervous. "I'm sorry, Mel. It was so lovely outside and . . ." She stopped speaking when she heard Mr. Blessing's tone. She turned to look at him as he stood toe to toe with the much larger gentleman.

"You can return now, Palmer. I am more than able to escort the ladies to their aunts. You need not trouble them again," Mr. Blessing said.

She had never expected him to possess such steel in his voice. She watched in awe as the larger man actually retreated a few steps.

"No trouble, meant no harm. Ladies, Peter, your servant." The big man bowed, then left.

"Thank you, Mr. Blessing," Melanie said. "I have been trying to break free from his escort since supper."

"I suggest you have nothing more to do with Lord Palmer, Miss Preston. He is not a good sort." Mr. Blessing offered his arm to Melanie.

Winifred bit back the hot retort she had ready to sling at him. What made him think he was any better? An unwanted stab of jealousy pricked her as Melanie took Mr. Blessing's offered arm.

"Thank you again, Mr. Blessing. I shall heed your suggestion in future." Her sister looked every inch the lady rescued from distress.

"What's so bad about him? I heard he is rich as Croesus." Winifred blurted and jerked her thumb in the direction that Lord Palmer had retreated.

Mr. Blessing turned to her, as did Melanie. "There are some things a man does not discuss with a lady, Miss Winifred. Please take my words of advice on faith that they are true. He is not kind to the weaker sex."

Melanie turned a little pale, and Winifred felt like an idiot. Mr. Blessing offered her his other arm, and Winifred took it grudgingly. When they entered the ballroom, Mr. Blessing proceeded to return them to their aunts, who looked none too pleased. Aunt Winifred thanked him, however, and he bowed graciously.

"Ladies, until we meet again," Mr. Blessing said.

"Yes, until then, Mr. Blessing," Melanie said eagerly. Winifred only nodded before he left.

"Well, where have you been?" Aunt Winifred asked. A much thinner woman than Aunt Augusta, she dressed in the height of fashion and carried herself with quiet dignity. Appearances meant everything to her. "It is not the thing to be missing from your first real introduction to society."

"We were in the—" Winifred started to explain, but Melanie interrupted.

" 'Tis a large ball, Aunt. We were just coming back from supper."

Winifred looked at her sister. Why did she not tell them that they were in the garden?

"Very well, girls, let us leave so you can be rested for your callers tomorrow."

Callers! Winifred sighed. No doubt, Mr. Blessing would be one of them and she would have to endure his presence again.

Peter sat comfortably in an overstuffed chair near the fire and swished the brandy in his glass. Liz sat across from him on her sofa and studied the list of eligible maids they had written down earlier in the day. Her dark hair, loosed from its style, hung softly. The silk dressing gown she wore slipped to reveal a bare shoulder. Peter was sorry to have to end their arrangement, but he could not very well keep a mistress when he was looking for a wife.

"What about Miss Drusilla Whent? She has plenty of money and seemed quite taken with you," Liz said.

"Yes, I shall call on her tomorrow. She's sort of a dull-witted girl, though."

"What matters is her dowry, Peter."

"What about the Turlington chit?" he asked. "She is a pretty thing."

"You would be barking up the wrong tree. Her father is a stickler and is hoping for a title."

"Well, then, that leaves the Misses Preston and Miss Whent," he said.

"There are a couple more ladies with modest dowries you may try. I am not sure about the Prestons, dear. You cannot court two sisters at once."

"I want a large dowry, Liz, more than just the ten thousand I owe. Miss Whent and the Misses Preston have more than enough, so I shall consider them my best prospects. As far as courting both sisters, I think I shall concentrate on Miss Winifred for now. If she proves too much to handle, I shall turn my attentions to her sister." He hoped he did not regret such a decision. He assured himself that he based his plan solely on the fact that Miss Winifred was strongly affected by him, physically. He would not admit to himself that he in turn felt an attraction for her.

"Why her? You haven't the time for dilly-dallying. Your payment is due in June, dear, and that is positively around the corner. Miss Winifred indeed looks like she may give you trouble. Only see what she did to you tonight at supper."

"You saw her trip me?"

"Yes. Luckily for her, I was apparently the only one. She is too much of a hoyden, I think. She is bound to mar her reputation with antics such as this evening's prank."

"All the more reason for me to pursue her. That way I shall have a clearer field."

"I do not think she has any admirers at all," she said.

"Not now, perhaps; they are all enamored by that diamond of the first water, Miss Melanie. But Winifred is a gemstone, sure to capture notice in time."

"Like she has captured your notice?" she asked.

Peter did not mistake the edge in her voice. When he did not answer, Liz went back to the list, scratching notes beside each name.

He considered her words. Winifred had in fact captured his notice, with more than just her fortune. First, he was aware of her obvious attraction to him. Second, he noticed her quick wit and sharp tongue, and now— he did not know what to think now. He had been more than shocked to find Winifred in his thoughts when he made love to Liz. He could not stop himself from picturing a slender goddess with reddish-gold hair lying entwined with him instead of the voluptuous form he had always preferred.

"Peter, are you listening to me?"

"Sorry. What did you say?"

"I have four ladies marked whom I think you may safely pursue with the best chance of acceptance. The Misses Preston, your choice not mine, Miss Whent, and a Miss Ann Collington, whom you have not met since she has not been formally presented at court. She's the daughter of an earl and likely out of your reach anyway."

"Fine, Liz, fine. I need to thank you for your help with all of this. John is too touchy about it, plus he don't know the society folk like you do. But, he's promised to help me get invitations where he can." Peter took a deep breath and let it out. "Which leads me to the subject of our relationship."

"I know, Peter. I know that you would like it to end. I knew it tonight." She looked at him with lonely eyes. "We have had some fine times, you and I."

"We have. But it's not as though we can't remain friends. We will see each other at parties and the like. I just can't be looking for a wife and . . ."

"I know." She held up her hand to silence his next words. "Believe it or not, you are an honorable fellow. Most men would not care. Dunstan certainly does not. He parades his light-skirts before my very eyes."

"Dunstan is a fool!" Peter said. That the man could ignore his beautiful wife and leave her to find what love she could with a rake like himself was despicable. It was not her fault she could not bear the lobcock an heir. "I'm sorry, Liz."

"No more so than I. But cheer up, you will catch yourself a rich bride and all your troubles will be over." She smiled at him, but warmth did not reach her eyes.

All his troubles were just beginning, he thought later after leaving Liz's townhouse on Curzon Street. He could not help but be disappointed in himself. He had hurt Liz, which he never wanted to do. And worse, he was planning his marriage attack on unsuspecting females for their dowries like any captain would spawn a military campaign. He only hoped he would not be one of the casualties. There was nothing to do but save his own skin and reputation. He had to carry out his mission.

He knew Winifred Preston was the best chance he had of getting a rich bride, and his chances with her were slim at best. And she already had a strong notion of what he was after. He supposed that her recognition of his character was better in the long run. She was not so terribly naive. Would she be satisfied with a marriage of convenience? Was it possible that they could find some sort of happiness together? Not if she knew exactly why he needed her hand in marriage. What woman would be happy knowing that she had been purchased, so to speak, for ten thousand dollars? Guilt pinched his conscience, but he pushed it aside. He had better seek out the other ladies Liz had told him about just in case he made a complete mull of it with Winifred.

He whistled softly as he walked along the darkened streets beyond Mayfair, toward his flat. The moon lay low in the sky opposite the lightening clouds of the on-coming dawn. He thought of Winifred again, and how much like the goddess Athena she had looked when she bent by the fountain to touch its water. With her face washed in moonlight and her slender form outlined by the fabric of her dress, she had appeared as elegant as any statue depicting the goddess.

She was not at all a beauty, but her clean looks appealed to him. And he was more than surprised at just how appealing he found her. Even her antics at supper made him think of Eton, when he and his friend Sheldrake had pulled any number of pranks upon each other. He could not remember when he had enjoyed a female's company more.

He walked up the steps to his rooms and pulled the

key from his pocket. Once inside, he took off his coat
and threw it on the chair. He had no servants other than
the cleaning staff and a man who acted as combination
butler, valet, and groom. He once had a housekeeper
sent to him from Sheldrake, but she cost him more than
he cared to spend, so he found her employment elsewhere and hired his man, Stark. Stark was obviously
sleeping off his own night of entertainment, since the
near elderly fellow did not awaken when he came home.

Peter scanned the list that Liz had given him. He
would make sure to call on the Misses Preston first, then
maybe swing by to visit Miss Whent. He emptied his
pockets of the money he carried. There was plenty for
him to buy each lady a bouquet of posies. And he'd do
the pretty as he must, bowing and scraping and giving
compliments where he could.

He only hoped he could delay the chance to meet with
Winifred for their ride. He wanted to lengthen the time
spent in her company and he wanted to further their
acquaintance considerably. He was surprised to find that
he wanted very much to see her in the out of doors,
galloping freely on horseback. She would no doubt have
a mischievous look upon her freckled face and he'd be
hard-pressed to stop her from causing him trouble. He
decided that he liked the kind of bedlam Miss Winifred
threw his way. In fact, he looked forward to it.

Chapter Four

Winifred sat at her vanity, brushing her hair with long
strokes. Her cup of chocolate sat ignored upon the
breakfast tray. Sunshine streamed in through the windows and the birds sang, but she cared little for the
beauty out of doors this morning. She stared absently
into the mirror, her thoughts filled by a handsome

charmer with eyes of softest brown and hair the color of spun gold.

"Win?" Melanie entered her bedchamber.

"Yes." Brought out of her daze, Winifred put the brush down and turned toward her sister.

"What should I wear today, do you think?"

"I care not what you choose, why ask me?"

"Oh, I do not know. We will have callers this afternoon and I do not know what I should wear," Melanie said with a vague air.

And Mr. Blessing would no doubt be one of them. Winifred swallowed hard before asking, "Is there a particular gentleman you have grown fond of?" She waited for her sister's answer. What if she had decided upon Mr. Blessing? She would have to tell her what he was about.

"Not really fond, not yet at any rate. There are a couple of gentlemen I find pleasing though. Mr. Thorn is very nice and Lord Stanley, and Mr. Blessing, of course."

Of course, Winifred thought with dread and jealousy and all sorts of undesirable feelings settling in her midsection. "Mel, Mr. Blessing is a fortune hunter."

"He is still a nice man," she said.

"No he is not! Melanie, he is after our money, does that not bother you in the least? You said yourself that you did not like the clingy, desperate ways of a fortune hunter."

"But he is none of those things. He is very handsome and charming and he did set us straight about Lord Palmer."

Winifred rolled her eyes. Leave it to her sister to think just because a man intervened on her behalf, he must be a gallant knight on a white charger.

"And I think he favors you, my dear," Melanie said.

"Only because you were busy." She knew it was only a matter of time before Mr. Blessing decided he would rather pursue Melanie. 'Twas what she wanted, was it not, to make him dislike her? She reminded herself again that she did, indeed, want Mr. Blessing to leave her alone. But she did not want him pestering Melanie either.

Her sister was far too forgiving of his motives and could not possibly ward off such an experienced charmer.

"We shall see this afternoon, will we not? What are you planning to wear?" Melanie asked.

Winifred thought a moment. It should be something awful, to be sure. Something that would make her look hideously ridiculous. "I do not know yet."

"Well, we have all morning to decide."

There was not much of it left, Winifred thought. Not used to keeping the late night hours of the *ton,* she had slept until ten o'clock. But it was not a restful sleep. She had had dreams and visions of Mr. Blessing biting her, and sometimes not in very proper places. Then he had taken her money and left her. She had come awake many times in a feverish sweat, only to have trouble falling back to sleep.

"Mel," Winifred asked, "why did you not tell Aunt Win that we were in the gardens last night?"

"Because, I did not want to risk her writing back to father to report it. After last autumn, I was afraid that he might send for you to come home." Melanie sat down upon the bed. "I do not want you to go home. Even though you do deserve a Season of your own, I want you here with me."

Winifred smiled at her sister's protectiveness. "But there were many couples walking about the gardens last evening. Mr. Blessing said there was nothing improper about doing so. We were in a public place, after all. We were not alone."

"Winnie, Mr. Blessing has his eyes definitely fixed upon you. He will positively say anything to get your attention. I watched you two at supper. He seemed quite taken with you. Do be careful."

Winifred was shocked at her sister's correct perception of Mr. Blessing's slyness. Did he not hesitate in giving her his word to behave? He was a scoundrel and yet Melanie was ready to defend him!

"Father would not like the idea of you walking in the gardens with any man. He wants no hint of impropriety to touch either of us. This is not the country, Winnie. You have to be very careful of appearances."

"I do not give a hoot about appearances, Mel. And I am not at all interested in capturing the attentions of a man like Mr. Blessing. How can you possibly like him? He is an outright fortune hunter, which makes him no better than David Stanton."

"He is nothing like David. Besides, I think Mr. Blessing is truly taken with you, and that makes him a perceptive man in my estimation."

Winifred looked up at Melanie, who smiled fondly at her, and Winifred rushed over to give her sister a hug. She felt like the lowest of creatures to constantly feel envious of her sister's beauty, when she knew Melanie wanted only what was best for her, what was best for them both.

Her sister always looked for the good in people before looking at the bad. She was, however, an excellent judge of character. Melanie had never liked David Stanton, a gentleman, who had fervently courted Winifred last summer while on leave from the army. At first, Winifred had thought that Melanie was simply jealous, since most of the gentlemen at home swarmed around her elder sister and rarely paid any heed to Winifred.

But that had not been the case at all. Melanie had never trusted him and Winifred wished with all her heart that she had not done so either. David Stanton had pretended to be in love with Winifred. He had tried to compromise her into marriage. Fortunately, her angry father had sent him packing and no one ever knew about her disgrace. Melanie had been a source of strength in helping Winifred pick up the pieces of her broken heart and they had become very close through the entire ordeal.

"Thank you. That was nice of you to say." Winifred released her sister with a squeeze. Whether Melanie was right or wrong about Peter Blessing, Winifred had no interest in finding out. He was simply not worth it.

"Shall we go through our new wardrobes and see what we can wear to make the very best impressions this afternoon?"

"Yes, let us do so." Winifred linked her arm with her sister's. She wanted to make an impression of course, but not a good one.

Entering the dressing room that adjoined their two chambers, Melanie opened the doors of the armoires. Their papa had spared no expense, and shimmering gowns of every style and fabric burst forth.

"We do have many to choose from," Melanie said.

"Yes." Winifred ran her fingers along her sister's gowns. Since Melanie was the elder of the two, her gowns were of the latest fashion styles, with low necklines and deep flounces and some with very long sleeves. Winifred's wardrobe was more sedate and simple. Her dresses were made in the classic Greek lines of the past few years with few trimmings or attachments. The modiste had said such ribbons and ruffles would only detract from her tall frame, making her look silly.

An idea formed in her mind. "Mel, do you think I could borrow one of your dresses?"

"But, they will be too short for you."

"Please?"

"I do not know, what if your ankles show?"

"If they do, I shall reconsider," Winifred said. She cared little about her ankles as long as she looked ridiculous enough to give Mr. Blessing pause in pursuing her further. Surely, there were other ladies he could bother.

"Very well. Which will you choose?" Melanie asked.

"I do not know yet. You go ahead and make your choice, I will make mine later."

Melanie proceeded to try on any number of outfits for Winifred's approval. Each one she cast off, Winifred considered for herself. Most were lovely creations, but there were a few fussy things with all sorts of ties and ribbons and lace and such. Two gowns were downright gaudy, and those were the ones Winifred knew she would choose between.

Peter trotted lightly up the steps to the Fitzhugh residence—home to the aunts bringing out the Misses Preston. He tugged on the knocker and pounded twice. A surly looking butler let him in and walked him to the drawing room where Miss Melanie Preston held court over her admirers. The room was rather full, considering it was nigh three o'clock.

He scanned the richly appointed interior but did not see Miss Winifred. He bowed to their aunt, who nodded stiffly toward him. "Good afternoon, Mr. Blessing. Winifred will be down directly."

Miss Preston waved to him and he walked over to her. "I have brought you these," he said, feeling ridiculous as he handed her a small bunch of violets. He nodded a greeting toward Lord Stanley, an acquaintance often found at the gaming tables.

"How lovely," she said. "And I see that you have also brought some for Winifred. I shall ring for two vases of water."

Peter nodded again, and took a seat near the fire. It was a cool day, and since he had walked the many blocks from his flat in Belgrave Square to Mayfair, he felt cold.

His chills were soon chased away when he saw her. Miss Winifred Preston appeared in the doorway. Even her aunt raised high an eyebrow at the picture her niece presented. The gown she wore was a blue beribboned confection with flounces starting at the knee all the way to the hem, which revealed Miss Winifred's exquisitely formed ankles.

Peter found himself raising his own brow when she gazed at him with marked mischief twinkling in her eyes. The dress was obviously the wrong style for her, but the color was perfect. It brought out the clear blue of her eyes, which were huge and shining. Her hair, looking more red than gold, was pulled into a loose knot with some of it falling in ringlets down her back.

"Miss Winifred," he said as he stood.

"Mr. Blessing, how nice of you to call," she said too brightly. She sat down directly across from him, which allowed him an excellent view of her ankles. He looked up to find that he was not the only gentleman to notice the shortness of her gown. Lord Stanley ogled her openly.

A raw irritation ripped through him. "My, we are showing a bit of limb today."

She leaned forward and Peter was awarded a different view. The neckline of her dress was scooped out deeply and even though she wore a lace fichu, the bodice gaped, since it was obviously designed for a more endowed figure.

"Do you think so?" she asked.

It took him a moment to recover his wits and look away from the firm swell of her breasts to her face. He still held the bunch of violets in his hand. Before he could answer her, Lord Stanley and another man gathered before his Athena.

They bowed, and she beamed up at them both, her smile wide.

"Miss Winifred, may I please introduce myself and my friend," Lord Stanley asked.

"Of course you may, sir."

"Miss Winifred Preston, I am Lord Stanley, and this is Mr. Oliver."

"How delightful. Please gentlemen, sit down."

Peter watched as she slid down the sofa, making room for the two men. Her movement dragged the hem of her gown a little higher and her ankles along with a good portion of her slender calves were fully exposed. Mr. Oliver sat next to her, but Stanley remained standing. The brazen hussy actually leaned into Mr. Oliver when he told her some idiotic story. She laughed aloud and Peter cringed. What was she doing, what did she think she was doing? A rare feeling of jealousy sliced its way through him. He could play her game, as well.

He rose and walked over to Miss Melanie Preston, who looked up at him.

He quietly asked, "I know Lord Stanley, but who is this Mr. Oliver?"

She smiled fully at him, then whispered, "Mr. Oliver is a very rich nabob, just back from India. And please, do call me Melanie."

"Very well. I guess that explains his darkened skin."

He did not like it one bit that the man seemed altogether enchanted by Winifred.

"I sent Lord Stanley over to introduce them, since Mr. Oliver kept asking about her."

Melanie seemed quite pleased by the situation. He considered it to her credit. She must know that she outshone her sister in looks and yet, she was genuinely happy that one of her admirers defected to Winifred's side.

"What do you know about him?" he asked.

"Why, Mr. Blessing, you are actually concerned for my sister."

Had he given something away? Whatever it was, it did not bear examination. But it was foolish thinking that he felt anything at all; he merely needed to know the competition so he could best it. That was all.

"Please, you must call me Peter. I simply would not like Miss Winifred to be gulled . . ." He stopped in mid-sentence. His conscience nagged at him. He himself was trying to gull her into marriage, for pity's sake.

"Perhaps you would like to go for a carriage ride this afternoon to discuss the subject." Melanie looked around quickly, then gave him a pointed look and nodded toward her sister.

Peter understood, and wondered if it was possible that he had Miss Melanie Preston in his corner. "Excellent idea, I shall ask your aunt for permission."

"Wait for a few more minutes, sir, as I believe some of the gentlemen will be gone by then," she whispered. "And Peter?"

"Yes?"

She hesitated, shifted in her seat, then asked, "How is your brother, Lord Blessing?"

"John?" Peter had not known that they knew one another. "Fine, I suppose."

"You will give him my regards?" She suddenly blushed and Peter knew that she was interested in his brother. That would explain why she looked a little disappointed when he had arrived alone. No doubt, she was hoping for John to call.

"I shall be honored," Peter said with a smile. He decided he liked Melanie very well. She obviously cared for Winifred deeply and despite the girl's beauty, there was no vanity in her.

Perhaps he should reconsider which sister he courted. He looked around and decided against it. Melanie had more gentlemen callers than he cared to compete against. And what if John decided to pursue her? His brother deserved a sweet-natured lady like Melanie Preston. Besides, he had an ally in her which could prove most helpful in his attempt to conquer Miss Winifred.

A loud feminine laugh caught his attention. It was not the cultured sound so many of society's ladies practiced, but an outright peal of real amusement. It was Winifred, and she was having far too much fun with Mr. Oliver for his liking. Nor did her aunt seem amused by her slightly less than maidenly decorum. He wondered if now might be a good time to ask the aunt for that carriage ride. She looked troubled by the scene her niece and Mr. Oliver presented. And she should, considering that Winifred had her hand resting on the nabob's arm.

"Excuse me, Lady Winifred, is it?" He stood before a woman not yet elderly, clothed in the finest of elegance.

"Yes, that is correct, Mr. Blessing. What can I do for you?"

"I should like to ask permission to take your niece—both your nieces, actually—for a carriage ride this afternoon in Hyde Park." He was glad he had added Melanie in his invitation. Surely, having both girls along would give their aunt no cause for alarm or concern. He hoped his occupation would not give her a reason to refuse his request.

He watched as Lady Winifred looked again in the direction of her younger niece, who now slapped her knee in a gauche manner as she continued to laugh. Peter happened to catch Winifred looking up at him. Her eyes twinkled with mirth. She wanted him to notice her bad behavior!

"Yes, Mr. Blessing, I believe I shall grant you permission. The girls will be ready to accompany you at a quarter past the hour of four," their aunt said.

"Thank you, ma'am." Peter bowed and realized he still held the bunch of violets. He approached Winifred.

She looked up at him, as did Mr. Oliver, who wore a frown at the interruption.

"Please excuse me, but I have engagements elsewhere and I wanted to be sure to give you these." He held out the bouquet to her. A couple of the flowers were sadly wilted, no doubt by his constant squeezing of them.

"Thank you, Mr. Blessing." She smiled triumphantly at him.

The imp. Was she putting on a show, then? As she took the posies from him, he could not keep from leaning closer to her and whispering, "I shall see you later, Athena."

He was glad to see the blush of pink that suffused her cheeks. He grinned at the annoyed Mr. Oliver. He might as well let the nabob know right now that she was his.

"Good day." He bowed and left.

Winifred held the violets in her hands. It was hard not to bring them to her nose and bury herself in the scent. They were simple street-seller flowers and yet she liked them all the same. She placed them in the vase next to Melanie's bouquet and wondered just who Mr. Blessing was trying to court. Had he not spoken to Melanie for an age? It was difficult to keep her eyes on Mr. Blessing and entertain Mr. Oliver at the same time.

She thought she had scored a win in this round, as she was sure she had made Mr. Blessing angry with her. He scowled enough at her, at least. But then when he had whispered to her, it was as if she had not acted poorly at all. What was she going to do? She certainly did not want Mr. Oliver; he was positively silly. She dared not encourage him too much, else she would have a whole new set of problems.

After all of the gentlemen finally took their leave, Winifred leaned back against the sofa and sighed. Flirting was hard work.

"Winifred," Aunt Winifred hissed, outraged.

"Yes?"

"You had better be ashamed of yourself!"

"What? Why?"

"Acting like an opera singer and dressed no better. What are you doing wearing Melanie's gown? It is too short for you and you look . . . you look fast, my dear."

She wanted to look absurd, not fast. She supposed letting her ankles show was a bit bird-witted, but surely no one would think her loose?

"You had the men positively at your feet today," Melanie added.

"But I did not mean to look fast. I only thought to give Mr. Blessing . . ."

"An eyeful?" Melanie teased.

"What do you mean!" Winifred demanded.

"Well, he could not keep his gaze off of you, dear."

"And can you blame him, showing your ankles like that," her aunt scolded. "I shall warn you now, Winifred, you must behave yourself and keep a modest front. I will not have you taint any of us with scandalous behavior. Your sister is trying to find a good husband, as should you. I will not have you appear fast or hoydenish."

"But Aunt Winifred, Mr. Blessing is obviously interested only in our money."

"Oh, pooh! Half of the *ton* is interested in the Preston inheritance. Even though you have the smudge of trade in your background, most gentlemen would welcome your dowries, and my side of the family has impeccable lineage," Aunt Winifred said.

"I do not see why you must slight Father, Aunt," Winifred stated. "He worked very hard to provide for us. Besides, you should have a care about Mr. Blessing. He is an outright fortune hunter!"

"What is this about Mr. Blessing?" Aunt Augusta walked into the room.

"He has asked the girls to go for a carriage ride in Hyde Park this afternoon," Aunt Winifred said.

"What!" Winifred stood up.

"And you did not give him permission did you?" Aunt Augusta looked positively shocked.

"Of course I did. He asked to take both of the girls, which is admirable, so I see no real harm. He is of good family. His brother is a prime catch and held in the highest regard among many."

"He asked us both?" A frown marred Melanie's forehead.

"But he is, he has been linked with . . . that is to say . . ." Aunt Augusta stammered.

"What she is trying to say, is that Lady Dunstan is his mistress!" Winifred blurted.

Melanie gasped in shock.

"Oh for heaven's sake, Winifred, you should never suggest or even know about such things," Aunt Winifred said. She coughed genteelly. "At least he finds his comfort with a lady instead of—well, never mind. He is most assuredly discreet, since I have never heard of this connection. And I have excellent sources. Pray, Augusta, tell me who told you this?"

Aunt Augusta looked down at the floor. Winifred noticed that they all waited with held breath to find out who would murmur such gossip.

"Well, I came by the information when I applied for vouchers to Almack's for the girls." She looked sheepish.

"And who said such a thing?" Aunt Winifred asked.

"Lady Jersey mentioned it to me. Well, she was not certain, but she wondered about it. And then there was Lady Dunstan, proud as you please, introducing Mr. Blessing to all the young ladies at Countess Sefton's ball and, well, I figured it must be true."

Melanie sighed and said, "But you do not know for sure that such a thing is true? You see, Winifred, he may just be friends with Lady Dunstan."

"And pigs might fly," Winifred answered.

Winifred played with the tassel of her reticule. She sat in the drawing room, wearing one of her own gowns topped with a short grass-green spencer, and waited. Melanie was still trying on several bonnets in her room. Was no one to oppose Mr. Blessing's attentions to them? Aunt Winifred was somewhat of a stickler, and she seemed unruffled by the scoundrel that was Mr. Peter Blessing.

Aunt Augusta gave over and allowed the carriage outing to go forward. She usually bowed to Aunt Winifred's will, regardless. The door opened and the butler announced Mr. Blessing. She looked up into his eyes and he smiled.

"I see you have changed into something more suitable for you," he said.

"Yes," she sighed.

"Are you going to tell me what your little theatrical production was about this afternoon?"

"No, I will not." She shrugged her shoulders. "And besides there was no 'production,' as you call it. I merely thought to wear my sister's gown."

"Oh, I see." He gave her a naughty grin and added, "Actually, I saw quite a bit."

She felt her cheeks grow warm. What was a pair of ankles to a man like him! Surely, he had seen countless parts of the female anatomy. "No more than anyone else," she shot back.

"Yes, and therein lies the trouble. I doubt Mr. Oliver will ever recover from his admiration of you and even Lord Stanley was quite content to appreciate your, ah, feet."

"Appreciate my feet! Oh please." Winifred rolled her eyes. "Why are you here, Mr. Blessing?"

"To take you for a ride in Hyde Park."

"Why are you really here, what do you want from us?" She watched his consternation at her question and there seemed to be a war waging within him. His expression turned slightly serious.

"Can you not believe that I simply enjoy your company?" His eyes were soft and genuine.

"No sir, I cannot believe that, nor will I."

"So cynical, my tall goddess." He walked over to the window and looked out over Park Lane, then he turned and faced her again. "Of the many things that can be said about me with a modicum of truth, lying is not one of them."

Winifred was not moved. She merely answered with an ungraceful snort.

Melanie entered the drawing room. "Peter, how charming to see you again," Melanie said as she gave him her gloved hand in greeting. Mr. Blessing took it to his lips briefly.

Winifred sat in stunned silence. *Peter?* Why was Melanie using Mr. Blessing's Christian name all of a sudden? She could not think it proper in the least. "Mel, I think you should refrain from using Mr. Blessing's given name."

"But he has given me leave to use it," Melanie answered, "and it is just us at present."

"You may call me Peter too, if you wish, Miss Winifred."

"No, I do not wish, Mr. Blessing." Winifred, suddenly irritable, turned and left the room.

Once outside, Winifred could not help but marvel at the beautiful high-flyer phaeton standing before her. The seat was at a great height and she wondered at its width. "Are you certain the three of us can fit?" she asked.

Peter jumped up onto the seat. "We can fit." He gave Melanie his hand and helped her up. "You are next, Miss Winifred." He held out his hand to her.

She grabbed hold and hoisted herself up. She sat next to Melanie and Peter was soon sitting next to her. They did indeed fit, but it was tight. Her leg had nowhere to rest except next to his. She tried to ignore the warmth she felt from his leather-encased thigh pressed against her own, but failed miserably. A tingling sensation flooded her body at the contact.

He appeared to know the reason for her discomfort and smiled down at her with his boyishly crooked grin. Flustered, she looked straight ahead.

He chuckled under his breath. "Shall we go?" he asked.

A thrill of excitement bubbled through her. "Yes, let us go, Mr. Blessing, and do not be shy about your speed."

He clicked the reins. The matched pair of grays he

had harnessed moved as one. They pulled away from the curb with complete grace. In no time, they were moving along at a smart pace and Winifred grinned with pleasure. The townhouses of Mayfair soon gave way to the lush green expanse that was Hyde Park.

Melanie did not share Winifred's enthusiasm for speed. She held onto both Winifred and the gig's side with a strong grip. But Winifred knew that her sister was trying to be brave as she managed a smile. They slowed considerably after they had gone deeper into Hyde Park. At the height of the fashionable hour, most carriages slowed to little better than a standstill. People nodded and stopped to gossip or visit.

"There is your Mr. Oliver," Peter whispered to her.

She looked across to see that he was perched atop a bright blue phaeton with Miss Whent. She caught his gaze and he smiled in greeting. She nodded politely in return.

"And there is your Lady Dunstan," Winifred said when she spotted the lady coming toward them.

He looked at her quickly, then waved as the lady's curricle stopped before them.

"Good afternoon, Peter, Miss Preston, Miss Winifred," Lady Dunstan said.

Winifred nodded and wondered if Lady Dunstan was in fact Peter's mistress. They seemed to be at complete ease with each other and there was no awkwardness when they spoke briefly of the fine weather. Winifred noticed that Lady Dunstan drove her curricle herself. A groom stood solemnly behind her, but she was otherwise alone.

"How are you enjoying London, ladies?" Lady Dunstan asked.

"Very well, thank you," Melanie responded.

"Lady Dunstan, is it very difficult to drive in town?" Winifred asked.

"In town?" Lady Dunstan looked confused.

"As opposed to the country. Is it very different?"

Lady Dunstan exchanged a glance with Peter, then she

answered, "I do not believe 'tis too different, except of course there are more people to look out for."

"Do you wish to drive, Miss Winifred?" Peter asked.

"I should like that above all things, Mr. Blessing." Winifred announced.

"Oh my, are you sure, Winnie? It is likely to be crowded." Melanie's voice quivered slightly.

"You may ride with me, Miss Preston, if you would like," Lady Dunstan offered. "We can make the rounds."

Melanie smiled and accepted.

"When shall we meet, say one half-hour back at this spot?" Peter asked.

"Yes, until then," Lady Dunstan said. She waited for Melanie to climb aboard before pulling her curricle away.

"Will she be all right?" Winifred asked.

"With Liz? Of course she will. No doubt she will introduce your sister to half the *ton* or more. Miss Melanie will no doubt have all the doors of the *haute monde* opened to her when she's seen with Elizabeth Dunstan."

"We have our aunts for that, sir." Winifred shifted uncomfortably and moved away from Peter. She wanted to know if Lady Dunstan was his mistress, yet dare she ask him? Of course, she dared. If he did not like her asking it, the better for her and her plan to give him a disgust of her. She gritted her teeth and forced herself to turn and face him. After taking a deep breath, she asked, "Is Lady Dunstan your mistress?"

Peter choked, then coughed, then turned in his seat to look at her directly. "Where did you hear that?"

"Simply answer the question."

"No. I shall not answer your question." His voice was slightly higher than normal as if he tried to control it. Fire ignited behind his eyes and she knew she had made him angry. Good, that was very good.

He ran a hand through his hair. "Winifred, you cannot ask a gentleman such a question, it is beyond the pale, it is simply not done. If you should ever ask any other man such a question, your Season and your reputation would be in shreds. You don't want that. You don't want your sister's chances diminished because of your forth-right way of speaking, do you?"

He sounded just like her Aunt Win, and yet there was a softness to his voice now. She had to look away. It was very hard for her to think about displeasing him when he looked at her with such caring in his eyes. But he was not *any other man,* and she would never dream of asking someone else this question. She had a perverse longing to hear what he had to say.

"Of course I do not want to hurt Melanie's Season, but I still would like to know." She kept her gaze upon the seat and the empty space that was between them. She felt his fingers under her chin, turning her head toward him. She looked at him then.

"No, Athena, she is not."

Winifred felt a strong sense of relief and almost smiled, but he looked guilty as he gazed into her eyes.

"Not anymore at least," he added.

Winifred's eyes widened. It had been true! Lady Dunstan had been Peter's mistress. She saw his eyes cloud over and he dropped his hand from her face.

"You asked for the truth," he said. "Do not be disappointed when you receive it."

She sat back in her seat. "You misread me, sir. I am not disappointed. In fact, I expected as much." But the knowledge indeed bothered her. When had he broken off with Lady Dunstan? She wondered how they could act so comfortably around each other after terminating such a relationship. An unbidden and wholly undesired thought wracked her brain as she wondered what it would be like to be held by Peter Blessing. What would it feel like to have his hands on her?

"Sweet wisdom, now what are you thinking?" Peter asked.

She felt herself flush to her roots. And he laughed, which eased the awkwardness of the moment. But she needed that awkwardness back, she needed to keep Mr. Blessing off balance, so she ventured another question. "Did you love her?"   .

"I beg your pardon?"

"Do you love her?"

"Love has little . . ." He broke off, clearly uncomfortable with the question. "I do not think this is at all an appropriate conversation." He shifted the reins and offered them to her. "Come, you wish to drive, don't you?" he asked.

"Yes."

She had made him uneasy. He actually withdrew from her, and that was very good, indeed. She had knocked his charming mask askew slightly, but unfortunately it did not take him very long to put a disarming smile back on his face.

"Here, move over here." He guided her with his hands upon her waist as she stood to take his seat while he slid down to her right. The warmth of his touch was soon forgotten when she felt pure exhilaration pump through her veins as she took the reins from him. She was more than grateful to have something other than his nearness to occupy her thoughts.

They pulled away from the crowds until they were before a wide sandy lane called Rotten Row. Used primarily for riding in the morning, it was almost empty since many of the carriages were further down, where everyone congregated to see one another and be seen.

"You have driven a gig before, correct?" he asked.

"Oh, yes. I have even driven Papa's curricle at home."

He nodded. "We are going to take it easy at first."

Winifred ignored him and clicked the reins with ease. The grays pulled forward gently and, with a switch of leather, increased their speed. In no time they were moving at a spanking pace heading south, about to leave Hyde Park. The cool wind in her face and the pure joy of driving such a smart vehicle left her practically breathless.

She looked over at Peter to see if he wanted her to turn and go back, but he appeared to be enjoying the ride almost as much as she. He motioned for her to continue forward. She smiled at him fully and gave the grays a chance to truly stretch their legs.

She was not sure exactly how it happened, but somehow a farmer's wagon appeared out of nowhere and Winifred reacted poorly. She pulled back too hard on the reins, and the horses jerked and fell out of sequence in their movement. She feared they would overturn the gig.

"Mr. Blessing, please, I need your help!" she shouted.

He took control in a matter of seconds. His arms came around hers and he coaxed the horses to slow their pace. Gently, he took the reins from her stiff hands and, with his arms still about her, slowed them to a walk and negotiated the narrow lane in time to swerve around the wagon. The phaeton came to a stop and she leaned back into his chest with a ragged, shuttering sigh of relief.

"Are you all right?" His arms tightened around her.

"I am so sorry, so very sorry. I could have gotten us killed." She started to shake.

"No, Athena. You did very well. You only misjudged the distance and acted too hastily." He turned her around and gathered her into his arms.

She grudgingly accepted the soothing warmth of his embrace. "But I pulled on the horses too hard," she mumbled into his cravat. "I have no doubt bruised their mouths and they will be no good to you for a week or more."

"Sshh, Winifred, it is all right, truly," he whispered into her hair.

Her trembling soon subsided and she considered how pleasant it was to be held by him. She was even surprised that he did not hold too closely. Nor did he try to take advantage of her weakened state, but merely calmed her down and patted her back. She knew she must pull away from him, even though she did not truly wish to.

"Thank you, Mr. Blessing," she said, stiffening. His hands slid down her arms to give her a slight squeeze of encouragement. "You are most kind not to give me the dressing-down I deserve for going too fast."

"Nonsense." He cupped her chin with his hand and forced her gaze up to his face, his eyes. "You are not a half bad whip, Winifred, and that is a compliment I rarely pay to many gentlemen that I know. My horseflesh will recover, and I promise to pamper them for you."

As she looked into his eyes, she was surprised to see nothing but kindness and understanding there. Her father would have had her hide for such a stunt, yet Peter had easily entrusted himself into her hands. Few men she knew would allow a lady the chance to drive in their presence let alone with such speed. David had never allowed her to drive in his company.

"Mr. Blessing, I do not know what to say."

"Say nothing, sweet goddess, only let me pay homage and worship you the rest of my days." He grinned at her and began to laugh.

"Oh, for heaven's sake." She leaned back in her seat, annoyed that Peter had retreated behind his mask of charm. She had to admit that she rather liked the glimpse of man that lay beyond the practiced rakehell that he portrayed to the world. "We had better return, for we are already late."

He nodded and clicked at the team. Grateful that they rode on in silence, Winifred wondered about his reticence in explaining his feelings toward Lady Dunstan. It appeared that he did not love her, but he was most unhappy at being asked such a question. Yet how could one possibly become involved in such a way without love, she wondered.

She cast a peek at him sitting next to her. His profile was every bit as handsome to look upon. Her body seemed drawn to him and she was more than tempted to feel the warmth of his embrace again. She chided herself as being no better than he and Lady Dunstan for having such wanton thoughts.,

"What has you so grim, Athena?"

"Mr. Blessing, why must you call me that?"

"Because it suits you." He looked at her and winked. "Now, what troubles you?"

Winifred hesitated. "I shall be quite truthful. I am bothered by your relationship with Lady Dunstan." She saw his eyes roll. Good, she was annoying him, she thought, and proceeded. "I do not understand. If you did not love her, then why—"

"Let me stop you right there," he started. "It is not always a matter of love. There is loneliness and a need to connect with another human being, if only for a moment here or there."

"But it is not right. She is a married lady," Winifred protested.

"Yes, and miserable." He released an exasperated breath. "Truly, this conversation is not appropriate."

"But, you did not seem to mind speaking to me in an inappropriate manner last evening at the Sefton's."

"That was different."

"How so?" she asked.

"It just was."

He looked a bit red around the collar, and Winifred knew that she was irritating him with her questions. Perhaps she was going about this plan of trying to disgust him the wrong way. Perhaps she should try a completely different tactic.

She leaned back satisfied that she had won this round with Mr. Peter Blessing, but she needed to think more about revising her strategy. She would continue to be as provoking as she could be with her normal hoyden antics. But if she could show Peter his faults as an attempt to push him away from her, then all the better. Surely, he would stand for only so much, and when she finally pushed him too far, he would be gone.

When they met Lady Dunstan and Melanie, they were a good half-hour late. Peter explained what had happened and Melanie immediately acted the mother hen and clucked over her little sister. Lady Dunstan merely raised an eyebrow, but Peter seemed to ignore it as he bid her good day.

They were oddly silent on the journey back to Mayfair but for Melanie's chatter about the people she had been introduced to by Lady Dunstan, whom she found very agreeable.

Winifred felt strangely deflated when Peter left them in their aunts' care. According to Melanie's description,

Lady Dunstan appeared to be a nice lady. She felt oddly disappointed by that.

When Melanie asked to hear all the details of her mad carriage ride, Winifred confessed to being sadly pulled and said she would rather rest before dinner. She did not wish to speak of the near accident, nor remember the feel of Peter's arms about her. She had a hollow feeling inside that she was not about to examine. She needed all her resolve to carry out her plan.

Chapter Five

Two days passed and Winifred had not seen Peter Blessing. This was a good thing, but she could only dwell on the fact that she expected him to walk into the drawing room whenever a gentleman caller was announced. When she took the air with Melanie, she looked for him on the street. It was horrible, this anticipation. She wanted only to see him again.

Melanie's praises of him were no help either. She thought Peter an even more gallant knight once Winifred told her how he had saved the day with the phaeton. Of course, Winifred conveniently left out any information regarding his arms about her. She kept that secret, alternately wondering why he had not tried to kiss her, then cursing herself a fool for doing so. It was an infuriating situation.

Although he failed to call, Peter had not forgotten her. Every day he sent her a small present. His card with a single white rose arrived yesterday and today he sent her a lock of the horse's mane tied with white ribbon and a white rosebud. He had included a note assuring her that the horses were well and completely spoiled. He informed her that their mouths were only slightly bruised, and that they were grateful to her for they had not been so pampered in ages.

She brought the clipped hair to her nose and breathed in deeply the fine scent of leather and horse. It reminded her of Hillie Park where she spent much of her time riding across her father's lands. She wondered when he would ask her to go riding with him as penalty for her prank. She hoped it would be soon so that she could be done with him. She caught herself looking forward to his company and cursed her desire to be with him. Surely, she was the weakest sort of female to be so affected by the physical reactions a man stirred within her.

Melanie had also received gifts from Peter. Each day he had sent her a white rosebud as well. Melanie teased Winifred about the lock of horse hair, stating that it was an odd thing to send but very sweet. Winifred tried to act aloof, as if it did not matter, but inside she wondered if he truly favored her over Melanie.

Perhaps he had not tried to kiss her when she was in his arms simply because he planned on fixing his interest with Melanie after all. Perhaps he did not like her physically and thought her too skinny. These ideas plagued her and she began to think herself touched in the head.

She would have no doubt considered him a creature lower than dirt had he kissed her when she was upset. Yet she was disappointed that he had not, even though she wanted to be rid of him.

Although Peter had not called, the last two days actually brought other callers for Winifred. Mr. Oliver and Lord Stanley and even a gentleman named Mr. Pratt, who had seen her driving skills in the Park, had called upon her. She found that she actually looked forward to the next ball where she would have invitations to dance.

One afternoon, after the callers had all left, Winifred and Melanie hurried to their abigail for a change of clothes. An evening at the theater was planned.

Winifred positively beamed with excitement. She had never been to the theater and could barely contain herself during dinner. She had chosen her gown carefully, deciding Drury Lane was no doubt a place to wear only the finest attire. She wore a simple gown of the palest lilac silk with a broad neckline that allowed her shoulders to remain practically bare. She donned long white gloves and fixed a pretty circlet of amethysts in her upswept hair. The same gems dangled from her earlobes. She was satisfied with her appearance, and even more so when Aunt Winifred complimented her.

They entered the theater amid a bustle of carriages and people. Winifred stayed close to her aunts as they walked up the stairs to their private box. Once seated, she breathed in deeply. The place smelled heavily of oranges with an undertone of stale beer, but she reveled in the newness of it all.

"Is this not wonderful?" Winifred asked.

"Completely," Melanie agreed.

Winifred gazed about the theater. Jewels glittered in the dull light, and she marveled at the stunning scene of members of the *ton* dressed at the very height of fashion. The lower classes and young gentlemen of town were crowded onto the floor benches and they jostled each other for room. Girls selling oranges sauntered between the rows of benches with an occasional squeal at being pinched or slapped on the bottom by a fresh young buck.

Above, however, the rulers of society were seated in boxes where various guests visited to pay homage. Diamond tiaras twinkled, ladies tittered and hid their smiles behind fans, while men of nobility stood tall and elegant in their evening dress.

She spotted Peter Blessing sitting in a box diagonally across from them. To her utter annoyance, her stomach lurched. He had not noticed her so she stared at him freely. She was struck anew by how indecently attractive he was. He sat next to an older man who must be the brother he and Aunt Win had spoken of.

There was a definite resemblance. His brother, also a handsome man, was much leaner than Peter and had darker hair. He seemed rather tense and kept pulling at his waistcoat. Peter looked positively dashing in a black evening coat and ivory waistcoat, but he fiddled with his cravat. She wished he were not such a gambler but an honorable gentleman. But there was no use in wishing for something that was not so. She finally looked away and it took her every bit of determination to keep her gaze from straying back toward him.

Hearing a slight commotion coming from the direction of the Blessing box, Winifred looked over to see that a group of people had entered it. She experienced an odd mixture of annoyance and jealousy when Peter placed a kiss upon Miss Whent's wrist and she playfully swatted him with her fan. Miss Whent fairly drooled as she leaned toward him and whispered something in his ear. Peter happened to look up and notice Winifred and he winked. She quickly looked away.

The play was about to begin. A gentleman approached the stage and announced that this evening's production was Mr. Shakespeare's *A Midsummer Night's Dream*. Winifred sighed her appreciation as she had often read the play as a child. Her mother never approved, but her father had always given his daughters license to read what they wished, even more so since their mother had died.

She had always identified with the tall, lovesick Helena who wanted Demetrius. Melanie was no doubt Hermia, who had both Demetrius and Lysander vying for her attentions. Bittersweet memories of boys upon whom she had had silly *tendres* flitted through her mind. She had always cast Melanie in the role of Hermia and had tormented her sister for it.

She leaned forward to better watch the play and in no time she was completely engrossed. Eventually the brightening of the oil lamps brought an intermission. Winifred glanced once more at the Blessings' box, but it was empty.

"How do you like the theater, Winifred?" Aunt Augusta asked.

"Very much." Winifred stood to stretch slightly, then stopped and stared as Peter Blessing and his brother entered their box. Her stomach lurched again.

"Good evening, Lady Winifred, Lady Augusta." Peter bowed deeply.

Winifred watched with dread as both her aunts smiled and welcomed Peter and his brother into the box.

"Miss Winifred, Miss Melanie, good evening," he said with a bow.

"Mr. Blessing," Winifred said stiffly. Melanie was also on her feet extending her hand in welcome to both men.

"I'd like to introduce to you my elder brother, Lord Blessing. John, this is Miss Winifred Preston and I believe you have met Miss Melanie Preston."

"How do you do, ladies." His brother managed a stiff bow over each of their hands. He was much more reserved than Peter.

"Lord Blessing, it is so very nice to meet you. I have heard that you are a paragon of goodness," Winifred said in an unsure rush of words.

"Oh, and who has been telling you these tales?" Lord Blessing asked.

"Why your brother, of course. He quite admires you."

Peter seemed uncomfortable with her statement and gave her a quick look, no doubt in hopes of silencing her.

"Does he now? Well that is news." Lord Blessing smiled broadly.

"There is no need to mock me," Peter started. "You are my brother after all, and well, there it is."

Lord Blessing merely slapped his brother on his shoulder and laughed aloud. He had a pleasant laugh, and Winifred realized that there was genuine affection shared by them.

"I am sure your brother did not mean to poke fun, Mr. Blessing," Melanie said. "Would you gentlemen like to sit down? We have two extra seats as you can see."

Winifred would have liked to sit by her sister, but it was too late. Lord Blessing helped Melanie to her place, then took the seat beside her.

That left two empty chairs in the front of the box for her and Peter. She tried to quell the panic that threatened to possess her.

"Miss Winifred," Peter said as he stood waiting for her to be seated.

She hesitated and knew her apprehension must show as Peter gave her a questioning look. She merely stood there, like an idiot.

"Are you all right, Athena?" Peter leaned toward her and whispered.

"Yes, yes of course I am." She recovered and quickly sat down.

"What is the matter?" he asked.

"Nothing." What could she possibly say? That now she was afraid of him? That after being held by him in the phaeton she did not trust herself around him? It was terrible, this out-of-control feeling that had suddenly come over her. She breathed deeply trying to calm herself. Absently, she noticed that Melanie and Lord Blessing were chatting amiably behind them.

"Are you feeling poorly this evening?" Peter whispered when the oil lamps dimmed.

"I am perfectly well." Winifred did not like her snappish response so she amended it gently. " 'Tis only that I had not expected to see you this evening."

Their box was cast in shadows but the glow from the lighted stage allowed her to see him. She did not mistake the satisfied smile that appeared on his face.

"I don't usually attend the theater, but I had hoped to see you here. We have, after all, unfinished business."

"Pray enlighten me, sir," she whispered.

"Our ride, Athena. We have yet to plan our early morning ride."

"I hoped you had forgotten," she lied.

He leaned closer to her and she could feel the warmth of his breath on her neck. "I don't forget penalties, my dear. Especially when owed by such an enchanting creature."

The panic intensified as she felt her body betraying her again. She felt all quivers and shivers inside due to his nearness. "You flatter me too much, I fear," Winifred said.

"Never."

He had taken hold of her gloved hand and brought it to his lips. He let his kiss linger. Winifred could not pull away. She sat motionless, staring at the stage without seeing. He mesmerized her with the worship he gave the back of her hand. Her insides threatened to melt to a boil when he turned her respectably gloved hand to nip indecently at her thumb.

She came to her senses. "Mr. Blessing, please. Melanie and Lord Blessing are behind us."

"So?"

"They may see us." She did not recognize her own voice for it had turned hoarse.

"Do not fret, Athena; we are angled in such a way that no one behind us can tell that I have hold of your hand."

Winifred found her strength at last and pulled her hand away from him. She feared he would in fact divest her of her glove and she doubted she could remain sitting upright if his lips touched her bared skin. "I think not, Mr. Blessing."

She clasped her shaking hands and placed them firmly in her lap. Mr. Blessing still leaned too close for her mental stability, but at least he was not touching her. She turned to watch the play, but again his presence invaded her peace and distracted her focus. The scent he wore tickled her senses with wicked thoughts of wanting to edge closer to breath deeply of him.

Winifred scanned the balconies in an attempt to pull her attention away from Peter and noticed Miss Whent was seated in her family's box. The young lady caught Winifred's gaze and held it. Winifred mused that at any moment, daggers would fly from that cold stare. She shifted in her chair and tried to focus on the play.

As the third act proceeded, Winifred still noticed every move Peter made. She was restless and longed to be away from him. How could she possibly pay attention to the stage when he drew her thoughts and gaze constantly away from it? She had to do something about her attraction to him. If she continued to see him, she feared she would not have the presence of mind to keep to her plan of disgusting him.

He certainly acted as if he had overcome his annoyance with her from their carriage ride. In fact, he had rallied considerably well. She had to cut him off completely and have nothing further to do with him while she still had sense enough to do so. After their ride, of course. She was honor-bound to ride with him.

"When did you wish to ride, Mr. Blessing?" she said quietly.

"Morning, I think. That is the best time to find enough space to do more than a sedate trot."

"Yes, but when?"

"Soon, very soon," Peter said.

Winifred wondered if he could possibly have read her thoughts. Why else had he not given her an exact date? What game was he playing with her now?

Peter noted the frustration that flitted across Winifred's face. He did not trust her eagerness to ride with him. She had an idea cooking in her fascinating head, he was sure of it. He had better keep the promised riding engagement as the proverbial carrot before the horse to be given only when all other calls and convenient meetings with Winifred had been exhausted.

His gaze took in her profile. She had a strong, straight nose and a proud lift to her chin. He quickly glanced back at his brother, who actually appeared to be enjoying himself as he chatted with Miss Melanie. The two were not in the least bit interested in the production unfolding on the stage below. He turned his attention back to Winifred. She, on the other hand, appeared completely immersed in the play. Only she would be so adorable as to come to the theater to actually watch the cursed thing, he mused.

"Is something amiss?" Winifred asked.

"No, why do you ask?"

"You keep looking at me."

She sounded vexed with him. He had to be careful not to overdo it with his pretty compliments and physical overtures. She was much too unsettled by his company this evening. But keeping her off balance by flirting outrageously with her was better than allowing her mouth to run its course. She asked too many questions for his comfort.

"Just admiring the view," he said.

"Please stop."

He did not bother to resist his urge to tease her. "Now that would be like asking the rain not to fall."

"It only rains on occasion, Mr. Blessing. I suggest that you admire your view at some other time."

"I am certain that I shall, but you do look ravishing this evening." He told the complete truth. The cut of her gown draped her slim form beautifully. Her bared shoulders enticed him with their smoothness and he had never before noticed how graceful the back of a woman's neck could be.

"Thank you," she whispered.

"You are most welcome."

He kept quiet the rest of the play. He supposed he owed her that much. She truly wanted to watch the production, so he tried not to be too much of a bother. But he sat as close to her as he could. He had to own that of all the ladies he had been courting since the Sefton ball, he found that he liked Winifred Preston best.

Despite her sharp tongue and probing questions, he guessed that underneath was a vulnerable young lady. That vulnerability had kept him from pouring on the seductive charm when she trembled in his arms after driving his phaeton. Somehow he could not bring himself to take advantage of her then.

Her opinion of him was already low, even though she was obviously physically attracted to him. Had he pressed her for a kiss or some such nonsense, no doubt he would have sunk beneath contempt in her eyes. He admitted that he did not wish to earn Miss Winifred's disgust for more reasons than just losing a good marriage prospect. To his shock, he found he actually wanted to please her. Even more so, it was pretty easy to be himself with her, and that was the real stunner of them all.

As much as he had to play games with Winifred in hopes of obtaining her hand in marriage, he wished that he did not need to. It gave him no satisfaction to use her and exploit her attraction for him, but what else could he do?

He could not keep blaming John for his situation, either. Peter had been playing deeper and losing more, that was true. He had known the time would come when John would finally refuse to pay his debts. Peter had not expected his brother to hold out as long as he did before making him clean up his own mess.

When would it ever end with him? Had he not gathered with his cronies last night at Brooks's to play a mild game of faro only to end his evening in a Jermyn Street gaming hell? He had lost nearly two hundred pounds when all was said and done. Not for the first time in his life, he felt tired of it all and wondered why he could not have been more like his brother.

As the play ended and the final curtain fell, he heard Winifred sigh.

"You enjoyed it, yes?" he asked her.

"Most definitely. 'Tis my favorite of Shakespeare's works."

"Is it? Now, why is that?"

"I do not know, I have always liked the story ever since I was in the schoolroom."

"You see yourself as the fair Helena, perhaps?" He had meant it only as a tease, but she looked at him with such a startled expression that he knew he had guessed correctly. When she did not answer, he added, "But of course, Demetrius was a fool not to appreciate the charms of Helena from the start."

"Of course," she stammered.

"Only a fool would fail to see the strength of character in Helena. Not to mention that her statuesque beauty rivaled a goddess."

She smiled almost ruefully, then said, "Mr. Blessing, you are absurd."

He smiled in return and counted this evening as successful in his pursuit of Miss Winifred Preston.

After the play, and much bowing and scraping over the two aunts, Peter rode back with John to his townhouse in Grosvenor Square.

"So, tell me." His brother's voice split the silence inside the coach. "Winifred Preston, is she your target for marriage?"

"Egad, John, you needn't make it sound so mercenary."

"But that is exactly what it is."

His conscience pricked him, but he pushed it aside. "She is one of the ladies I am pursuing, yes."

"Do you like her?"

"What the devil does that have to do with it?"

"If you are going to spend the rest of your life with

someone, you may as well make sure you at least like the woman."

Peter had already considered this, which was why Winifred was at the top of his list of prospects. He pulled at his cravat and wiped his hands upon his knee breeches. "Yes, I like her just fine."

"Good. Make sure that you treat her with utmost respect," his brother said. "I would not like to have you upset either of the Misses Preston."

"And who made you their champion?" Peter asked sarcastically. He did not look forward to his brother's interference in this matter.

John held his hands up in defense. "What has your scruff up? I merely do not want to see either of the ladies hurt by your antics to find a wife. If Miss Winifred is as demure as Miss Melanie, then it would be a crime to trifle with her affections if you have plans to find your bride elsewhere."

"First of all, it's none of your concern," Peter said. "And secondly, Winifred is nothing at all like her sister. She is very capable of following her own wishes. She knows which way is up."

John looked as if he were about to say something else on the matter, but merely nodded, then added, "Would you care to come up for some cognac? I have just received a new shipment."

Since Peter had no other plans, he accepted his brother's offer. They drank far into the night and Peter could not remember when he and his brother had so enjoyed each other's company. They spoke of nothing in particular, but sat about like a couple of hens discussing the latest bits and scraps of gossip. John proudly displayed the new guns he had purchased for target shooting and the two settled into a comfortable evening.

It was very late by the time Peter finally rose to bid his brother goodnight. John persuaded him to stay until morning. Peter soon found himself in the room he'd had as a child, when his father had been up to Parliament. His father had always wanted his boys close to him when they were not in school or at university. Peter had not realized how fortunate he had been to have a father who actually cared about him until it had been too late and his father was dead.

He laid his head upon the pillow and drifted quickly into a deep sleep. Sometime before dawn, he was wakened by a dream. It was the dream he always had, but this time it was slightly different. He sat up, sweat dripping from his forehead as he recalled every detail. He was at his estate in Kent and he was happy. He was the kind of man he wanted to be—respected, responsible. And his children raced about him.

Thus far it was the same as it had always been. It changed when a woman, his wife, walked into the idyllic scene with a frown. Her face was fuzzy and unclear as she held a slip of paper in her hand. Peter snatched it from her only to find that it was his IOU for a debt he owed. All he owned had to be sold in order to settle the debt. He was completely ruined. He looked up into the face of his wife, and her features became solid. It was Winifred.

"Oh Winifred, is he not grand?" Melanie whispered as they sat around the dying embers of the fire in the grate of their shared sitting room.

"Who, dear?" Winifred turned the page of the novel she was reading.

"Why, Lord Blessing. Who else, silly?"

Winifred put her book down. "You favor Lord Blessing?"

"Well, I do not know quite yet, only I do know he is the most comfortable gentleman."

"Comfortable?" Winifred raised her eyebrows.

"Yes, I felt most at ease with him, and did you not notice that we chatted all evening?" Her sister reclined against the settee with a sigh.

Oh no. She could not fall in love with Peter Blessing's brother. It simply would not do. Were the two to form something lasting, it would mean that Peter Blessing would be in her life forever! It did not bear thinking about. "Mel, you hardly know the man. And besides, he is too old for you."

"He is not!" Melanie sat up straight.

"Did you not notice the gray in his hair?"

"But 'tis only on the sides by his temples and I think it makes him look quite dashing."

Winifred leaned back against the cushions on the couch and closed her eyes. This was the last thing she wanted to hear.

"Would it not be famous if we were to marry the two of them? We would be able to see each other often since we would still be in the family and all."

"Melanie, have you lost all sense in your head?" Icy cold fear lodged itself in her throat to glide down and freeze its way to her gut. "Besides, how do you know if his feelings for you are returned?"

"Of course I do not know. I only hope that they may be."

"Well, there is nothing to do for it but wait and see. But I shall not marry Peter Blessing. He is only after money."

"We shall just have to wait and see," Melanie agreed, but with a wide smile as if she knew something that Winifred did not.

Winifred hoped that Lord Blessing had not taken a liking to Melanie. But if Melanie truly did care for Lord Blessing and her affection was returned, how could she hope for anything other than Melanie's happiness? If Lord Blessing was part of that happiness, then who was she to discourage it?

Chapter Six

An uneventful week flew by and Winifred collected the calling cards she had received. She bound them with ribbon and placed them on her desk. Mr. Oliver was a regular caller as was Mr. Pratt and Lord Stanley. She also had two new callers. After a ball at Almack's, Winifred received Lord Huntley and Lord Sustane. Both gentlemen, she believed, were with pockets to let, but she had to admit that they were fairly agreeable in personality if not in age. Lord Huntley was older than her father and Lord Sustane was not far behind.

She had seen Peter at only two of the evening engagements she and Melanie had attended. He was more than attentive to them both as well as to Miss Whent. He called the day after each event, but stayed only a short while. Again, he divided his time between herself and Melanie. Of course when he sat with Winifred, he teased her on her newly acquired group of admirers and filled her head with pretty compliments.

She had asked him when they would take their morning ride, but still he had put her off. He stated that he wanted to be sure the weather was warm and dry when they went. It was nearly the end of April and the weather had greatly improved, so she expected his invitation would come soon. After their ride, she planned to cut off any further contact with him.

Melanie had not received a call from Lord Blessing, and although she would not admit to it, Winifred knew it bothered her sister. Every day when callers were announced or cards were left, Melanie looked disappointed that Lord Blessing had not been among them. He had sent a polite note after the theater, but that was all. And they had not seen him at any of the social events they attended. Winifred was relieved.

She looked up from her desk, out into the morning sunshine. It promised to be a fine day and Winifred was glad not to have to spend it indoors. She and Melanie, along with their abigail, had planned a day of shopping. She turned as Melanie entered her bedchamber.

"Are you ready to go?" her sister asked.

"Yes, in a moment."

Melanie stood next to Winifred's desk and tapped her finger absently on its top as she stared out of the window. "Perhaps a day of shopping is just what we need," she murmured, then looked down at the calling cards bound with ribbon. "Winnie, what are these?"

Winifred took them from her sister's hands and placed them in the drawer. "Nothing, just calling cards."

"Whose cards are they?"

"Why, everyone's. Well, the gentlemen that have called or left them for me at least." Winifred shut the drawer.

"Oh, let me see." Melanie opened the drawer and tried to pull them out.

"No," Winifred said quickly. "That is, you already know who they are."

"But I thought you did not want to find a husband while we were here."

"I still do not," Winifred said.

"Then why keep them?"

Melanie did not understand. How could she when all she had to do was simply enter a room to have the gentlemen turn their heads and notice her. To Winifred, these cards represented a hope that perhaps she was not so terribly plain after all. Not every man who visited her did so only to win her hand for her money. Mr. Oliver was very wealthy in his own right, but merely enjoyed her company, as he said time and again. He did not press her for anything more than friendship.

Winifred felt relaxed around Mr. Oliver. Not trembling and upset, like when Peter Blessing was near her. Actually, none of her gentlemen callers made the least impact on her nerves as Peter had. David Stanton had affected her this way, but then she had loved him and near disaster had resulted. All the more reason to cease spending time in Peter Blessing's presence, she thought. She did not wish to know him or come to love him.

"Win, you have not answered my question." Melanie's voice intruded on her thoughts.

"I just wanted to keep them, as a memory, I suppose."

"I see. And is Peter Blessing's card in that bundle?"

Winifred hesitated. She had Peter's cards and the now-pressed flowers he had given her stored separately. Like a goose, she cherished them. "I do not know for sure, I cannot remember where I put his card," she lied.

Melanie merely nodded her head with a knowing look that Winifred found quite irritating.

Winifred fetched her bonnet. "I am ready."

Bond Street hummed with a flurry of activity as ladies and gentlemen perused the various shops lining either side of the street. Winifred and Melanie entered practically every boutique, store, and mercantile to purchase new bonnets, stockings, and various accessories they found they could not bear to be without. By afternoon, they were hot, tired, and longing for a break.

"Shall we go to Gunter's for ices?" Winifred asked.

"Yes. I should like that above all things." Melanie handed the last parcel to their abigail who proceeded to place it with the other packages in the waiting carriage. They promised the coachman to send their abigail back with ices. After looking about the crowded street, Winifred steered her sister into Gunter's, the famous confectionary shop.

Once they were seated with lemon ices in hand, Winifred sighed with delight. "I tell you, my poor feet shall never recover from this excursion."

"We did not walk all that much, Winnie."

"No, but more than enough for these slippers, I am afraid." Winifred reached down to adjust the tie of her shoe and slipped it off, stretching her toes demurely beneath her gown.

She looked up and saw a gentleman with gold hair at the counter ordering ices. She sat up quickly. Peter Blessing stood not twenty feet from their table. The familiar panicky feeling stole her breath away as she stared at him hoping both that he would see her and that he would not. She turned her head aside and concentrated on her ice.

"It's Peter Blessing," Melanie announced. When Winifred only nodded as she continued to eat her lemon ice, Melanie called out to him and waved.

Winifred wished she had not looked up. Peter turned and smiled warmly at them and her insides turned to jelly. He proceeded to the table where Miss Whent was seated. She tried to feel glad, but failed miserably. She had wanted him to bother someone else with his charm which, it appeared, was exactly what he was doing. Miss Whent enjoyed Peter's attention to the extreme. Winifred cringed when she heard the lady's tinkling laugh.

She had no reason to feel such jealousy, but she did. Peter was on the hunt for a rich wife and Miss Whent had a prime dowry. It was obvious what he was about. She would simply finish her ice and try her best to ignore his presence. She was grateful that he had chosen another to court. Things were just as she wanted them.

Peter offered the ice to Miss Whent and took his seat. He nodded politely now and again as the young lady across from him rattled on about the latest style of dress she had had made by her modiste. Peter could not have been more thoroughly bored. His gaze wandered to the Preston table where Melanie and Winifred enjoyed their ices with smiles and laughs.

He let his thoughts once again ponder the dream he had had a week ago. The dream that prompted him to back off in his pursuit of Winifred Preston. In it, Winifred had been his wife, and he had failed her with his gambling. He could not decipher if the dream revealed only his guilt for pursuing Winifred to pay for his current debt or if it foretold his future.

The fact that Winifred had played a major role in the dream scared him somewhat. She fit too perfectly into the rosy bliss that was his secret desire. Trenton Manor made into a prosperous home with children and a loving wife was his innermost wish. Winifred appeared to be a piece destined to make the puzzle complete, save for his failure to her at the dream's end. He did not like the fact that Winifred, whether in the flesh or in his dreams, had made him look at himself and what he had become.

"Mr. Blessing." Miss Whent's voice broke through his musings. "Did you not hear me?"

"I'm sorry, my wits were scattered for a moment. Please, what did you say?"

"Are you are planning to attend our rout? My mama

has been planning it this age, and I made sure an invitation was sent to both you and Lord Blessing."

"Yes, I shall be there," he answered quickly. He looked at the Preston table and it appeared they had finished their ices. Winifred was standing, eager to leave. He suddenly stood as well. "Miss Whent, I see the Misses Preston. Come, let us join them."

Miss Whent sputtered genteelly but could do nothing but take his offered hand without making a scene.

"Here, give me your ice, if you are not finished," he said. "We can enjoy them at the Preston table."

"It appears that they are preparing to leave, Mr. Blessing."

He ignored her statement of the obvious and practically dragged her out of her seat. Something within him had snapped. He would not take Miss Whent to wife, not when he could barely stand the sound of her voice any longer. Money or no, debtor's prison would be infinitely better than spending a lifetime in her company. He made his decision—he would set his sights firmly upon Winifred Preston, whatever the consequences.

He soon stood before his Athena, careful not to let his admiring gaze linger for more than a moment. She looked deliciously fresh in a pale yellow muslin with her cheeks pinked by the day's sunshine. "Miss Winifred, Miss Melanie." He bowed. "May we join you?"

"We were just about to leave," Winifred said.

"There, you see," Miss Whent said to Peter. "We do not wish to keep them."

"Nonsense," Melanie said hurriedly. "I have not yet finished my ice, even though Winnie is trying to hurry me along. Please sit down and join us, do."

Peter pulled out a chair for Miss Whent and he turned to do the same for Winifred, who cast him a churlish look. He could not keep from whispering close to her ear as she sat down, "How pretty you are today."

Winifred's expression only grew more sour, and he laughed aloud.

"Why, Mr. Blessing, please do tell us what is so amusing?" Miss Whent asked.

Melanie turned her attention toward him and Winifred raised a haughty brow as she gazed expectantly at him. He was cornered by three ladies' questioning stares, as they waited for him to share his joke with them. He sat down.

"Why nothing, really." He shifted and thought quickly. "I noticed Miss Winifred's shoe ribbon is untied. I was about to inform her of the situation which brought to mind the Sefton ball where I tripped and dropped a supper plate upon the floor." He looked at Winifred and winked. "May I assist you with your shoe? I would be loath to see you fall when you leave."

He smiled when color suffused Winifred's cheeks and she looked down. The ribbon to her shoe was in fact untied.

"Thank you, but I am sure that I can manage," she said.

"She was complaining of her poor feet and the punishment our day of shopping has inflicted. Winnie is forever kicking off her slippers," Miss Melanie informed them.

"Oh my." Miss Whent looked scandalized.

Peter was sure Miss Whent had never considered kicking off her slippers anywhere other than her own bedchamber. As Winifred bent down to remedy her ribbon situation, Peter let his napkin fall below the table. "Now I've done it. I dropped my napkin. Excuse me, ladies." He nodded before ducking under the table's linen cloth. He heard Miss Whent's gasp and Miss Melanie's soft quip for him to take his time.

His head brushed against Winifred's as she studiously tied the ribbons of her shoe.

"Here, let me help you." He reached toward her foot, only to have his hand pinched.

"I will not have you tying my slippers in public, sir."

"Yes, undoing them in private would be much more pleasant," he murmured.

He heard her gasp of outrage and chuckled. He grabbed his napkin, but not before viewing her perfectly turned ankle. He sat upright before Winifred had finished her task.

"Did you find what you were looking for, Mr. Blessing?" Melanie asked with a sly smile.

He raised his napkin with a grin of confirmation. Melanie smiled in return. It was quite plain that she favored his pursuit of her sister. They sat for some time chatting amiably while Winifred tried to look bored and Miss Whent looked frustrated. He and Melanie carried the conversation.

Finally, Miss Whent rose from the table. "I had better return home, Mr. Blessing."

He stood as well. "Yes, of course. Miss Melanie, Miss Winifred, I trust I shall see you both at Miss Whent's rout this evening?"

"Yes. Until this evening, then." Melanie said.

"Until then." He bowed, then turned to offer an already out-of-sorts Miss Whent his arm to escort her home, but she had proceeded to the exit before him.

"Winifred," Melanie hissed after they had gone.

"What?"

"Why did you not talk to Peter?"

"Oh for heaven's sake." Winifred rolled her eyes. She did not know which was worse—Peter in the company of Miss Whent or his obvious enjoyment in speaking with Melanie. "I certainly did not need to say anything, you were completely capable of handling the conversation."

"Of course I had to, since you sat like a bump on a log." Melanie stood as it was time they took their leave. "Sometimes, I wonder why he bothers with you," she mumbled.

But Winifred heard her sister. She had been trying to make Peter Blessing go away, but instead, he merely turned his attentions to Melanie after flirting scandalously with her. It only made matters worse knowing she would see Mr. Blessing again this evening.

Winifred entered the Whent townhouse accompanied by her aunts and sister. The large number of people jammed into the stately townhouse was almost unbearable and the evening was as yet young.

"Quite a crush, is it not?" Melanie said.

"Quite." Winifred looked about for a place to sit once they were in the upper floor's drawing room. She saw no good reason for holding such an event where the more guests were crowded, the more fashionable the party. Routs typically were not considered a success unless far more people than could comfortably fit into your home, attended. She shook her head at the silliness of society as she searched for a place to hide. She spotted a chair near an opened window and smiled at her good luck. She and Melanie could take turns sitting upon it. Their aunts were on their own.

"Come." Winifred took hold of Melanie's hand and made her way through the throng of people. She bumped into various ladies and gentlemen along the way, excusing and pardoning herself more than she cared to count.

Once she arrived at her goal, she sank into the chair with a flourish and fanned herself. "I dare say 'tis hot enough to bake a cake."

"Yes, but we must not stay hidden for long. We must mingle, Win. 'Tis the point of these gatherings."

"How can one possibly carry on a conversation over this din?" The noise grew in swells due to chatter from various groupings of people coming from every direction.

"I believe there may be musicians that will play, and that should solve some of the problem. The music shall make a good background for the hum of conversation." Melanie stood on tiptoe as she looked about.

"For whom do you search?" Winifred asked her sister.

"No one in particular."

Winifred watched as Melanie's countenance soon changed into a glow of happiness. She turned her gaze to discover the reason for her sister's glee and found it in the form of two gentlemen. Peter Blessing and his brother stood not too far away from them, speaking with Lord Stanley.

Almost as if sensing her gaze on him, Peter turned to look directly at Winifred. He smiled and excused himself from Lord Stanley. She could not take her eyes off of him as he walked toward her, his look intent upon hers. He was a man born to wear evening dress, as the black of his jacket and ivory of his knee-breeches and waistcoat only enhanced his golden hair and chocolate-brown eyes.

When he reached her, he bowed to Melanie, then bowed to her. "Good evening, Miss Winifred."

"Mr. Blessing."

"And why are you sitting here, so far away from everyone?"

"It is too hot, and this was the only chair near a window."

"They have a lovely balcony. Perhaps a stroll in the night air will cool you," he offered.

Winifred looked at Melanie.

"Yes, do take a turn upon the balcony, Win, I will be fine here," she said.

"But you must join us," Peter said to Melanie.

When she looked ready to refuse, Winifred hurriedly agreed. She did not wish to be alone with Peter Blessing if she did not need to be.

"Come."

Winifred reluctantly took his right arm, leaving Melanie to take his left.

They wove their way through the crowd, occasionally stopping to say their hellos to acquaintances. Miss Whent approached them and Peter cleverly dodged her by slipping behind a large matron and then ducking down until they reached the balcony.

Laughing, Melanie finally said, "Peter, you have considerable pluck."

"Nay, I am a coward. I have been running from her ever since I arrived."

"You have taken a dislike of Miss Whent?" Winifred whispered. "What has she done to earn your scorn?"

"Oh no." He shook his finger playfully at her. "I shall not tell you that or else you will no doubt try the same in an attempt to be rid of me."

Winifred made a face at him and turned to lean over the balcony's edge to watch the carriages continue to arrive below. She paid no heed to the silly conversation between Peter and Melanie about Miss Whent's obvious distaste at having to sit with them at Gunter's earlier in the afternoon.

"Peter," Lord Blessing called as he walked out onto the balcony. He noticed Melanie and his expression softened. "Oh, hello."

"Lord Blessing, good evening," Melanie said.

"John, pray join us." Peter motioned with his hand for him to come closer to them.

Winifred turned to watch her sister's reaction to the appearance of Lord Blessing. A pink blush spread over her sister's cheeks as she smiled her welcome.

"Well, yes, of course. Too dashed warm in there." Lord Blessing's color seemed a bit heightened as he gazed at Melanie.

Winifred knew then that Lord Blessing had tender feelings toward her sister and she nearly rolled her eyes. She chided herself as being cruel, but her sister was truly a living Hermia and the Blessing brothers were becoming her Lysander and Demetrius.

Of course, Peter did not display the characteristics of Demetrius. He divided his attentions between Melanie and herself. He chose to flirt outrageously with her, but Winifred could not be certain that Peter did not also tease Melanie in such a fashion. And of course, Winifred could not claim herself in love with Peter as Helena was with Demetrius.

Just give it time, her unruly heart seemed to whisper in her mind. Flustered at such an unbidden thought, she turned her attention back to the guests still arriving below.

"What has so captivated your interest, my fair Athena?" Peter leaned close next to her.

"I do not believe there is any more room for the guests arriving below."

The sound of his soft laughter caressed her ears. "Miss Whent will be in alt to have such a crush at her rout," he said.

"Yes."

"Would you like to make our way to the refreshment table? I know how fond you are of food," he teased.

She felt her cheeks redden. She glanced over at Melanie, who looked quite content to be in conversation with

Lord Blessing, and nodded to Peter. "To the refreshment table," she said with forced gusto.

"You promise not to trip me this time?"

"I suppose, if I must." She smiled as she took his offered arm.

The crowd was thick and it took some time to reach the food tables, which were across the room opposite the balcony. Since they were unable to walk side by side, Peter had grasped her hand so they would not become separated. Winifred tried not to dwell on the warmth of his hand, nor the firmness of it. Even through the silk of her gloves she felt the heat as his bare fingers threaded securely through her own.

They made it to the refreshment table and literally bumped into Mr. Oliver.

"Miss Winifred," Mr. Oliver said, then added with a look of disgust, "oh, and Mr. Blessing, too. How do you do?"

Winifred tried to pull her hand out of Peter's, but he merely held on a moment longer than necessary, then pulled her hand firmly into place around the crook of his elbow.

Mr. Oliver did not mistake the possessive gesture, and raised a brow toward Winifred. She awkwardly pulled her hand away, but it was too late. Mr. Oliver looked offended.

"Oh, hey! Peter, good fellow." A heavy-set gentleman standing near Mr. Oliver turned and slapped Peter on the shoulder. "Tell me something, what is this nonsense I hear about your brother coming to the defense of some yokels trying to stir up another Luddite riot?"

"I did not hear of it," Peter stated.

"I cannot blame these fellows really," Mr. Oliver started with a bored drawl. "Had not the merchant class gotten these ideas of grandeur into their heads to invent these blasted machines that rob a poor man of his job and wages, there would have been no cause for riots."

"Why that is positively archaic thinking, Mr. Olivier," Winifred interjected. "Progress is what makes a civilization grow and stretch. I would think that you of all people, returning from India, would think thus." At his look of confusion, Winifred blundered on, "My father backed one of the manufacturers who made spinning machines automatic. He says these machines have in fact bettered the lot of laborers. It has made the cotton mills run that much smoother and become more profitable, hence bettering the wages."

The gentlemen stared at her as if she had grown a second head. Mr. Oliver was clearly displeased with her rebuttal to his statement in front of other men. She refused to cower and looked each one of them in the eye despite the uncomfortable silence.

"Yes, well, your father is from the merchant class, is he not?" Mr. Oliver asked with a sneer.

Winifred was shocked at his rudeness. That he, whom she had called friend, would try to insult her was beyond fair. If he thought he could shame her regarding her father's background in trade, then he was sadly mistaken. She lifted her head higher. "That is correct, Mr. Oliver. My father was the son of a very successful cotton mill owner."

She took a deep breath, ready to do further battle, when Peter interjected, "Yes, and your father was a genius for knowing where the future of textiles lay. I say, Oliver, can't you stomach a good argument from a lady?"

"But I . . ." Mr. Oliver stuttered.

"Tried to put her firmly in her place," Peter finished for him.

The heavy-set gentleman laughed and his belly jiggled. He slapped Peter on the shoulder again. "Aye, she does have a good point there, Oliver. I say, Miss Preston, you have more in your noggin than just the pretty trappings of feminine interests. You do your father proud, gel."

"Thank you, sir."

"Miss Winifred and I were on our way to the punch, Sir Giles," Peter informed the heavy man. "Can we fetch a cup for you?" Winifred noticed that he had left out Mr. Oliver from the invitation.

"Lord no, boy, I'll be having brandy with Lord Whent. I bid you good evening." Sir Giles tottered away, leaving a disgruntled Mr. Oliver, who gave them both a look of disgust before walking away.

"I'm sorry, Athena, but I think you've just lost one of your admirers."

Winifred was still a little stunned. She had considered Mr. Oliver a good friend, and yet the moment she spoke of economic matters, he tried to insult her for speaking her mind. "No great loss, I suppose, Mr. Blessing." She turned toward him with a grateful smile for coming to her defense.

"You have again spoken the truth. Beauty and brains. I am impressed. Now, let us get some punch."

"Mr. Blessing." Winifred placed her hand upon his sleeve.

"Yes?"

"I fear I must thank you."

"There is nothing to thank me for. Oliver is a dolt and he tried to insult you. And I happen to agree with you and your father." He captured her gaze with the warmth of his brown eyes. "May I ask you something?"

"Of course."

"I am more than just curious, I am quite interested to know. Is that how your father made the infamous Preston fortune—by financing a manufacturer's endeavor?"

"Yes. It is quite a romantic story, really. My father met and fell in love with my mother. She was the daughter of a duke, but my father was beneath her in both social and financial status. My father had inherited mills from his father which he had been running at a fine profit. But in order to win my mother's hand and her family's approval, my father entered a business venture with a Scotsman, who took Mr. Crompton's spinning invention and made it automatic. My father gained a percentage of every machine sold and within no time, he was a very rich man."

"Too rich for your mother's family to refuse his offer?"

"Yes."

"Your father must have loved your mother very deeply to have risked so much for her. He could have just as easily failed."

"He could have. I like to think that my mother would have run away and married him anyway," Winifred said.

"Miss Winifred, I had no idea that you held such romantic fancies." He smiled his boyish grin.

"True love, sir, is worth more than money, or should be."

"My proud Athena, how easily you say that. Would you think the same if your funds were ever depleted?"

"But they shan't be. I have no intention of delivering my father's hard work into the hands of any man who would lose it." She gave him a pointed look and was not as satisfied as she would have liked when she saw him stiffen.

"And how will you safeguard yourself against such a thing?" he asked.

"That is quite simple. I come into control of my funds at the age of twenty-five. I shall remain unwed until then, at least."

Peter burst out laughing.

"I do not see what you find so amusing," she said.

"I am sorry, but my dear, how do you expect to rule your heart so? Should you find your true love before this time, will you have the poor man wait?"

When she did not answer, he lifted her chin with his finger so she had to look him in the eyes as he spoke ever so softly to her. "What if you have already met this man and are destined to love him, what then, Athena?"

She stared into his molten chocolate-colored eyes and nearly drowned in their sweet depths. When she did dare speak, her voice was low and ragged. "I do not believe that has happened sir, as I have yet to meet a man worthy of my love."

He let his hand drop from her and he actually took a step back. She had intended it to be an insult and she found no satisfaction in seeing the barb hit its mark.

"But until then," she added, "I shall guard my heart."

"Then guard it well, my dear, because I will try my best to capture it." He looked serious as he said the words, and she could hardly believe such a solemn statement had been uttered by him. Then he gave her such a charming grin that her insides became unsettled. "Let us get our punch," he said.

She followed him, but she felt weak inside. Something

had happened between them and she was not sure what it was. Her strong words to Mr. Oliver did not phase Peter in the least, he rather seemed to admire her for them. And now he knew about her father and his love for her mother and how much Winifred held that dear.

Her inheritance was a representation of that love. It was something to be protected. And if Aunt Augusta's words about Mr. Blessing's time spent playing cards were true, then he was the type of man who could easily lose what her father had worked so hard to provide. She became chilled at the thought of the threat he posed to not only her fortune, but her heart.

Melanie had been correct about one thing: Peter was nothing like David Stanton. He was far more dangerous.

Peter handed a cup of punch to Winifred and tried to quell his conscience. She deserved far better than him. If he were a good man, instead of the worthless good-for-nothing he knew himself to be, he would walk away from Miss Winifred Preston and never look back. But he would not. Not now.

He did not have the time to cultivate another marriage prospect. Miss Whent was out of the picture; he would not consider marrying her. He feared she would make his life a living hell, which was no more than what he deserved.

He straightened just in time to see his brother with Melanie upon his arm, heading for the refreshment table as well. He forced a smile upon his face and pushed his dreary thoughts aside.

"Miss Melanie, John." Peter nodded. "May I pour each of you some punch?"

"Yes, please do," Melanie said, and she reached out her hand.

John spoke with Winifred so Peter and Melanie perused the table laden with delectable tarts and watercress sandwiches.

Melanie drew closer to him. "How are you progressing with Winnie?" she whispered.

"Fine, and you with John?"

She looked surprised, then merely smiled. She leaned closer still. "I have a proposition to make to you, Peter."

He could not help but grin. "I do so love propositions."

She smacked his knuckles with her fan, then said, "I shall do all that I can to aid you in your pursuit of Winifred, but you must do me a favor in return."

He knew what she was about to ask. He was no fool. He had noticed how Melanie lit up from within when she looked upon John, but he wanted to hear her ask it, to see just how she would word it. She had more pluck than he had ever given her credit for.

"I should like you to help me capture your brother's notice," she whispered.

"Oh, I think you have already done that," Peter said.

"But he has not called, and just this evening upon the balcony, he was most reserved. I surely cannot chase the man."

"Heavens no," he said in mock horror. "I think John could use a little feminine chasing, my dear."

"Peter, you are no help at all."

Again, he received a rap upon his hand with the fan. "Egad, please do not beat me within an inch of my life with that thing. Miss Melanie, I shall be honored to do everything in my power to bring the two of you together as often as possible. But I shall leave the magic of luring him to you and your loveliness."

"Thank you, Peter, truly."

"Thank him for what?" Winifred asked when she and John rejoined them.

"Why, for the punch of course," Miss Melanie said. She handed a cup to John. "Lord Blessing, this one is for you."

John took the cup and Peter noticed that his brother's fingers brushed Melanie's in the process. She did not give up the cup too fast, thus allowing the touching to linger. And he thought he had moves!

He exchanged a knowing smile with Melanie and nearly laughed at the gleam in her eye. He turned his attention back to Winifred. No, he would not walk away from Miss Winifred Preston. In fact, he would exact the penalty ride from her just to see her again.

Chapter Seven

Winifred woke with a start. The sun's rays peeked over the eastern horizon allowing pale pinkish light to stream into her window. She sat up and reached to her bedstand for the note from Peter that she had found last night in her reticule. He wanted to call upon her this morning to go for their ride in Hyde Park. His note read that he would provide her with a horse and that he would call at nine o'clock.

She stretched her arms above her head and then lay back on her bed with a sigh. She had well over two hours before he would arrive. She pondered her current situation.

She could not help but like Peter Blessing and she feared that she looked forward to his company far too much. This outing would release her from any promise or obligation to him and if she used her head, she should sever their relationship and ask him to discontinue seeking her out. An ache at the thought of no longer seeing him lodged itself in the center of her chest. It was the only way, she told herself.

For all his charm and handsomeness, there was something deeper in him that drew her. She could not explain what it was. He seemed to show her glimpses of the real Peter Blessing, not just the rakish gambler and ladies' man, but a restless soul longing for something. She shook her head to clear such fanciful thoughts. She had to end it now, while she still could.

She sat up again and opened the drawer of her bedstand. Safely tucked inside a book of the Psalms, lay the pressed flowers and calling cards from Peter. She pulled out the book and opened it. Unbinding the ribbon, she added the note from her reticule, then gently tied the bundle back together and placed the book into the drawer for safekeeping. She would have these small mementos to look back on and be glad of her escape from him.

Once dressed in a riding habit of azure blue, she sat at the breakfast table with a strong cup of coffee and a muffin and perused the day's copy of the *Morning Post*. She tried to focus on the various articles and gossip columns but could not. She had an hour yet to wait. She rehearsed the speech that she planned to give Peter. She had to own that she was nervous.

When the butler finally announced Peter's arrival, Winifred thought she would lose her courage. She stood, rather weak in the knees, and asked that he be shown to the breakfast parlor. Melanie was still abed, but Aunt Winifred had since joined her and was sipping chocolate.

When Peter entered the room, it seemed as though he had brought the sun inside with him. His golden hair shone and his smile was easy and bright.

"Good morning ladies." He bowed.

"Why, Mr. Blessing," Aunt Winifred said. "You are here early to take my niece for a ride in the park, I am told."

"Yes, ma'am. I do hope that I have your permission," he said.

"You do." Aunt Winifred nodded.

Winifred merely stared at him. He was so thoroughly handsome and his boyish charm seemed to surround him like a cloak, it was so tangible. What was truly underneath it?

"Miss Winifred, are you ready?" he asked.

Brought out of her stupor, she nodded, then bent to kiss her aunt good-bye. "We shall not be gone overlong."

"Enjoy the ride, dear. Mr. Blessing, I shall expect you back no later than one hour."

"Yes ma'am." Peter offered Winifred his arm and she took it after only a slight hesitation. He noticed, however, and raised his brow as if to question what was wrong.

She merely smiled at him. She would wait and tell him her request later, after their ride.

Once outside, Winifred admired the prime bit of horseflesh he had brought for her to ride. The horse was a large mare with a dappled gray coat. "She is beautiful," Winifred said. "What is her name?"

"Helen of Troy."

"Truly?" Winifred looked at him to see if he was joking.

"Yes, a rather odd name, but she's a lovely girl and lives up to her beauty in manners as well as appearance. She has much spirit, but she is as well trained as they come, so she will obey your every command."

"Where did you get her?" Winifred stroked the horse's nose.

"Actually, I won her," Peter said. He offered his cupped hands as a step for Winifred to mount the mare.

"Won her?" she asked. She placed her foot into Peter's hands and grabbed hold of the reins and saddle. She hoisted herself up, as at the same time Peter gave her a push. She sat firmly in the side-saddle and looked down at him. "How did you win her?"

"A wager with Lord Stanley. He lost."

"My goodness." She patted the mare's neck. "What on earth would make a man wager such a fine animal?"

" 'Twas on the outcome of a race. We were both in our cups at the time, but he wagered Helen of Troy and I won."

"And what would you have had to give up if you had lost?"

He stopped and thought before mounting his own fine gelding. "I honestly do not remember."

"But why wager at all?" she asked.

He did not answer straightaway, but then finally said, "Winifred, I must say that there is a certain amount of thrill involved."

"But how thrilling can it be when you lose?"

"My wise Athena, as always, you have a point. Shall we?" He gestured with his arm toward the park which lay directly across from her aunts' townhouse.

Winifred clicked her reins and Helen of Troy danced her way across the street to the grass of Hyde Park. She was a sweet goer, but Winifred kept the mare at a sedate pace until the sandy track of Rotten Row was in sight. "Shall we race, Mr. Blessing?" she asked.

Peter smiled fully at her and agreed. "To the track and once around. But first, let me introduce to you the thrill of the wager, my dear Athena. Shall we decide here and now upon the winner's prize?"

"What shall we wager then, Mr. Blessing?" she asked.

"A kiss," Peter announced. "A kiss bestowed upon the winner by the loser anywhere the winner chooses."

Excitement seemed to skitter its way down her spine, and Winifred understood the type of thrill he spoke of. She needed to win so that she did not have to give him a prize that would no doubt cost her dearly. "Agreed."

She lightly jabbed the horse's side with her boot and Helen of Troy jumped at the chance to stretch her long legs into a canter. She looked back to see that Peter had taken little time to coax his dark chestnut to follow in pursuit. In no time he was gaining on Helen of Troy.

Winifred smiled with abandon at the warm spring sunshine on her face. She urged the mare faster to a full gallop and she cried out with pure pleasure. She looked back, to see that Peter's gelding was nearly beside her. She leaned further in the saddle to let Helen of Troy race at full speed. The spunky mare was encouraged by the gelding that gained on her and, with a sudden burst of energy, Helen of Troy dashed faster toward the curve of Rotten Row's track.

Winifred leaned as Helen of Troy took the curve at a lightning pace. Years of riding allowed her the skill to remain in the saddle as the horse whipped around the bend of the track and blocked Peter and his chestnut from overtaking them. At the straightaway, Helen of Troy was a full neck length ahead of Peter's gelding.

Winifred felt as if she were flying. The mare's hoofs beat into the ground with a rhythm that echoed in Winifred's ears and pounded through her body. They moved as one. Human and horseflesh merged into one force and one mind. Their only wish—to win.

When Winifred rounded the second curve, she looked

back. Peter was not far behind, and the look of serious concentration on his face proved that he was as intent upon winning as she. The gelding's nose was nearly past Helen of Troy's midsection.

"Come on, Helen, my girl, now is the time to give it your all," Winifred yelled into the wind.

The mare seemed to understand her words and she pulled ahead, out of the gelding's range again, and they sped into victory. Winifred slowed the horse to a trot and turned the mare around toward Peter. "I believe I have won our wager, sir," Winifred said with genuine glee.

He trotted up alongside the mare. "You have, and as the loser of our race, I owe you a kiss. I do hope you have an interesting place upon your person where I may bestow it."

Winifred had the grace to blush. "You will be sorely disappointed, I am afraid. I will choose only a proper place, sir."

"Then I shall endeavor to make what is most proper seem interesting." He grinned at her. "You ride very well."

"Thank you. I have been doing so since I was a small girl." She slowed the mare to a walk.

"It shows. This gelding is supposed to be the faster of the two, but you proved me wrong on that score. Helen of Troy obviously responds to you. You move together with total grace. Had I not been trying so hard to win, I would have watched you more."

Winifred's insides were a jumble of emotions. She had completely enjoyed racing against Peter, but she had to admit to being more pleased by his reaction to her win. He was not surly, nor did he blame his loss on some mishap or bad luck. He had actually given her skill the credit for her win. She smiled. They walked the horses to the farthest corner of the park.

"Why do you gamble?" Winifred asked.

A shadow crossed his features but he did not try to charm, he merely looked her straight in the eye and said, "It is the only thing I do well."

"Did you not have other occupations to try?"

"My sweet Athena, I have tried many things and failed, to both my father's and my brother's utter disappointment. Besides, there is the thrill of the game involved. As I said before, I am a scoundrel."

Winifred noted the sad wistfulness behind the gallic shrug and charming grin. "And what if you found something equally thrilling, would you stop?"

His charming facade was firmly back in place this time when he said, "For your kiss, I would gladly do anything."

She laughed, but still she wondered. Could he stop if he wanted to?

She looked up to notice that Peter had led them to a large tree. The huge canopy of leaves shielded them completely from the sun. He slipped off his gelding, and let the horse munch at the grass. When he reached up to her, she slid off the mare and let his hands grasp her waist to guide her to the ground. She stood still when he brought her close to him. She gazed up into his eyes and noticed that the corners crinkled as he smiled down at her, his hands still resting upon her waist.

"You have to choose a place for my kiss, Athena, and do choose wisely." His voice was a mere whisper in the wind.

Her mind reeled at the sensation of being so close to him. The questions raging in her mind about his gambling vanished as if they were nothing but a puff of smoke. His hands burned through the wool of her habit and scorched her skin. He was leaning toward her as though he planned to bestow his kiss upon her lips. Instinctively, she licked them and swallowed hard.

"Wait," she cried, and put her hand up to shield her mouth. "I have to choose where you will kiss me."

"Yes, you do." His eyes darkened.

She feared that if she stared at him any longer, she would let him kiss her wherever he wished, and that simply would not do. She backed away from him and raised her hand in front of her. "You did say to choose wisely, and so I have. You may kiss my hand, sir."

"Athena, you have faltered in your wisdom, for I can kiss your hand just about any time. I shall simply have to work hard to make this kiss memorable to you and hopefully the best you have ever received."

Winifred felt a sudden fear at his words, but it was magnified tenfold when he grasped her hand and tenderly pulled the glove off slowly, one finger at a time. Once divested of her glove, Peter cradled her hand between both of his own and raised it to his lips.

As his mouth touched her bare skin, he looked up into her eyes and did not look away. She thought she would swoon. He dragged his lips across the back of her hand to turn and press sweet kisses upon her palm. He teased her with the tip of his tongue, all the while staring directly into her eyes. The heat that emanated from his gaze made her weak and she feared that her knees would buckle.

Peter continued to torture her poor hand. He bit his way to the base of her thumb and tasted her skin. It was evidently not enough for him as he ran his tongue along the swell of flesh there until he nipped the tip of her thumb, then suckled it fully.

A moan escaped from her and she closed her eyes. Her insides were pure fire and the heat threatened to consume her at the very center of her being.

"Sweet Athena," he whispered raggedly.

Winifred opened her eyes and suddenly pulled away from him. She stumbled in her steps and leaned against the tree's trunk for support. Her breath came in deep gasps and she held up her hand to keep him from coming closer. "Thank you, Mr. Blessing," she breathed. "That was indeed quite a kiss."

"Peter," he whispered.

"What?"

"Call me Peter." He stood close to her but did not try to touch her. She noticed then that his breathing was not nearly steady either.

"Peter." Even his name sounded sultry to her ears. She had to gain her composure, fast. "I must speak to you."

"You are speaking to me." He smiled at her and she felt almost light-headed.

This was absurd, she scolded herself. "May we sit down, a moment."

"Whatever you wish," he said. He sat down once she was seated and waited.

"Well, that is what I need to speak to you about." She tried to remember the speech she had planned to deliver, but found that her wits had scattered. She looked at him and he stared at her with an expression of almost surprised awe. "What is it?" she blurted.

"What?" he said.

"Why are you looking at me like that?" she huffed.

"How," he demanded, sounding almost defensive, "am I looking at you?"

"I do not know, almost as if you are seeing me for the first time."

"Perhaps I am," he said, then looked away. "I had no idea."

She had barely heard him, but asked, "No idea about what?"

He looked her straight in the eye and said, "You, my dear, are a passionate woman."

She felt her cheeks redden and looked away. "Mr. Blessing, may we please discuss something else. We need to speak on the matter of our, ah, acquaintance."

"I am listening."

She could barely look at him and everything in her body and soul cried out to her to halt and forget about what she had planned to say to him. But her mind forced herself to forge ahead on its own, giving words to her voice. "I would like you to stop calling on me."

"I beg your pardon?"

"I no longer wish to, that is to say, I do not wish to see you anymore."

"Why? If I have frightened you, I am indeed sorry."

"That is not the reason."

"Then what is?" His voice sounded alarmed.

"We both know what it is," she said.

"Then explain it to me." Now his voice sounded angry.

"I will not." She stood up and cast a glance at the watch pinned to her habit. "We are late, Mr. Blessing. It is time to go."

He scrambled to his feet and grabbed hold of her arm, and faced her. "Why? You want me and I want you. Why can we not continue and see where our desire takes us?"

She shook off his touch and cried, "Because I cannot go there, not with you! All that you truly want is my money, not me! 'Tis all anyone has ever wanted, and I'll not be destroyed because of it."

She stomped off toward Helen of Troy and without any assistance she climbed into the saddle while Peter stood as if he had been slapped. It was true—at least it had been true when he first sought her out, but now it was different. He was shocked at the longing he still felt for her. It had taken all his willpower not to take her mouth and feast upon the passion that she held back from him with iron control.

What would she be like if she let go and gave in to her desire? All Peter knew was that more than even the fortune she promised, he wanted to find out. But he could not, he could not use seduction and have any hope of winning her hand. It would not work, it had not worked. Time was running out, and he did not want anyone else as he wanted Winifred Preston.

She turned the mare around to face him and she looked close to tears, by Jove. He could not press her. He breathed in and forced the anger that swelled within him down. He mounted the gelding and without a word, followed her back to Mayfair.

At her aunts' townhouse, Peter reined in his horse and dismounted. He turned to Winifred and reached up to help her down. She would not look into his eyes, but did not refuse his aid. A drop of water splashed upon his glove and he knew they were her tears.

He cursed.

She looked at him then, and he was appalled to see another tear ready to fall from her beautiful eyes. He helped her to dismount and gently he cupped her chin.

"Please, Athena, don't," was all he could manage, and he wiped her tear away with his fingertips.

She tried to smile at him, and he wondered if he could possibly feel more worthless. What was he doing to her? What had he become that he could reduce a fair maid to tears? Had he any decency, he would leave her alone.

"My aunt is waiting," she said. She plastered a false smile upon her face and wiped the remaining moisture from her eyes with the back of her hand.

His proud Athena. Did she regret his motives for pursuing her as much as he? It was not possible. At that moment, he swore he would have given anything to be the kind of man worthy of her hand. Was it too late for him to change his ways? He had never before tried.

He followed her into the entry and gave his hat to the butler. He had some apologizing to do to the aunt, at least. He followed her up the stairs to the drawing room, where both aunts and Melanie were seated.

"Mr. Blessing." Melanie smiled as she got up to offer him her hand.

He bowed over it and straightened. "A moment please, Miss Melanie." He turned to Lady Winifred and Lady Augusta. "Madams, I humbly beg your forgiveness in returning your niece late."

"Oh, bother," Miss Melanie interrupted. " 'Tis only a few minutes."

"Even so, Melanie, keep quiet if you please." Lady Winifred raised her gaze from the needlework to look daggers at him. "Thank you for your apology, sir. I trust this shall not happen again."

"Of course not," he replied. He knew he had been dismissed when Lady Winifred returned to her needlework and Lady Augusta nodded politely.

"I must change," Winifred said. "Mr. Blessing, thank you for the ride and for providing such a wonderful mount."

She looked tense, so he did not keep her. The last thing he needed right now was to have her break down into tears in front of her dragon aunts. He would not be allowed to set foot near her again, no doubt. And he wanted to be near her. His arms positively ached to take her into an embrace and soothe her as he had done in the phaeton.

"Miss Winifred, you are most welcome. The honor was mine." He bowed stiffly and watched her go.

"Come, I shall see you out," Melanie said, and took him by the arm to lead him. When they were out of the aunts' hearing, she turned to him. "How did you do?"

"Not well, I am afraid."

"What happened?" she asked.

"Winifred asked me to stop calling on her. She wants nothing more to do with me."

"But why?" She suddenly turned a fierce look upon him. "Have you done something to upset my sister, sir?"

"No, Miss Melanie, no. I've done nothing but be my worthless self." He laughed when he saw the look of pity in her eyes. "Cheer up, I shall not quit, even though today I go home with my tail between my legs."

"Good for you." She clapped her hands demurely. "What do you plan to do?"

"I do not know." He had no idea how he should approach Winifred now. He looked up at Melanie and had to ask her, "Why do you favor my pursuit of Winifred?"

"Because I think you are a good sort of man. My sister needs someone to cherish her for who she is. I believe you will do that."

"How can you be so sure of what sort of man I am?"

"I am an excellent judge of character. And besides, I think Winifred truly cares for you. She is simply scared of being hurt again."

"Again?"

"That is not for me to discuss," she said.

He reeled at her admission of Winifred's feelings for him. He also could not fathom why she would consider him good for Winifred. It made no sense to him, other than that Melanie Preston was a kind young lady who seemed to give him the benefit of doubting his motives. "Are you not bothered by my lack of wealth?" he asked.

"Oh pooh. You are no fortune hunter, even if you do need to marry money. You truly care for my sister. That is what is important to me."

Peter smiled at Melanie as she handed him his hat. He dared not contradict her, as he needed her help in furthering his position with Winifred. But the thought that perhaps he did care for Winifred Preston was not an unwelcome one.

She gave him a reassuring squeeze, then added, "Call on me, Mr. Blessing, and let us see if we cannot get Winnie to join us."

"I will." He bowed over her hand before he took his leave, and added, "And next time, I will bring John with me." Even if he had to bind him and drag him.

Winifred watched from the hallway above and nearly choked. She did not hear the words between them, but Peter had obviously turned his charm on Melanie. A tear worked its way down her cheek and she angrily brushed it aside. It mattered not, she thought. She did not care whom he chose to flirt with or pursue as long as he stayed away from her.

She slid down the wall to sit upon the floor and another tear ran down her face. That was not true, not true at all. She did not want Melanie to flounder into his clutches. Besides, Melanie was enthralled with Lord Blessing, not Peter. And she did not want Peter to spoil any chances Melanie had with his brother by luring her away from him. She had to keep her eye on Melanie and Peter. And that would be very hard indeed, since she had hoped that she would not have to endure his company any longer."

Peter sat at his favorite table in Brooks's and ordered another brandy. He was not sure what to do or how to proceed with Miss Winifred Preston. He did not like the idea that she had possibly given her heart away before only to have it broken.

What had Melanie said, that she was afraid of being hurt again? The idea of Winifred Preston hurting did not sit well with him. What was it about her that made him long to be better than he was?

The memory of her response to his kiss flooded his brain and heated his loins. The fact that he could reduce her to moans of ecstasy just by kissing her hand proved to him that she smoldered with passion that waited only to be unleashed.

Surely, she felt something for him, else why would she cry after telling him to cease courting her? But she was afraid. Afraid that he would lose the inheritance that she held as some love pledge between her parents. And she was afraid to let her heart be broken by him.

Somehow, he had to find a way not to hurt her. She had openly admitted to believing that true love was more important than money. The key to winning her hand was to make her fall in love with him. But how? She had to be with him to fall in love with him.

He took another sip to wash away the bitter taste that had settled in his mouth. Which meant that he had to give her something to fall in love with. He had played the charming rake for so long, he worried that there was nothing left worth loving inside of him.

Lord Stanley stopped by his table and asked him to join a few men for a game of faro. The stakes were not high, but even so, Peter declined. He had more important matters to deal with. He needed help and the only person he knew to be completely deserving of a woman's love was John.

"Sorry, Stanley, old fellow, but I have to pay a visit to my brother," Peter said as he stood.

"How is the old chap? Still pining away for his lost wife?"

Peter had never considered his brother in this light before. "Actually, I believe he may be getting past his loss." He had always kept himself from thinking about Anne and how much John must miss her. Thinking of her only made him feel miserable. He wondered, had he not coaxed her out into the rain, would she have suffered her fatal infection? John had never blamed him. He did not have to. Peter did enough of that for himself.

"Give Lord Blessing my regards, would you?" Lord Stanley asked.

"I will." Peter left his club with a mission.

* * *

"What kind of help do you need?" John asked.

Peter paced the drawing room floor. It was not so easy putting into words what he had considered at dinner.

"If it's money, Peter, you know where I stand."

"No, it is nothing like that."

"Then what? Spit it out before you wear a hole in my carpet."

"I need to know how to make a woman fall in love with me." Peter stopped to stand near the fire.

"By George, what would I know of the subject? I have not had near the encounters you have. Why are you asking me?"

"Because you were married once. How did you make Anne fall in love with you?"

John closed his eyes briefly and Peter knew that just the sound of her name caused his brother pain. But when John recovered his composure he said, "You have already made your first mistake."

"What is that?"

"You cannot make a woman fall in love with you." John poured his brother a cup of tea and offered it to him. "Is it Winifred Preston that you are trying to persuade? I did not think you cared about a love match."

"I don't," he answered quickly. "That is to say, I don't have to love her. But I am afraid I cannot even think of being accepted if I ask her to marry me unless she is in love with me."

"And you are determined to marry Miss Winifred?"

"Yes. Blast it! John, I am running out of time here. The first of May is tomorrow and I'm no closer to an offer than I was when I first met her."

"Oh, by the looks of it, you appear to be seducing her quite nicely." His brother smirked.

"That's the problem of it; I can't just seduce her into an offer. She won't stand for it. The more I press her physically, the more she backs away."

"Indeed." John put his hand over his mouth to hide his mirth.

"It's not funny. I'm in a real coil."

"The infamous Peter Blessing, charmer of women, lover to Lady Dunstan no less, is against a wall of brick in the form of a maid of only eighteen summers?"

"Nineteen."

"Even so." His brother continued to laugh.

"I am glad you find this amusing."

"Little brother, just be yourself. I have seen how the fair Miss Winifred looks at you. You are farther along than you think."

"Not so far. She has asked that I stop calling upon her," Peter said.

"Did she now?"

Peter did not offer a response. He remained deep in thought until finally he asked, "What about Melanie?"

"What about her?"

Peter detected a note of concern in his brother's voice. "You find her to be pleasant company, do you not?"

"I do," John said.

"Would you mind accompanying me to call upon her?"

"Why, what are you trying to do? I shall not let you use Miss Melanie to make her sister jealous. 'Tis a cruel thing to do."

"Even I wouldn't stoop that low. But I need you to go with me. If the three of us were to plan something, no doubt Winifred would concede to go along with us."

"Plan what?"

"I don't know. A picnic or some such thing."

"Where?"

"John, for the love of all that's holy, you act as if you are afraid to be in Melanie's presence."

"I am not." This time John stood and walked over to stand in front of the fire. Peter had never seen his brother so defensive where a lady was concerned.

"Where would we go?" John asked.

"I thought Trenton Manor might be a good place. It is not too far."

"Your estate? You have not been there in an age, are you sure you know the way?"

"Stop, you are killing me with your humor," Peter said dryly.

"All right, I will go on this picnic. When is it to be?"

"That I do not know. We have to call upon the Misses Preston together and find out their immediate plans. Shall we call tomorrow afternoon?"

"Oh, I forgot to tell you. We have received an invitation to the Fitzhugh residence for a musical the day after tomorrow. We can speak to them then," John said.

"I did not receive any invitation."

"It came only a day or two ago and it was addressed to me, but your name was added."

"As an afterthought," Peter grumbled.

John merely smiled, then said, "It was an open invitation, no response was required."

Peter sipped his tea, wondering why Winifred had not mentioned the musical. Perhaps she did not know that he had been invited. He saw Melanie's hand in this and chuckled to himself. Perhaps it was best to leave Winifred alone for a day, before seeing her again. He needed a break from courting as well. His nerves were shot.

"What say you to an afternoon spent at Gentleman Jackson's for a bout of sparring tomorrow?" Peter asked. He needed all the practice he could get before coming to blows with his proud Athena, even if her jabs tended to be of a verbal variety.

"Yes, that would be most welcome," John agreed.

Chapter Eight

May 1813

Winifred pulled an evening gown from her armoire with little enthusiasm. She did not care if she stayed in her room all night and wallowed in her own self-pity. She could not shake the empty feeling she had had ever since she told Peter Blessing not to call upon her. Her heart ached, her soul ached and her mind screamed in frustration that she was the biggest sort of fool for feeling so low. Perhaps the musicale would give her some reprieve from her gloomy thoughts.

She donned the pale peach silk gown. The style was simple with a scroll pattern embroidered in gold along the hem, a squared neckline, and short puffed sleeves. She sat down at her dressing table and sighed heavily as the abigail she shared with Melanie transformed her unruly curls into a sleek, simple coil encircled with gilded leaves.

She told herself that she had done the right thing, that furthering her acquaintance with Peter Blessing could only cause her pain and heartache. Had not Melanie and her father warned her to stay away from David Stanton? She had not listened to reason then, and almost ruined her life over it. She would not make the same mistake again.

She made her way down the stairs and noted that the guests had already arrived when she saw him. Peter Blessing stood in the entry with his brother. Winifred stopped in mid-step and tried to swallow the panicky weakness that took hold of her upon seeing him. She had not known that her aunts had invited them. It was to be only a small gathering of their closest friends, most of them close to their aunts in age. She stood as still as a stone statue, unsure of what to do or say.

Melanie skipped past her down the stairs with words of welcome upon her lips. She obviously knew they had been sent an invitation. The Blessing brothers both looked up and Winifred caught Peter's gaze. A gleam of appreciation shone in his eyes and Winifred wondered for the first time if he truly found her attractive. She did not think he could fake the expression he wore. But then David had. Winifred shook her head, trying to clear it. Would she never stop comparing the two?

She descended slowly, careful to avoid his gaze. Melanie chatted with Lord Blessing and drew him into the parlor where the musicians were tuning their instruments. When she reached the bottom step, Peter was there, offering her his arm.

"You are lovely this evening," he said.

"I did not know you had been invited, Mr. Blessing. You said nothing of it before."

"I did not know myself until I visited my brother the evening of our ride in Hyde Park. He received an invitation for us both."

"I see." Winifred knew then that it had to have been Melanie.

"You are not happy to see me, are you?" he asked quietly.

She hesitated. The truth of the matter was that she was pleased to see him. Indeed, she felt alive again for the first time in a day and a half.

"Give me another chance, Athena," he whispered. "I am not anything like whoever he was that hurt you."

She looked at him sharply. "Who has said such a thing?"

"Do not be cross. Melanie would tell me nothing other than you have been hurt before. You said as much in Hyde Park. Believe me when I say that I do not for the world wish to hurt you."

Temptation to give in to him was overwhelming. So much so that she did not trust herself to speak. She shook her head and guided him to the drawing room and a seat next to Melanie and Lord Blessing.

Aunt Winifred soon approached and beamed upon Lord Blessing. "So nice you both were able to attend upon such short notice, my lord," she said. "Melanie was most insistent that we send an invitation. We had but one left and so we had to squeeze you both onto it."

Lord Blessing stood and bowed over her aunt's hand. "Delighted, Lady Winifred, thank you."

Peter also stood and placed a kiss upon Aunt Winifred's hand. She tut-tutted and rapped him with her fan before taking her leave to greet other guests. His charm worked even on Aunt Augusta, who also stopped to welcome the brothers.

The musicians and songstress seemed to entertain forever. Winifred constantly shifted upon her chair. The nearness of Mr. Blessing was no comfort to her and she cursed herself for not sitting elsewhere. The conversation she did not offer him, he received from Melanie as she sat between the two brothers.

Winifred tried not to sulk. Melanie whispered back and forth between Peter and his brother. Every smile and chuckle out of Peter caused Winifred to despair more deeply. He was charming and amusing and treating Melanie as if she were a dear friend, but that was all. He did not flirt or tease or do any of the things he did with her.

When the applause for the last performance finally died down, Aunt Winifred rose to announce that refreshments were offered in the dining room across the hall. Everyone made their way out of the drawing room, but the Blessing brothers remained seated.

"A moment, if you please," Peter said when Melanie rose.

"Yes?"

Peter moved his chair back, so that the four of them could easily see each other while they spoke. "John and I have planned an outing and we would like you both to join us." He directed his statement to Melanie.

"What kind of outing?" Melanie asked with barely concealed excitement.

"A picnic, at my estate in Kent. It's not more than fifteen miles from here, but we shall need to leave in the morning."

Melanie clapped her hands and Winifred knew she was doomed. She cast an angry glance at Peter. He was not playing fair. He used her own sister against her. "I do not know, Mr. Blessing," Winifred said. "Melanie and I have a full calendar of social engagements now that the Season is at its peak."

"Winnie, we can make the time, I am sure of it. Oh, please say you will join us, for I do not believe our aunts would allow just me to accompany them to Kent."

"Of course they would not," Winifred said.

"You need not give us a date and time today," John blurted. "Think on it and let us know."

"Very well, my lord," Melanie said. "Will you both be

present at the breakfast given by the Donnors the day after tomorrow?''

"We can be," Peter said.

"Then we shall give you the date there, after we have discussed the matter with our aunts." Melanie folded her hands in her lap and looked at Winifred as if daring her to disagree.

Winifred said nothing. She did not have the heart to spoil such an outing for her sister when Lord Blessing was to accompany them. Indeed, she found herself interested in seeing Peter's estate. He had never mentioned owning a country house before and she was surprised that he did. Especially since he chose to remain in London year-round except for his visits to his friend in the Cotswolds.

"Very well. It is agreed. I shall drop a hint to your aunts to be sure that they are agreeable to the idea. We shall be properly chaperoned with Peter's caretaker and his wife. You may bring your abigail, of course," Lord Blessing said.

"Of course," Melanie agreed with a smile. "Shall we see what the refreshment table offers, my lord?"

Winifred thought that her sister looked very much like the cat that had just swallowed the cream. She had never seen her so animated in the company of a gentleman and she looked all the more beautiful for it. Lord Blessing gazed admiringly at Melanie as he escorted her from the room, which bode well for her. Melanie had a sweetness that seemed to draw men to her side. Her inheritance was simply the icing to the cake.

Winifred could not cast Melanie in the role of Hermia and herself as Helena this time. The difference was that Peter, her Demetrius, wanted his Helena but Winifred did not want him. No, she corrected herself; she did not want to want him.

Peter looked intently upon her and she became instantly uncomfortable.

"You are very quiet this evening," he said.

"I have nothing to say, sir."

He pulled his chair a bit closer to hers. "Now how can that be? My clever Athena always has something to say."

She leaned forward and hissed, "Mr. Blessing, you must know that the only reason I concede to accompany you to your picnic is for my sister's sake."

"Yes, I figured as much. That is why I have engaged John's help in the matter of the picnic."

"Do you ever play fair, Mr. Blessing?"

He also leaned forward so that his elbows rested upon his knees and his hands were clasped in front of him. Their heads were so close as to almost touch. "Not where you are concerned I am afraid." Candlelight shone in his eyes as he looked at her and whispered, "I will not give you up, you may as well know that now."

She retreated by leaning back in her chair, away from him and his disturbing nearness. "And you must also know that I question your motives in pursuing me. I cannot trust you, sir."

"Yes, I have known that since we met. But I have not lied to you, my dear. I promise here and now that I will not do so in the future. And I do enjoy your company."

"As you enjoy every other lady's company with a large dowry?"

"Never one to mince words," Peter said.

"I simply cannot afford to. The stakes are too high for me." She hoped he understood her. Of course he must, she spoke clearly enough.

"They are for me as well and yet you keep raising them constantly. There is no other lady, large dowry or no, that I enjoy spending time with more than you or that I want more than you. That is the honest truth."

It was not the response she'd expected from him. Was he trying to tell her that he cared for her? Or was he simply telling her he planned to offer for her? 'Twas absurd. Surely he must know that she would refuse him. She searched his eyes for some glimmer of deceit from him, but could not find it.

Perhaps she had best try again at her plan to dig into his persona and show him his faults to prove his unsuitability. She took a deep breath. "Mr. Blessing, one thing that troubles me immensely is that you gamble."

He stiffened slightly, but did not flinch or look away. "Yes, I suppose that it must."

"Why, sir? Why have you fallen prey to such a dangerous vice?"

He coughed. "I do not believe I have 'fallen prey,' as you put it. It was my choice to gamble."

Winifred cocked an eyebrow. "Are you telling me that you can simply walk away whenever you choose? That there is no need for you to play other than the simple thrill and uncertain living that you derive from it?"

He was quiet for too long.

"I thought as much."

"What do you think?" he asked.

"You can no more stop gambling than a fish could stop swimming." There, she thought, what could he possibly say to that?

He became defensive. "I have never tried to walk away, Athena. I never had a reason to." His voice gentled when he added, "Until now."

She did not feel confident in the implication that he would stop gambling for her. Was it possible for him to do so? She wanted to believe his words more than she should. But she had to complete her task at hand and dig deeper. "What of your family, surely they cannot be pleased by your gambling."

Nosey, probing questions, Peter thought with a sigh. She was at it again; asking him things he did not wish to discuss. But at least she was talking to him instead of trying to avoid him. He looked her in the eye. "John hates what I do. My father would no doubt be disappointed as well, had he lived to see it."

"And your mother?" Her voice had softened.

"My mother died when I was born," he answered. "Is there anything else you wish to know?"

Her eyebrows shot up and he realized he had snapped at her. "Winifred, I am sorry. I merely am not used to baring my soul."

"I hardly think what we have discussed sheds any light

on your soul, sir. But if you are so determined to court me, then I warn you, there are a great many things I wish to know."

"Yes, I suppose there are. What is next on your agenda of questions?"

"You still have not told me why you gamble for a living when it obviously is a source of stress for your family. Surely there are other occupations you could have chosen."

She would not let go of it. "I had no interest in entering the clergy. I am hardly suited for it. Nor did the military appeal. John had lost enough of his loved ones in his life, I did not want to be another casualty for him. The man has had enough grief."

She reached out her hand, almost as if she had not meant to, and touched his sleeve. "Yes, his poor wife. Melanie mentioned to me that he was a widow. What was her name?"

"Anne."

"Your poor brother. How did she die?"

A tension inside his head that had started when she asked about his gambling was getting stronger by the minute. Why did the minx have to make him so uncomfortable with her blasted questions, her sweet concern.

He shifted under her gaze. "A fever." His throat felt tight.

"How terrible. Were you very close to her?"

Was there never to be an end to her infernal questions? "Yes, I was," he found himself saying. "I loved her dearly because she let me be who I was and laughed with me. She enjoyed life to the very fullest. I got sent down from university and knowing John would be furious, I made a big joke of it. I bellowed out my disgrace as I came charging up to their home in Surrey. Anne ran out, of course, to see what was the matter. It was raining, and she had been sick." He stopped in disbelief. Why was he telling her this?

"You could not have known she was ill," Winifred whispered. "And contrary to popular belief, rain does not cause a fever or a cold or any such malady. Peter, you cannot blame yourself."

She was looking at him with an expression he had never seen her wear, and he was not sure he liked it. Pity, he thought, he certainly did not want anyone's pity. "No, of course not," he muttered, then abruptly stood and held out his hand to her. "What say you to finding the refreshments?"

Winifred took his hand. He was smiling his charmingly boyish grin, but it did not steal away the pain from his eyes. He was trying to pull his mask back in place, but she had effectively torn it aside and he was struggling to retrieve it. She had tried to push him away with her questions, make him irritated with her, which she had done. But she never expected to see what she found lurking behind Peter Blessing's practiced charm.

A man who hurt.

Was it that hurt that drove him to be what he was? She felt slightly unsettled, and worse, she felt more drawn to him than ever.

Melanie turned her attention to her food. Lord Blessing was terribly quiet and he seemed preoccupied with the bit of poached pear on his plate. She had thought things were moving along perfectly when the brothers had invited them on a picnic, but now she knew better. The outing was merely Peter's way of getting close to Winifred. John had been pulled along as an excuse to keep Winifred from refusing.

She sighed and wondered if perhaps she should stop trying to capture Lord Blessing's attention. He clearly was not over his dead wife, and wanted nothing to do with her.

"Is something wrong?" he asked.

Melanie realized she had been absently stabbing at her ham. She looked up at him. "No."

Silence.

"Sometimes it helps if you talk about it," he said.

Melanie smiled. He had used her words when they had

first met. She swallowed before boldly stating, "I thought that perhaps I was boring you."

"Not at all. Whatever gave you that idea?" Lord Blessing wore a truly stricken look upon his face.

"Well, I know that Peter is trying to court Winifred and that he engaged your help in securing Winifred's agreement to the picnic."

"Yes, well . . ." he sputtered.

She laid her hand upon his sleeve. "It is quite all right. I too wish to help further your brother and my sister's relationship. He is good for her."

"And she can be nothing but good for him," he agreed.

"Exactly. And so, the very least we can do is help them along. But you need not entertain me, my lord. Feel free to bring along something to read."

He looked offended. "Miss Melanie, how can you possibly think that I should rather read when in your presence?"

That was good, at least she had gained a response from him other than a polite comment. She thought at times, when she had glimpsed him looking at her, that she saw longing in his eyes. But he would quickly look away and she often wondered if she had only wished it there. Lately, when they were together, he became quiet, reserved, thoughtful. He was nothing like the congenial gentleman at the theater. "Well," she started—she might as well be honest and jump in with both feet—"you seem to have nothing to say to me and so I thought . . ."

"By George," Lord Blessing interrupted, "that is not it at all."

When he said no more and looked thoroughly miserable, Melanie asserted, "What is it then? I truly wish for us to be comfortable with each other again, like we were at Drury Lane."

"My dear Miss Melanie, I am afraid that I have done you a great disservice and I humbly beg your pardon."

"You are forgiven, my lord, but please tell me what I may do to make amends."

"Amends? Sweet child, you have done nothing but be your sweet self and I find that I . . ."

"Yes?" She leaned forward eagerly.

"Very much wish to be in your presence, against my better judgment."

Hope soared in her heart. He wanted to be with her, but something was wrong. Why would he think his judgment in question? "Now, sir, I accept your apology, but you are digging yourself in deeper. Please explain to me why I am poor judgment?" She had meant for a light, teasing tone, but Lord Blessing again wore that stricken expression.

"I beg your pardon, that is not at all what I meant." He pulled at his cravat in a gesture similar to his brother's fidgets.

Melanie cocked her head in a manner to let him know that she was still listening.

"Miss Melanie, surely there are younger gentlemen you would rather spend time with?"

"Younger? Lord Blessing, do you think yourself too old, or me too young?" She was treading dangerous ground here. She was actually letting him know that she thought him a potential suitor. What would he do with the knowledge that she hoped him to be much more?

"There is a large difference in our ages. I am thirty-five, my dear. If I were your father, I would prefer that your suitor was closer to your own age."

"But you are not my father, sir. Besides, my father is nearly fifty and I think him a young man still."

Lord Blessing shifted uncomfortably. What was she doing? Inviting him to pay his addresses to her? He was more than tempted to do so. She was like a breath of fresh air to his otherwise stale life, but how could he betray his memory of Anne?

She reached out and touched his hand this time, casting her glossy eyes with their absurdly long lashes at him. It was all he could do to keep himself from taking her into his arms right there.

"If the memory of your poor wife causes you distress, I understand, my lord. I value our friendship, is all."

She had given him an out for him to take if he wished. To claim merely friendship and be done with it. But friendship was the furthest thing from his mind where she was concerned. She was pulling feelings from him that he had thought long dead and buried with Anne. He did not know what to do about it or how to react to them. He only knew that his confusion was hurting her, and that he could not do.

He took her hand in his own and looked deeply into her eyes that glimmered a grayish-blue this night. "I simply need some time."

"Time, Lord Blessing, I have in abundance."

Later that evening, Melanie came into Winifred's room and sat upon her bed. "What do you think of Lord Blessing?" Melanie asked.

"He appears to be a very nice gentleman."

"Yes. Do you think him too old for me?"

"Do you?"

"No. I do not. But I think our age difference bothers him."

"Melanie, you are twenty, soon to be twenty-one. You are no green girl but a woman grown."

"Yes, that is what I think as well." She twirled the ends of her braided hair between her fingers.

"Did he speak of his late wife?" Winifred asked. She wondered if Melanie knew that a memory may be her biggest competition for Lord Blessing's affection.

Melanie's smile faded as she answered, "Yes. It still pains him, his loss of her. I wish I could make it better for him."

Winifred was relieved. Lord Blessing had obviously been honest with her sister. "I am sure that you will."

"Did you know Papa is coming to London the end of the month?" Melanie asked.

"He is? I suppose to prepare for the onslaught of offers you shall receive." Winifred smiled.

"I will tell you the truth of it, Win. I want only one offer from one man."

Winifred knew she spoke of Lord Blessing. "How can

you be so sure? You have known him only a short while. Melanie, do you love him?"

"Not yet, at least I am not sure. But I do know that I could love him."

"And how do you know that?"

"I do not know how. I just do." Melanie inspected her fingernails, then asked, "What of you, Win? Will Papa be receiving an offer for your hand?"

Winifred was quiet. Dear Heaven, it was entirely possible that he could. Peter said he wanted her, which could only mean that he wanted her hand in marriage. What would she do if he asked her father? What answer should she give him? She had always thought that she would refuse. But after tonight she wavered in her conviction.

"Winnie?" Melanie reached out and touched her arm. "What is wrong?"

"Nothing, I am just cold and tired. Can you go to your own room now? I would like to go to sleep."

"Of course, dear. Of course." Melanie leaned over to give her a goodnight kiss on the cheek, then she proceeded to tuck the covers in for her.

Winifred snuggled down into the warmth of her blankets. "Thank you, Mel."

"You are welcome." Her sister left the room.

What answer would she give should Peter ask her father permission to pay his addresses? He wanted her, he had been more than open about that. He did not want Melanie, or any other maid, he wanted her. An unexpected thrill in that knowledge raced along her spine, causing her to shiver and burrow deeper under the coverlet.

He was not a bad man, she supposed. He treated her with respect and seemed to value her thoughts and opinions. And no matter what she did, she could not chase him away from her. And he was nothing like David Stanton, who had proved to be false in his protestations of love. He had cared for nothing other than the Preston fortune. And yet, Peter Blessing wanted the same thing.

Winifred stared at the low flames of the banked fire in the grate. It was not terribly cold, but still she felt chilled. What on earth was it about Peter Blessing that drew her? He genuinely liked her for herself—she knew that to be true. And now she knew that underneath his charming facade, lay a terrible vulnerability.

She had seen glimpses of what she believed was the real man behind the mask of charm—a caring man with a kind and soft heart that was hurting. But a man who loved the thrill of gaming and considered himself a scoundrel. How could she possibly allow herself to love such a man and not be hurt, eventually? She had loved David Stanton and he had brought her misery and made a mockery of her affection. Would Peter do the same if she let him?

Winifred decided she could no longer think as her head was swimming. She could only continue to guard herself against falling in love with Peter Blessing. If she remained adamantly intent upon getting to know the real man, he would either go away and leave her alone or perhaps change completely into a trustworthy man who loved her. Both were extremes she doubted would happen, but then she could only hope.

Chapter Nine

The day of the Donnor breakfast continued with fine weather. Winifred sat in the tiny garden behind her aunts' townhouse reading the *Morning Post* to while away the short time before they were to leave. The sunshine was brilliant and the air quite warm with a gentle breeze. A perfect day for an event out of doors, she thought.

She had had an enjoyable evening the night before at an informal dinner party and ball. Peter Blessing had not been in attendance, so she was able to relax and enjoy the company of the many partners she found herself to have. Lord Stanley, Mr. Pratt, and Lord Huntley were among the guests and she danced with them as well. Mr. Oliver also attended, but he took care to avoid all contact with her.

She had given herself little time to dwell upon Mr. Oliver's rudeness, however, as she had been whisked into one dance after another. There was no need for dance cards since the affair was small. Perhaps that helped with the gentlemen's generous invitations to all the ladies present. No young maid was refused at least one dance.

She stretched out her long legs before her and rested her head against the bench back. She raised her face to the sunshine and hummed along to the memory of music from last night as she wondered what she would do about Peter Blessing.

It was this way that Peter Blessing found her. "Good morning, sweet goddess," he said.

Winifred jumped at the sound of his voice. "What are you doing here?"

"We have come to escort you to the breakfast. John has brought the berline, so there is room for us all. You need not get up. In fact, I preferred you as you were Stretched out in worship of your brother Apollo, you looked temptingly pagan."

But she sat all the more straight when Peter sat down beside her on the bench. He was positively delicious-looking in buff-colored pantaloons and a bottle-green morning coat. His hair gleamed in the sun like spun gold.

"Are you not speaking to me, Athena?" he asked.

Winifred felt her cheeks grow warm. She was merely staring at him. It had been a day between sightings of the handsome Peter Blessing, yet she knew she looked upon him as if she were starved. She looked away, flustered. "Of course, I am speaking to you."

"Good, because in another moment I thought you might eat me, so fierce was your goddess gaze."

"Not with displeasure, I assure you," she blurted. She put her hand up over her mouth, shocked at her saucy words.

His eyes darkened and he slid down the bench, closer to her. "Then I am glad that my presence pleases you," he whispered. "Is there anything else I can do to bring you pleasure?"

A shiver of excitement and desire and temptation raced along her spine. He wore a positively wicked expression and Winifred knew that all she need do was ask, and he would kiss her. She looked at his lips, then to his eyes, then back to his lips which were turning into a seductive smile.

"Yes," she said, overloud, and stood quickly. "You may escort me inside, Mr. Blessing. I have only to get my shawl and bonnet and I am ready to leave."

"As you wish," he said and offered her his arm.

She took it carefully, trying not to let him notice her tremble as she rested her hand upon his forearm. But it was no use hiding her physical reaction to him. He knew how he affected her and, blast his eyes, he no doubt reveled in it, she thought.

She felt his fingertips graze her neck and pulled back with a gasp.

"A leaf, my dear. A leaf had got caught in your hair." He lifted his hands with an expression of innocence.

She felt like a ninnyhammer to be so jumpy, but her emotions were in turmoil at seeing him so unexpectedly. "I shall return directly." Winifred turned and dashed up the stairs.

Soon, they were piled into the crested carriage and on their way. Lord Blessing sat between Melanie and herself. This forced Peter to sit beside her aunts. It was close quarters, but as they were only driving to Kensington, they could manage. Winifred thought herself very smart to have rushed to sit next to Lord Blessing. But, now she knew the error of her ways. Worried about having to sit next to Peter, she had given no thought to sitting across from him.

Every time she looked up, he was there, gazing back at her. Although he entertained Aunt Augusta and Aunt Winifred with silly stories of when he and Lord blessing were children, his eyes constantly strayed to look into her own. His gaze had a caressing effect and she wondered what it would be like to be held by him and kissed senseless. If it was anything close to his treatment of her hand in Hyde Park, she would no doubt faint with pleasure.

When the carriage pulled into Lord and Lady Donnor's estate, Winifred was eager to leave the space of the carriage that was so charged with Peter Blessing's energy. She stepped out lightly and proceeded toward the lawn, which had been transformed into a marvel of beautiful canopies with urns of flowers placed positively everywhere.

Ladies strolled along the edge of an ornamental lake; their parasols like exotic flowers rustling in the wind. Gentlemen either lounged in chairs, escorted the ladies, or played games of skill on the open lawns. The early afternoon sunshine bore down upon them from a perfectly cloudless sky.

Winifred shielded her eyes as she looked out over the lake where some gentlemen rowed small boats with ladies reclining against the pillows stacked inside of the craft for comfort.

She hesitated only until her party had exited the carriage, then she grasped Melanie's hand in her own. "We must see if we can have use of the boats."

"Is this not the most beautiful place?" her sister asked as if she had not heard Winifred's comment.

"It is lovely." She cast a longing glance at the boats, then turned her head to spy Peter. He and Lord Blessing each escorted their aunts, but he noticed her gaze and smiled in return. Warmth spread through her.

It was a short walk to the gathering where various canopies sheltered tables and chairs for cards from the sun as well as tables laden with food served alfresco. Many of the guests were filling their plates and Winifred had to admit that she was ready for something, since she had eaten only a light repast this morning.

Peter came up behind her after delivering her aunts to a table of other matrons nibbling at the delicacies provided. "Are you hungry?" he whispered.

"Yes," she said simply.

"Then let us eat and then we can track down a boat."

Winifred whirled to look at him. "You heard me?"

"Yes, and I would be most honored to row you about." He bowed with a flourish.

She giggled. "Well then, let us hurry, as I am sure many of the guests will take them once they have eaten." Surely she could not get into any trouble in a small boat with him in view of the entire party.

In no time they were at the lakeshore. Winifred did not even bother to look for her sister. She was in Lord Blessing's care and so she knew her to be safe and happy. She watched as Peter tore off his jacket and draped it across the bench of the rowboat as he gingerly stepped into it. The deep fawn-colored waistcoat complemented his golden skin and hair. Truly, she had never seen him look more handsome.

He reached out his hand to her to step in. When she did so, the tiny boat tipped and lurched. She reacted to the wobble and lost her balance, nearly falling into him. Suddenly his arms were completely about her.

"Careful," he whispered, "or we shall be dumped."

She looked into his eyes but did not pull away from him. He let his arms loosen and his hands traced a heated path from her back to her waist, then he pushed her from him gently. "I believe you shall need to sit there."

She came to her senses and sat down at the rear of the boat, which was covered with large pillows.

Peter smiled at her and began to row.

She leaned back against the cushions. Neither of them spoke. She watched his muscles strain under the linen shirt he wore as he rowed. And he kept sweeping her with a scorching gaze from her toes, which had been freed from her slippers, to her head.

"Your cheeks are turning pink," he finally said.

"I do not care. The sun feels marvelously divine." She stretched her arms above her head and actually yawned.

"Are you sleepy, my Athena?"

"I should not be. But the motion of the boat and the warmth of the sun have made me so." She closed her eyes.

He swung the oars back into place and let the boat

drift where it would. They were across the lake and the soft breeze would carry them back. He looked at Winifred draped upon the cushions like royalty and felt an incredible desire to nestle down next to her.

When he saw her hand fall limply from her lap, he knew she had fallen asleep and he nearly laughed aloud.

It was just as well. Then she would not ask him any more questions that made him uncomfortable. She had the terrible habit of making him regret what he was and what he had done with his life. Could he walk away from gambling? Surely he could, he simply had never felt the need to do so before. Rather, the need to walk away had always been less than the need not to fail at something else.

She seemed even more aware of him today. That was good. Very good, indeed. Was he succeeding in making her fall closer to love with him? He hoped so. He wanted to offer for her, but could not be sure of her acceptance. In fact, he feared she would reject him outright. He had to work on that.

The afternoon was quite warm and the clear blue water looked more than inviting. He gazed at Winifred's sleeping form. Her cheeks did indeed look pink. He had better get her out of the sun.

He looked about when he heard his name called. John was rowing Melanie, who sat underneath a dainty parasol. They were heading his way, and he waved. John rowed his boat toward him until he was next to him. Their boats bumped.

"Sshhhh," Peter put a finger to his lips. "She is sleeping."

John's eyes rounded in surprise. "Sleeping?"

"Yes."

"Good heavens," Melanie said. "She will be burned to a crisp if you do not get her out of the sun. She is always doing this, and pays dearly the next day."

"She falls asleep in the sun?" John asked.

"At home, she often takes a blanket out into the garden to read. She falls asleep and ends up with a very red and freckled face. Peter, you have to wake her."

He looked back at his sleeping goddess and considered that perhaps waking her would, indeed, be an enjoyable thing to do. He felt a grin spread across his face at the thought of how he should do it. He looked back at John, who had let his boat drift slightly away.

He stood and bent over the reclining form before him and whispered her name. When she did not stir, he bent down to place a feather-light kiss upon her brow. She swatted at him and turned to nestle further into the pillows. He looked back at John, who smiled like a fool at him as did Melanie. He became aware that a small audience of sorts had formed.

Another boat stopped rowing, and then another. His audience was growing. He stood and grinned, then bent again to wake his sleeping goddess. She would be more than angry with him when she did wake to find that many watched the prince try to awaken his princess with a kiss. Some of the gentlemen yelled out where he should plant his lips and some wagered with each other regarding where he would do so.

Peter had not meant to make such a scene, but perhaps it was a good thing to have word about town that he was officially courting Miss Winifred Preston. He bowed to the small crowd, causing the boat to tip and wobble. Then he bent to bestow a chaste kiss upon her lips. He could not help but apply more pressure with his mouth and Winifred moaned softly. Heat surged within him. And then she opened her eyes with a flutter.

"What are you doing?" she cried.

"Why, waking you with a kiss, my sleeping beauty." He grinned.

She sat up and looked about, her already flushed cheeks becoming hot when the surrounding rowers began to clap and whistle.

"Oh!" She put her hands to her flaming face. "How dare you!"

Peter remained standing, staring at the enraged Winifred. She looked like an angry kitten, and he could not help but chuckle. He soon realized that he had made a mistake when she pushed him with a strength he should have known that she would possess. He tried to catch his balance, but could not. He fell into the water with a splash, but not before tipping the small water craft over with him.

He came up to the surface expelling a burst of air. Then he looked about for Winifred. What if she did not know how to swim? The crowd jeered and their applause was nearly deafening as was their laughter. Where was she? He looked at Melanie, who smiled and pointed to the water. He dipped back down under the water's surface, fear lodged into his heart when he saw her.

He could have been spying a mermaid, he thought as he watched her gracefully dive to the bottom in a ray of sun shining through the water. What was she after? He dove down as well, keeping his eyes open and riveted upon Winifred. Her hair had come loose and its reddish locks swirled around her head. She grabbed her slippers. When he reached for his jacket that was laying nearby and tried to help her, she pushed him away. The water was not overly deep. The bottom could not have been more than five or six feet from the surface.

He burst out from underneath the water as she swam deftly to the capsized rowboat. Peter looked about, hoping he had not disgraced both himself and her, but then he noticed that gentlemen were jumping out of their rowboats to the horror of the ladies and gentlemen on the shoreline. Peter grinned from ear to ear.

"See what you have started?" John said with a laugh as he rowed toward him. Melanie looked amused as well.

Peter swam to their boat and draped his arms over the side. It tipped dangerously and it did not appear stable enough for him to board from the water, nor was there enough room.

"Do not even try," John warned. "I am in no mood for a swim, and neither is Miss Melanie."

"The water is cool, but fine once one gets used to it," Peter said. He glanced over at Winifred, who bobbed about their overturned boat. "Here, take my jacket," he said as he handed the sodden mass to John. Then he swam over to Winifred.

"Well? What are we going to do now?" she asked. "I do not think we can turn it right side up."

He tried to push the boat over. It turned, rolled and righted itself with half of the boat filled with water. "I do not think we can row back. Can you swim to shore?"

She gave him the foulest look he had ever seen on a woman. He thought perhaps that he heard her mutter an oath under her breath. "Yes, I can swim." Then she eyed him with an evil glint. "In fact, I shall race you."

Peter grinned. She was no shrinking violet. "And the winner shall receive what, pray tell?"

"Mr. Blessing, must you always turn everything into a wager?"

"Yes, just as you turn everything into a competition. You like to play as much as I do, Winifred."

She did not answer him but swam to her sister's boat to give her the sodden slippers. "I shall need my shawl when I emerge from the water. Can you row back and have it ready for me? I left it on a bench near Aunt Augusta. Goodness, Mel, what will they think? I shall be in a deep coil."

"Do not worry, Winnie. Look around you. Everyone has joined in the fun and Lady Donnor will no doubt be proud as a peacock to have such carrying on at her breakfast. 'Twill be the happening of the Season and no doubt talked about for ages to come."

"I hope you have the right of it. I would not want to cast any blemish upon your Season or your reputation," she said.

"Have no fear," her sister assured her.

Peter continued to listen to the sisters' exchange. Poor Winifred, he thought. He would make sure that he and John smoothed any of the aunts' ruffled feathers. He watched his brother laugh at the antics of those splashing about. Obviously, he did not care a whit about the impropriety of the whole thing. He only hoped John could use his excellent diplomacy with the Fitzhugh ladies.

"Are you ready?" Peter asked Winifred.

"Yes." She turned to John and asked if he would give them the start.

When he did so, Peter gave Winifred a modest lead. Her strokes were long and graceful, one arm coming out of the water at a time, her feet kicking furiously. She swam with the strength of someone used to the exercise.

He started after her and quickly gained on her. In no time he overtook and passed her. He climbed out of the water and turned to watch Winifred. Melanie came running with the shawl, but it was too late. He had more than a glimpse of her slender form exposed by the wet, clinging dress hanging shamelessly about her legs as she splashed her way to shore.

He grabbed the shawl out of Melanie's hands and trotted back into the water. He did not want anyone else's gaze to feast upon her body. The cotton muslin left little to the imagination.

"Here," he said as he wrapped the length of fine cashmere about her shoulders.

"Thank you." She looked up at him. Rivulets of water ran down her face, her pink nose covered with freckles. "You have won, sir, and I do not believe we named the prize."

He wiped a drop of water from the tip of her nose with his finger and whispered, "No, we did not. I shall surely think of something." But at the moment he could think of nothing decent to ask for, so he let the matter drop completely.

Before she could respond, Peter heard the shrill voice of Miss Whent from the shore. "Goodness, Miss Preston, you are a veritable tomboy."

It was meant to be a snide comment and Peter felt like splashing the obnoxiously arrogant look off her face. Instead he turned, offering Winifred his arm as if they were merely taking a stroll and said, "Ain't she grand?"

Several of the gentlemen who had joined in the swim were making their way to shore as well. When they heard his comment, they clapped and shouted their agreement. Peter felt more than satisfied when Miss Whent was struck speechless by the male appreciation of Winifred Preston's swimming expertise. The disgruntled young lady left in a huff.

Winifred's aunts were rushing down the lawn to help, but before they reached them, Winifred turned to him and with genuine gratitude in her eyes she whispered, "Thank you, Mr. Blessing. Again, you have helped me out of a scrape; even though 'tis your fault that I find myself in this condition."

"There was no need to push me over, my dove." He grinned.

"You are mistaken, sir. There was, indeed, every need." She did not look back at him when she was enveloped in her aunts' embrace and hurried up the lawn and into the house.

Winifred followed Lady Donnor to a private chamber. She kept her large shawl firmly wrapped about herself as she started to shiver in the coolness of the house. She ran a finger across her lips, remembering the warmth of Peter's mouth on hers. She was glad that she had not done something utterly inappropriate like wrap her arms about his neck and drag him down next to her for a more thorough exploration. An unbidden swell of heat burned through her at the thought of how thorough they could have been.

"Right this way, Miss Winifred. I shall have a maid sent to you with a change of clothes." Lady Donnor opened the door to a beautifully appointed room.

"Lady Donnor, I am terribly sorry for the trouble," Winifred said, feeling awkward.

"No trouble at all, dear. I tell you I do not know when I have laughed so hard as when you pushed that rascal into the lake."

Winifred smiled weakly. She worried that her behavior may have been too much for the delicate sensibilities of the *ton*. Aunt Winifred had given her a stiff scold, warning her again to curb her antics lest she bring shame upon them.

"Do not hesitate to ask Briggs, my abigail, for anything you may require. She will be with you in a moment."

"Thank you. You are so very kind." Winifred's voice faltered.

Lady Donnor took Winifred's cold hands in her own. "Do not let such a thing upset you, dear. 'Twas merely an accident that the boat tipped over."

"But do you not think that I shall be outcast for my behavior?"

"Outcast?" Lady Donnor smiled. "Heavens, child, no. I am sure some of the ladies are green with envy since most of the young gentlemen present think you a marvelous sport. And then, of course, the other ladies shall dislike you immensely for capturing the interest of Mr. Blessing, who is truly the most handsome of men. But you shall not be outcast, dear. I suppose some of the highest sticklers will look upon you with censure, mayhap, but that in and of itself may make you something of a rage. You have bottom, Miss Winifred, and every Englishman adores bottom."

Winifred was not entirely convinced, but she liked Lady Donnor all the more for giving her hope.

Lady Donnor took a seat upon a chaise, guiding Winifred to sit next to her. "And my breakfast shall be the rage as well. Any hostess wants such a spontaneously amusing thing to happen at her party. Do stop worrying about your reputation, my dear. It is entirely safe, in my opinion."

Moved beyond words, Winifred reached out and gave Lady Donnor's hand a squeeze. The kind lady patted her arms and left when Briggs entered with a change of gown.

Perhaps Lady Donnor had the right of it, and she need not fear. She had not expected Peter to be so well known among the *ton,* but then his brother was a highly respected and wealthy baron. The Blessing name was a good one. It suddenly dawned on her to wonder why, if his brother had so much, Peter found it necessary to marry money. He was obviously on a crusade for a good dowry and she had become his mission. He had admitted as much to her at her aunts' musicale. Why? she wondered.

She knew that it was a question she must ask him when they were next alone. The picnic to his estate provided the perfect opportunity. They had given the Blessing brothers the date of Tuesday, which was a mere four days away. She hoped her sadly guarded heart would allow her mind to make a proper decision once she heard Peter's answer to her most important question.

Winifred was soon dry and changed into a pale yellow muslin gown that was slightly short for her, but not daringly so. The matching slippers were a tad tight, but would do. Her hair had been arranged into a relaxed crown of curls atop her head. She was passable if not perfectly presentable, and she felt ready to face the crowd.

When she stepped outside, Peter Blessing turned from the gentlemen he spoke with to greet her with a smile.

"You look fresh as a daisy," he said.

"You, sir, look like a wilted dandelion," she responded. His unmentionables were sadly wrinkled and still damp. His shirt looked passable beneath his waistcoat, but his cravat had been taken off completely and she found the revealed skin of his strong neck was enticing her gaze to linger far too long.

"There are far too many of us that took a swim. Lord Donnor could not be expected to outfit us all. Perhaps we shall start a new fashion trend." He twirled around for her to further inspect his damaged clothes.

She laughed and he joined her, until a group of young men surrounded them to offer their comments on how prettily she swam. Compliments abounded and Winifred positively blushed in embarrassment. It was truly an odd sensation to be surrounded by gentlemen vying for her attention. She looked about for Melanie to come to her aid, but her sister was nowhere to be seen.

Peter must have sensed her discomfort and he gently extricated her from the swarm to guide her to a chair. Tea was served and Peter announced that she needed to be left alone. Winifred heard various guffaws and mild accusations that Peter wanted to keep her for himself.

"Thank you," she whispered when he brought her a cup of steaming Bohea.

"Not at all. I could not possibly stand by and watch you besieged by a bunch of star-struck lads. You will be quite popular, you know." With an expression of mock indignation he added, "I can't say that I am happy about it."

" 'Tis all of your own doing, so now you will have to endure the punishment," she said.

"But it is too harsh a sentence for my crime. Now every other gentleman will try to sweep you off your feet."

"Come now, Mr. Blessing. They were only interested in the novelty of my swimming abilities."

"You underestimate yourself, my modest Athena. Your fresh natural beauty shines like the sun when you are out of doors. Anyone with half their wits could see what a lovely nymph you made coming out of the water."

She was caught off guard by the seriousness with which he delivered his flattery. She looked down into her cup. She hoped that no one else had been privy to the view of her gown clinging to her skin. She was more than grateful to Peter for coming to her aid and wrapping her shawl about her so quickly. He had held the wrap up before his face in consideration for her state. For that, she was truly appreciative, even though she knew he had been given an eye-full when he had trudged toward her.

"What are you thinking?" he asked.

"I am thinking that I should like to play a lawn game," she said.

"More games? Shall we place a small wager?"

"Honestly, Mr. Blessing." She rolled her eyes heavenward. "I still owe you from the swim."

"No, my dear. I have let you off the hook with that one."

"Whatever for? Surely you know the folly of forgiving my debt, for I shall not let you win again. You shall have no second chance for a prize."

"Trust me, Athena, I have already seen my prize, and that was more than enough for now."

She blushed to the roots of her hair. The heightened color on his own cheeks suggested that he had quite enjoyed the view.

*   *   *

"Oh, I have done it again!" Melanie nearly threw the bow down upon the ground and stamped on it. "I tell you, I have never been any good with a bow and arrow, my lord."

"You need only practice your aim and refrain from closing your eyes when you let go," Lord Blessing said.

"But I fear the string will catch my face when I let go." She tried to explain to the already exasperated man. She had lost an entire quiver full of arrows into the Donnors' woods. No matter the instructions given, she failed to hit any part of the target, let alone get near the rings of the bull's eye. She had never excelled in sports like Winifred.

"Here, let me show you." Lord Blessing walked up close behind her. Taking another arrow, he said, "Take up the bow."

Before Melanie could complain, she felt his arms come up around her. His hands rested on her own, as she held the bow. She held her breath as his warmth caressed her back. She leaned into the solid wall of his chest.

"Now," he started, his mouth close to her ear, "set the arrow and pull back the bow string."

She did as he asked, keeping her elbow bent out straight as he had told her earlier, but it wavered. His hand slid to support her elbow and she thought her knees would buckle at the contact.

"Keep your eyes open, my dear." His voice was soft and slightly hoarse.

Melanie wondered if he felt the current of excitement that swamped her body. She did as she was bid, and with Lord Blessing's guidance and strength, they pulled the arrow back to let go with a snap. It stayed straight and hit the straw target. Outside of the rings, of course, but at least the arrow stuck fast in the object instead of missing it completely.

"Thank you, sir, that is quite an improvement." She turned her head toward him and looked up into his eyes.

He stared back at the beauty still in his arms. All he need do was bend down and his lips could easily brush her own. Blast! He needed to put some space between them, and fast. She felt too pliant, too willing, as she leaned against him.

Recovering his wits, John tucked a stray curl behind Melanie's ear. "Yes, a definite improvement." He rallied his strength and pulled away from her. "Now, Miss Melanie, let's see if you can try again on your own."

He did not miss the disappointment in the girl's eyes. She wanted him to kiss her! A good thing he had not. All the playfulness in the air of this party was keeping him from remembering his age, and his position. He dared not act upon the desires of his flesh, else he would be forced into making amends.

Miss Melanie Preston was a delectable young lady, who was decidedly clear in her wish that he pay his addresses to her. And he was very close, indeed, to fulfilling her wish. Only, he needed to be sure that this was what he wanted before he offered for her. He had to be certain that he could keep the memory of his Anne in its proper place. He owed Melanie his whole and undivided heart. Until he was ready to give that to her, he needed to keep a gentlemanly distance. And that was proving to be a difficult task with a sweet siren whose touch enflamed him and whose eyes conveyed invitations he desperately wanted to accept.

Chapter Ten

Winifred rushed about her chamber trying on bonnet after bonnet with no hope of being satisfied. Melanie was waiting for her downstairs as the Blessing brothers were expected at any moment to take them to Peter's estate in Kent. She had to own that she was anxious to see him.

She had beat Peter soundly in archery at the Donnors' and the wager that she had won was a promise from him to answer one special question truthfully when she asked it. He had agreed, although reluctantly. She explained that she would give him fair warning before she asked her question. And today seemed like as good a day as any to ask why he needed to marry for money.

There had been plenty of opportunities these past few days, when she saw him at dinner parties and the theater and again when he had called upon her, but there had been any number of distractions and she needed his utmost attention. There were always other people about and within hearing distance. Perhaps her reluctance in asking was that she dreaded his answer. She was growing more and more fond of his company. But it was eating at her and she knew she had to know what prompted Peter Blessing to look for a rich wife.

She had received more callers. Most of them were gentlemen who had also taken a swim at the Donnors' breakfast. The entire event had been practically catalogued in the gossip column of the *Morning Post.* Of course, only one's initials were used, but she had to wonder just how many Miss WP's there were this Season to confuse the reader as to just who was being singled out.

Lady Donnor had been correct; it appeared her reputation was intact. She had become quite popular among the Corinthian set. These sporting gentlemen hailed her as something of a marvel because of her excellent swimming ability which, evidently, was rarely found among the ladies. Even at Brighton, many gently bred misses entered the waters from bathing machines only to splash about, not swim as the gentlemen did.

Melanie had also become a target of popularity. It was being said that she had brought Lord Blessing out of his eight-year absence from society, and many whispered that she would be his next baroness. It amused more people than Winifred cared to consider that the Preston sisters, with their fortunes made by business dealings, were fast becoming the latest toasts of the Season.

A knock at her door brought a footman to inform her that Lord and Mr. Blessing were in the drawing room waiting. They were here! She swiftly grabbed her comfortable chip straw bonnet and tied a new ribbon of bishop's blue under her chin. The purplish-blue color complimented her pale lavender muslin printed with blue flowers and its matching spencer. She dashed out of the room and down the stairs in time to see Peter coming toward her.

"I heard you coming," he said as he offered her his arm.

She peeked at her aunt, who scowled at her less than decorous descent.

"As did everyone, I see," she whispered.

He winked at her and led her to the crested berline that belonged to Lord Blessing. "What is this?" he asked. He took the basket as he handed their abigail into the carriage.

"Just some tartlets and such made by the Fitzhugh cook." Winifred took her seat next to her abigail.

Peter smiled and peeked into the basket. A bigger smile spread across his face and Winifred thought he looked very young and boyish and her heart lurched. She looked away.

Lord Blessing helped Melanie into the carriage, but the men did not enter. They had decided to ride alongside the carriage in order to add to the number of mounts kept at Peter's estate in case the four of them wished to ride together.

The journey was not overly long, and yet Winifred was more than happy to exit the carriage to stretch her legs when they arrived in Kent. She looked about Trenton Manor, Peter's estate, and smiled. It was lovely. The lush countryside they had passed through had not prepared her for the simple beauty of Trenton Manor.

The manor house stood tall and proud amid beautifully manicured lawns. Woodlands canvased the rear and the right of the house, while an old apple orchard with a large brook babbling alongside lay directly east of the soft gray-stoned structure. Vines climbed about the small west wing which led to gardens that Winifred noticed were the only thing that did not appear to have been maintained.

"What do you think?" Peter had stepped beside her.

"Absolutely charming. I cannot believe you would

rather stay in London, when you have such a lovely place to live, here."

"But I have no one to share it with," he teased.

She looked sharply at him, but he had turned to help Melanie as John proceeded to the stables with their horses.

"No one, indeed," she uttered under her breath. She wandered ahead to the small fountain in the middle of the circular drive.

"My mother loved fountains," Peter explained as he caught up to her. "The baronetcy has a huge fountain, much more elaborate than this. Would you like a tour?"

"I should like that above all things," she said, and meant it most heartily.

John and Melanie joined them and they entered through the double oak doors. The entry was small but charming. A young maid took the ladies' bonnets and the gentlemen's hats and gloves. Peter ushered them all through the manor which, for all its neat and tidy appearance, lacked the warmth of a home. There were no personal items that Winifred could see. In fact, the furnishings were sparse, the excellent carpets were nearly threadbare with age, and the bedchambers still had their Holland covers over the few pieces of furniture inside.

"Do you never come here?" Winifred asked.

"No." His answer was quiet.

"Why not?"

Winifred thought she saw a trace of wistfulness which he quickly covered as he shrugged his shoulders. What made him not want to live here, she wondered.

The tour was almost complete as the manor was not overly large. She could not keep her mind from visualizing all the changes she would make if it were her home. She stood in the breakfast parlor, which she decided was her favorite room as it overlooked the orchard and brook. She could imagine watching the sunrise in such a gloriously cozy room with a fire crackling in the large grate.

"What are you thinking, my Athena," Peter said when

she hesitated to leave the parlor. Lord Blessing and Melanie had already exited to tour the stables.

"I was just thinking this the perfect spot to watch the sun rise while enjoying a cup of coffee or chocolate." At the look of surprise upon his face, she added, "Oh, Peter, this is such a pretty and cozy room. You could do so much with it."

Shock registered on his face, then turned to a look of approval. He stepped closer to her. "You have finally called me by name."

She looked up at him. She had, hadn't she. Somehow Mr. Blessing did not fit him here, in his country estate. He was just Peter. A wisp of warmth curled itself around her insides and grew as she looked at him and he at her.

He reached out and ran his finger along the side of her cheek. "I imagine that you could make this place a real home."

She was stunned by the depth of sincerity she saw in his beautiful brown eyes. Her mouth suddenly went dry as she let her gaze drop to his lips.

"Say it again," he whispered, and stepped even closer to her.

"What?" A sense of panic mixed with expectancy filled her.

"My name, say it. Let me hear my name from your lips."

He was standing directly in front of her, not touching her, but scorching her skin all the same with the intensity of his gaze upon her. "Peter."

"Hey, Peter, Miss Winifred, come, the meal is ready." Lord Blessing stuck his head in and the spell was broken.

Winifred stepped back from him as if she would burn up at any moment. She looked at Lord Blessing, disappointed but grateful that he had intruded. He only smiled at her, then disappeared back the way he had come.

"Let us go and feed my brother's empty stomach," Peter said with a lopsided grin. "And I imagine yours is ready for filling as well."

She nodded.

He held his arm out for her to take, and she did. Peter

tried to calm his insides. She belonged here. He could not shake the truth of that statement and the bit of fear that went with it. With every room they viewed, he could see her pleasure with the place and it drove the nail in deeper. She belonged here and he knew she was his chance at happiness and his dreams. She was the one he would marry, no matter what he had to do to make it so.

When he had dreamed about her as his wife, here, in this place, it must have been a premonition or omen or something. It was almost eerie, the way she took to Trenton Manor. He wondered if she saw herself belonging here.

They walked through the kitchens and out the back hallway. Winifred stopped to admire the fishing poles hanging along the wall and he could not refuse her when she asked if she could borrow one and try out the brook. He loaded his pockets with lures and flies and grabbed a pole for himself.

Her aunt would no doubt think it highly unladylike for her to fish, but Peter found it only endeared her to him more. No matter what hoydenish behavior she displayed toward him, he did not care. He liked her far too well to be shocked at anything she did. She was no more a society miss than he was—he looked around with a sense of defeat stealing into his thoughts—a decent man.

Was he fooling himself? Could he possibly be the kind of man he wished to be for her sake? Would he fail her as he had in his dream? They walked out into the sunshine, but he did not feel its warmth. He wondered if it was not too late for him to be more than what he was.

"What are you thinking?" Winifred asked. They were headed toward the orchards, where the picnic had been laid by the few servants he kept.

"Is this your 'special question'?" he asked. He did not want to have to share his thoughts.

He saw the smile go out of her eyes. "No, this is not the one. I will warn you, remember?"

"And I have to answer?"

"Yes, truthfully. 'Tis a matter of honor, you know. I won the wager squarely."

"Yes, yes. It is quite lowering to be so completely beaten by a woman with all her admirers looking on and cheering." He rolled his eyes heavenward in mock disgust.

"Yes, well you are truly a terrible archer. It was not so very difficult to win."

"Never interested in the thing. Standing about, sending arrows into stuffed targets seems like a waste of time."

"But 'tis a matter of skill and control. What sporting activities do you prefer?" She had stopped walking and now looked at him, patiently waiting for him to answer, her expression slightly indignant, challenging.

He leaned closer and whispered, "I prefer sports with contact, very close contact."

He watched the blush rise from her neck to cover her cheeks. Yes, he would enjoy such contact with her.

"Mr. Blessing, you are truly reprehensible."

"Have I not told you time and again that I am a scoundrel?"

"So you have said." She looped her arm back into his, but she did not sound quite like she believed him.

Luncheon was served and they ate well. His caretaker's wife had prepared a marvelous meal and served it under the shade of a white canopy by the brook. The ladies commented often how lovely everything was, and Winifred looked so relaxed that he had a mind to keep her here forever and never return to London. He had never considered Trenton Manor as paradise before, but the presence of his Athena was quickly changing his view.

"Shall we try out the pole?" she asked with a twinkle in her eye as she raised the reel and rod high.

"Win, where on earth did you get that?" Melanie asked.

"In the back hall behind the kitchens."

"It belongs to my caretaker," Peter informed them. "He is very fond of fishing and says the trout are plentiful in the stream here."

"Well then, what are we waiting for?" Winifred stood up, pole in hand.

"You two go on ahead," John said. "Miss Melanie and I shall remain here."

Peter noticed the content expression on his brother's face and turned to look at Melanie and winked. She was making progress, of that he was certain. He had never seen his brother look so carefree in eight years.

"We shan't be far, only up a few yards or so, where the stream widens and is deep," Peter said.

John watched his brother go, and a sudden wash of nervousness stole over him. He glanced at Melanie, who was sitting prettily in her chair, nibbling a tartlet. Her abigail and the caretaker and his wife were not far off playing a game of cards. "Miss Melanie," he started, then stopped and swallowed hard. Egads! He felt like a green lad again. She was looking at him, waiting for him to continue. "Would you care to take a stroll with me about the grounds?"

"I should like that above all things, my lord."

She rose with grace and took his arm, her cheeks a soft pink.

Blast! She knows, he thought. She looked very much like she expected his offer. Well, how could he blame her. He had held her hand as they walked through Peter's house and he had done very little but gaze upon her all morning like a lovesick puppy.

Which he was. He was overjoyed with the knowledge that he loved her. It filled him with promise, and hope that he could make a new life for himself. Sweet Melanie understood his love for his first wife and her memory did not threaten her. All the more reason he loved her, she would not require him to forget Anne.

"You are very quiet, my lord, is there something troubling you?" She had stopped walking and had turned toward him, her eyes a beautiful shade of blue. He loved the way her eyes changed depending upon what she wore. Today she dressed in a powder-blue gown that displayed her figure to advantage.

He swallowed again. He was more than tempted to pull her to him and ravish her pretty little mouth, but he held himself in check, his desire under steely control. If he dared unleash his passion upon her, he feared he would frighten her, or worse, he would not stop with just a kiss.

"I would like to ask you, Miss Melanie . . ." he started. No, this was all wrong. He could not ask her here, standing near the drive. "Come, let us go into what is left of the gardens. There is a bench there, where we may sit and be more comfortable."

"Very well." Melanie followed demurely, even though her heart soared and she felt like dancing a jig. He was going to offer for her, she just knew it. The poor man was trying to be so proper about the whole thing. She just wished he would ask her and be done with it. Otherwise, she would soon burst with excitement.

They walked into what was left of the Trenton gardens. Although mostly overgrown with wild roses, Melanie thought it a lovely, secluded place. A perfect place for a proposal and other things. . . .

Lord Blessing brushed off the bench before she sat down. Then, he placed his handkerchief upon the ground and knelt on one knee. Melanie thought she would explode from waiting. Finally, he took her hand in his own and looked up at her.

"Melanie," his voice was soft, almost a whisper.

"Yes," she interrupted.

"I would be most honored if you would consider becoming my wife."

She started to answer but before she could even take a breath he continued.

"I will ask your father's permission, of course, and I would not dream of distressing you with this offer if I did not think that you cared for me and would consider my suit."

"Yes," she interrupted again.

He blinked, then a smile split his handsome face. "You will?" He seemed almost surprised, then thought better of it, coughed, and added, "Yes, of course. You will. You have made me the happiest of men."

She reached out and took his face between her hands and stared deeply into his brown eyes. "You, sir, have made me the happiest of women."

He leaned forward and looked ready to kiss her. Melanie concentrated on his lips moving closer to her own, then she closed her eyes. But instead, he gathered up her hands and placed a reverent kiss upon her palms. Disappointment seared through her momentarily. She could hardly force him to kiss her. He would be shocked at her forward behavior. He was a proper man, after all, so she would simply have to wait until they were officially engaged to kiss her betrothed. For now, she would be satisfied with his offer.

"Melanie, please do not tell anyone until I have had the chance to get permission from your father. Perhaps I should have asked him first."

"No, I am glad that you asked me. My father will approve. He must, for I am determined to have you. In fact, he is coming to town so we can make it official very soon."

Peter could think of nothing more pleasing than watching Winifred land a trout. His smile grew wider when they reached the widest part of the stream up ahead. At the water's edge she kicked off her half-boots and demurely stripped off her stockings. "What are you doing?" he asked.

"Well, I have to wade in a bit. Are you terribly shocked, Mr. Blessing?" Her cheeky grin made him laugh.

"With you, nothing is a shock. I like it better when you call me Peter," he said. He let his gaze wander over the delectable barefooted goddess he pursued. He tore off his coat and waistcoat and decided to enjoy the heat of the day.

When she turned and glanced at him, she was the one who looked shocked as he too, pulled off his boots and waded barefoot in after her.

"Two can play at this game, Miss Preston," he said.

"Whatever can you mean?" She looked innocently at him.

"You think you can scare me off with a little fishing? And taking off your stockings? For shame, what would your aunts have to say?" He practically ripped his cravat from around his neck and threw it to shore.

He watched her swallow and stare, when he unbuttoned his shirt.

"What are you doing, Mr. Blessing?"

"Just getting comfortable, my dove."

She actually breathed a sigh of relief when he stopped and rolled up his sleeves. Until he got closer to her. He knew she stared at his neck and the bit of chest exposed for her view. He should have taken the blasted thing off entirely! She almost dropped the fishing pole in the water as she stood gawking at him. He smiled. He liked the way she looked at him and felt his own pulse race. If he could distract her enough with her own desire, perhaps he could offer for her, here and now.

She had failed to retrieve her bonnet. With the sun shining off her hair, he wanted more than anything to offer for her. But he was consumed by fear that she would say no. An unwanted ache hit his chest as he thought about her rejection. If he could just pretend, even for a moment, that he was worthy of her, perhaps he could find the courage to ask.

Instead, he held out his hand to her. "Here, you're going to need these." He had pulled a couple of tied flies out of his coat pocket before wading in toward her. He could not ask her, not yet.

"Thank you." She took the lures, and adjusted the pole in her grip to affix them to her line. She bit off the excess with her teeth and he just stood there watching the breeze play havoc with the tendrils of hair that had come loose. "How can you not live here, Mr. Blessing?"

She was trying to distance herself from him. He knew it every time she called him Mr. Blessing. "My presence would only ruin the place, I'm sure."

"How can you say such a thing?"

"I'm no farmer, for heaven's sake."

"Have you ever tried?"

She sounded like John. "No, I have not tried."

"Then how can you know?"

He gritted his teeth; he did not want to get into another one of her discussions. "I don't know the first thing about soil and crop rotation and all that nonsense."

"Does your caretaker know?"

"What are you suggesting Miss Wisdom, that I have my own servant teach me how to plant?"

"You need not be so touchy."

"I'm sorry. It is just that . . ." He did not finish his statement that he did not want to fail. He was not Lord Sheldrake, his friend, who studied the latest techniques in agriculture and enjoyed putting them into successful practice with his tenant farmers. Peter did not care. Let his tenants do what they had always done, and their fathers before them.

"What, what is it? What makes you gamble for a living when you could easily make a go of it here?"

"Easily? My dear, turning this place around could hardly be easy. I make only a small income from it, I assure you."

"But that is because you are not here to try things, to bring it up to modern standards and the like."

He stayed silent, considering her words. Her dowry would no doubt provide Trenton Manor with the funds to do just that. Many of his acres had not been farmed nor used for years. His manor was not nearly working at a quarter of its potential.

She cast her fly and it fell neatly into a calm pool, downstream. "You said before that your brother hated what you do. Surely, he could find no fault if you managed your own estate."

"I am sure that he could, my dear. It's one thing to be a disappointment when you're a gambler. It's expected, in fact. It's a whole different matter to be a disappointment in managing one's estate."

She turned and looked at him directly, as if seeing through him. It made him dashed uncomfortable to be looked at in such a way. He concentrated on tying a fly onto his own line.

"How did you come by this place?" she asked.

"I inherited it from my mother's side."

"Oh, I see. It must have been terrible for you not to have known your mother. My mother died four years ago, and although I miss her dearly, at least I was able to know her."

"But I cannot miss what I never had. It was far worse for my brother and father. No matter what I did or tried to do, I could not ease their sadness. They missed her."

"But it was not your place to ease their hurt, you were but a child."

Not his place? He was the reason for their sadness. It was his first grand failure, was it not? Nothing he did could ever erase the loss, so he had stopped trying. "Winifred," he began, "can we not speak of something else?"

She looked troubled, but nodded her head in agreement. "If you wish." She suddenly gasped as her line pulled and bent. "Oh, 'tis a big one!'

He waded back to set his pole down on shore, then he was behind her in a trice. He steadied her with his hands resting upon her waist, helping her keep her balance on the moss-spotted and slippery rocks. She bent toward the fish, then back, reeling furiously.

"Easy, easy," he chanted.

The line snapped and she fell backward into his chest. They both staggered, but managed to stay standing. Then she turned in his arms.

He pulled her close.

"He got away," she whispered.

"Lucky for him." He looked deeply into her eyes and pushed a strand of reddish-gold hair off of her face. It was the most natural thing for him to do. He leaned closer, ready to take her lips, which were ripe and waiting for him. But what he found in her gaze before she closed her eyes made him weak in the knees. Pure love beamed from her like a beacon in turbulent waters.

It shocked him. He could not quite revel in his success

at making her fall in love with him. He was glad, he was almost elated. The only emotion he never expected to feel was fear and that fear held him back. He let his lips brush only lightly against her own, then he pushed her slightly away. "Here, it's getting late, and we must have you and your sister in Mayfair before it is dark."

She opened her eyes and gave him an odd look, almost as though she was sorry that he had not kissed her thoroughly. "I should like to ask you my special question now, Mr. Blessing, while we are still alone."

He felt dread spread through him like ice, snuffing out the fire that she had already started in him. "Shall we make it to dry land first?"

She nodded.

When they were sitting upon the bank of the brook donning their shoes, she turned to him, very serious. "Why is it that you are so determined to marry money? What makes it so important?"

He nearly choked. Why, indeed, he thought sarcastically. He had given his word that he would answer truthfully and that he would never lie to her. But his answer could take her from him. She would see him as the scoundrel he was, and in her disgust and contempt, he would lose her. "You never mince words, Athena, never."

She sat quietly, though, awaiting his response. Where should he start? "I have a large debt that I must pay and I do not have the funds to do so."

"A gambling debt?" she asked.

He nodded, not able to look her in the eye. He hoped to God that she did not ask him how much.

"And Lord Blessing would not help you?"

"Not this time."

"I see," she said, and stood. "Thank you for the use of your fishing pole, Mr. Blessing."

Hurriedly, he slipped into his waistcoat, but he did not bother with his coat or cravat. He pulled his timepiece from his waistcoat pocket and checked the time. It was indeed late. They walked back to the picnic area in silence. He cursed himself as a fool to have been truthful with Winifred. But what else could he have done? She would have found out once they were betrothed, and then she would have known he had lied to her and she would not have forgiven him for it.

What difference did it make now what he could have or should have done? He doubted that she would ever agree to accept an offer of marriage from him after hearing her own fears confirmed. He was a gambler, one who was in deep for a large sum owed. And she did not want her fortune put at risk by such a man as he.

He looked at her, but she seemed deep in thought and there was a furrow to her brow. Obviously, she was not in the least pleased with his answer.

He rubbed the back of his neck. What was he going to do? It was the middle of May and he had to have ten thousand pounds plus interest by the end of next month. He looked around his grounds and wondered if he should just concede failure. He could sell Trenton Manor, and it would serve him right to lose it.

He pushed his self-pity away long enough to consider his options. He could not bear the thought of returning to court Miss Whent; besides, he had insulted her at the Donnors' breakfast. Melanie was in love with his brother and they belonged together. The deuce! He did not want anyone else. He wanted Winifred and he'd have her.

There had to be another way of gaining Winifred's hand in marriage besides asking her directly, or her father for that matter. Peter refused to listen to his conscience as a brilliant idea formed. He need only to thoroughly compromise her to gain her hand. It was perfect!

He had only to get her alone, amid a large group of people, and kiss her senseless. That could pose some difficulty. A dinner party or a ball would be the place to carry out such a thing, but when and where? He had never seen her wander off where he could take advantage of her and be caught. She was always in the company of Melanie if she stepped away from the main crowd.

He rolled the idea around in his mind, cursing to him-

self when he realized that such an action would crush
the look of affection in his Athena's eyes for a long
while. He would simply work all the more hard to make
her happy later. She loved him, so he would seek her
forgiveness afterward.

He had to have her. He knew he needed her far more
than just for her money. His debt was nearly due and
his word as a gentleman was on the line, so he had to
act fast in order not to lose his nerve. He looked about
his grounds as they approached the orchard. He could
see the outline of Trenton Manor against the sky. It
needed Winifred Preston as well. It was high time he
gave his inheritance its due.

"Did you catch anything?" John asked when they
came to the small canopy.

"I had a big one, but it broke the line," Winifred said.

Peter noticed that Melanie wore an expression of concern as she looked upon her sister. Peter hoped that she
would not turn her sweet blue eyes upon him for any
answers. He felt like a heel contemplating the compromise of Winifred, but he did not have any other choice. It
had to be done. He would make it up to all of them later.

"I was just informing Lord Blessing that our aunts will
be hosting a huge ball in honor of Papa's return to London. Please say that you will both come," Miss Melanie
said.

"When?" Peter asked calmly. The place and time were
about to present themselves. This was the chance he was
looking for, and with Mr. Preston in attendance, Winifred's fate would be sealed. He winced at his own bold
terms of thought. He was foul, but then what else could
he expect from himself? This was one game he intended
to win, and failure was not an option.

Winifred lay upon her bed, a soft breeze blowing the
curtains about the windows. Sleep would not come. She
had almost given it all away. Her love, her dreams, her
fortune, they were offered up to Peter Blessing, who
could destroy them. She had wanted him to kiss her
senseless in that stream. She had wanted him to offer for

her. And she had thought he would, but then he had held back. She was grateful that he did. And then she asked her question and her warm and wonderful daydream ended.

Peter Blessing was a gambler. It made no difference that the reason he gambled was merely to hide. She believed that he could walk away from it, if he truly desired to do so. But he was so afraid to try something else, that she wondered if he would ever stop gambling. In so many words, he had admitted to a fear of failure at managing his own estate.

Needless to say, it did not matter. He had lost at the tables before and would no doubt do so again. His debt must indeed be considerable if his brother refused to settle it for him. She wondered how they could stay on such easy terms with each other. Lord Blessing clearly adored his younger brother and Peter admired him in return. There seemed to be no grudge between them, yet Peter felt that his brother would find fault with him, no matter what he did.

And so, he had turned to gambling where failure was merely part of the odds, an expected thing.

Winifred rolled over and fluffed her pillow. Perhaps when her father arrived, he would let her return home straightaway. She had to get away from Peter. Her heart ached at the thought, but she pushed it away. In time he would only bring her pain. Was she up to the challenge of trying to reform a rake? Could her love for him be enough or would he come to resent her for her efforts to change him?

She could not bear the thought of Peter hating her for nagging at him to stop gambling, yet she could not possibly stand by and let him gamble if she were to marry him. In the end, she would resent him for his weakness and he would hate her for meddling. She could not let her funds be misused in such a way, especially when Trenton Manor begged to be attended to. Would he even agree to reside there?

If she married him, would he leave her at Trenton Manor, alone, while he returned to London and his rakish way of life? And when he tired of her and her demands, would he pick up where he had left off with Lady Dunstan? If that happened, she knew she would simply die inside. She pounded her pillow with her fist, but it was of no use. She could not spare herself the agony that was raging inside of her.

Her heart longed for Peter, her mind cursed him, and her soul was so confused it did not know what to do. If she could leave and go home, she would save herself and Peter the grief that was bound to come to them if they continued on this course.

Chapter Eleven

Winifred dressed carefully in a white muslin gown with an overdress of spangled silver net. Tiny diamonds hung from her earlobes to wink and sparkle in the candlelight. She could not help but feel a bit nervous due to the tension of expectation that surrounded her. Peter would soon be there and she could barely wait to set her gaze upon him.

She had seen little of him the last week and a half and she knew he was staying away on purpose. He played the game of courtship to perfection, knowing full well that his absence would further incite yearning for him in her heart.

She twirled in the cheval mirror, pleased with her reflection. She did not feel so awkward as she had when she had first arrived in London. She admitted that Peter had much to do with her newly found confidence. He made her feel like a desirable woman, not at all the tomboy she had often been called. She supposed she had him to thank as well for her success this Season. Had he not brought her to the attention of the Corinthian set?

It was amusing that she cared little about such attention when she had always craved it. Instead, she loved

Peter, a man who most likely did not love her in return. Again, she reminded herself that marriage to him would only court disaster for them both one day. She knew that as sure as her own name.

But tonight was different. She would put away her reservations and make it a night to remember. Her papa had given her permission to leave early and return home with him in a few days. Melanie would remain in town and plan her wedding. Melanie had received their father's approval to Lord Blessing's offer of marriage and tonight, they would announce their betrothal to the *ton*.

This was to be one of the last evenings she would spend with Peter Blessing for a long while, and she promised herself she would enjoy every moment. She planned to take advantage of each opportunity to make memories that she could cherish for always.

She took a deep breath and released it slowly before descending the stairs. The guests had not yet arrived, so Winifred sauntered through the empty halls to the ballroom. It looked like a fairyland with all the candles and twinkling little lights that her aunts had used. Two balconies which overlooked the small courtyard garden had their doors opened wide to let the warm night air mingle with the scent of beeswax candles and hothouse roses. The musicians tuned their instruments while the servants filled the punchbowl.

"Your aunts do know how to give a party," her father said.

She turned and smiled. "Yes, they do."

"And Miss Winifred Augusta Preston, are you sure you will not regret missing more of these to return home?"

"No, Mr. William Jacob Preston, I shall regret nothing. You know I do not care for society whirl and the like. Besides, Melanie will be in a whirl of her own with wedding plans. She has Aunt Augusta and Aunt Winifred to help her."

"Melanie tells me there is a young man who has been seeking your attention. What about him?"

She turned away from her father to study a bouquet

of pink rosebuds. Leave it to Melanie to tattle about Peter when she had asked her not to. "Actually, I have had more than one gentleman caller, Papa. But I assure you there is no one who will miss me overmuch when I leave." She looked up at him with a smile, hoping to convince him that she had no ties to keep her here.

Her father narrowed his gaze as he looked at her, but he said nothing further of the matter. "You look so very pretty," he added. "You would have made your mama proud this night."

"No mud or tangles." Winifred grinned. Her mother had always been at her wit's end when it came to her daughter's boyish pursuits. She had tried in vain to steer her toward the gentler, ladylike activities Melanie had excelled in and enjoyed.

Her father laughed, the warmth of it filling the room and her heart. He was such a dear man. Even after the grief she had caused him with David Stanton, her father had made her promise not to be anyone other than herself. He had always encouraged her in her pursuits and told her to enjoy her youth. He had often said that once it was gone, it was gone forever. She wondered if her father regretted the path that he had been forced to follow. He had spent his young days working in cotton mills for his father.

"Aye, no mud and no tangles. A lovely young lady has taken up residence where my little girl once was. You have turned into a grown woman—a lovely one."

Winifred did not mistake the bittersweet note to her father's voice. She threw her arms around him and squeezed tight.

Her father returned the embrace. His voice thick with emotion, he whispered, "Go now and take your place beside Melanie. I want everyone to see my wonderful girls when they enter."

Winifred did as she was bid. She stood next to Melanie as the guests arrived. After welcoming what seemed like hundreds of them, Aunt Augusta gave them leave to mingle. Winifred hurried into the parlor and looked out of the window at the line of carriages, but she did not see Lord Blessing's coach. But then Peter had said his brother's townhouse was but a block or two away. Perhaps they had decided to walk.

"Looking for someone?"

Winifred whirled around to find Peter standing in the doorway, his charmingly boyish grin spread across his handsome face. She stared at him a moment, memorizing every feature, every elegant line of his evening clothes. "When did you get here?"

"Just now." He walked toward her, his gaze never left hers. "I missed you," he said.

Her stomach flipped over and she felt so warm, so tempted to throw her arms around him and tell him that she, too, had missed him. If only he were not a gambler, were not a fortune hunter, if only she could trust him with her future. " 'Twas not my fault you stayed away."

"So, you missed me too." He took her hand in his and raised it to his lips for a lingering kiss.

She let her eyes close briefly at the feel of his touch upon her skin, but thought better of herself. She need not dissolve at his feet this early in the evening. "Come and see the ballroom," Winifred said as she pulled him along.

Peter followed obediently, but he could not keep his eyes off of her. She looked beautiful in her white dress. She had been out in the sunshine again, as her cheeks and nose had a tell-tale rosy glow and her freckles shown clearly. But her bright blue eyes sparkled and she stared at him as if she had indeed missed him. He glanced around the ballroom, wondering where he could get her alone for a compromising kiss.

The thought of kissing Winifred Preston senseless thrilled him, but he had to keep pushing his conscience firmly into a place where it would not bother him. Guilt gnawed at him for what he had planned. He had been over it many times and still the same conclusion faced him. It was his only chance of success.

He could not back out, not because of a code of honor that frowned on taking advantage of a young woman who loved him. He vowed to himself that he would make it up to her, he would find a way to make her happy once they were married.

Winifred stopped in her tracks before an older, distinguished-looking gentleman who could be none other than her father. He had the same reddish-gold hair and brilliant blue eyes as his daughter.

"Mr. Blessing, may I introduce you to my father, Mr. William Preston," she said.

Preston had not failed to notice that Winifred held onto his hand. Peter had to force himself to look into the man's eyes, so thick was the shame he felt. He was grateful for the chance to bow and look away from that piercing gaze. "How do you do, sir."

William Preston extended his hand. "Mr. Blessing, I have heard many good things about you," her father said as he shook Peter's hand vigorously.

Good things? Peter wondered what they could be and who could have been the teller. Surely not Winifred, since she looked almost embarrassed at her father's statement.

"Have you, sir?"

"Aye, Melanie tells me that you have shown a marked interest in Winifred."

Peter noticed the strength behind the friendly smile and began to sweat. He looked at Winifred, who rolled her eyes but overall seemed unconcerned. The man obviously hinted at Peter's intentions. Heaven help him, but his intentions were not honorable. He planned to ruin his daughter!

He cleared his throat and pulled at his cravat. It was deuced uncomfortable to be under the steel gaze of Winifred's father. "Yes, sir, your daughter is a most captivating young woman."

"Aye. Perhaps we can sit down over dinner while I am in town and discuss it." It was not a request, but a demand, and Peter knew he was in deep trouble if he failed tonight. Once Preston found out what kind of man he was, he would no doubt forbid any further contact with Winifred. Perhaps John had already warned his future father-in-law.

"Papa, please," Winifred interrupted.

"Sorry, my dear. I am certainly keeping you from the dancing," her father said with a slight bow.

"Your servant," Peter responded with a bow of his own before he allowed Winifred to whisk him farther into the ballroom. Couples were already forming sets for a country dance.

"Well, what do you think? Is it not beautiful?"

He looked around and noticed that the ball had already become a mad crush. The Preston ladies were considered very good *ton,* and the turnout of guests only confirmed it. He glanced at her face. She was so enraptured with the scene before them. "But I thought you did not like London, nor society," Peter teased.

"But this is different as it is a welcome tribute to my father and a celebration of Melanie and John's engagement."

He took hold of her hand to raise it to his lips. He too was glad for John and Melanie. He had not seen his brother this happy in ages.

Winifred could not help but shiver at the feel of Peter's lips upon her skin. He had an expression of longing in his eyes. Surely, he could not fake such a look, she thought as she pulled her hand away from him.

"I see the first dance has already started, but may I have the next one?" Peter asked.

"Yes."

"And you must save a waltz for me, as well," he said.

Winifred tried to get control of the shiver of excitement racing along her spine at the thought of waltzing with him. She had gained permission to dance it earlier in the Season, but had never done so with Peter. "Of course," she managed as he tucked her hand into the crook of his arm. They made their way around the room stopping to converse with various guests.

When the first dance ended, Peter leaned toward her and whispered in her ear that it was time for their dance. She nodded and without a word, she let him lead her to the floor for a cotillion.

They barely touched, but Winifred was aware of his

every move. She did not take her gaze from his as they bowed and twirled. As if following her example, Peter did not look away from her, even when the steps took him beside her. Winifred wondered if the other dancers in the set noticed the intensity between them. She felt it as if it were a tangible thing, this connection between them. Was it possible that Peter knew what she wanted— a memory to cherish after she had gone?

They came together again, and their hands touched. Peter looked at her with such desire that she missed her footing and nearly faltered. She regained her balance but her composure was beginning to suffer. She felt warm and short of breath and it had nothing to do with a lack of fresh air. A welcome breeze blew steadily through the opened balcony doors. When the dance finally ended, Winifred felt as though she had climbed a mountain.

"Miss Preston, may I have this next dance?"

Winifred pulled her attention away from Peter and turned to see Lord Stanley waiting for her reply.

"Certainly," she said, and was soon whisked back onto the floor.

"You look very well this evening," Lord Stanley told her.

"Thank you, sir." Winifred barely heard the rest of Lord Stanley's chatter. She knew she responded, but for the life of her, she could not remember what she had said. Her gaze kept drifting to Peter.

Dance after dance, Winifred twirled and conversed amiably with all her partners, but her gaze often found Peter's. He seemed content to watch her.

After light refreshments had been served, the announcement of John and Melanie's engagement was made to the approving cheers of the guests. Her sister beamed and Lord Blessing looked as proud as a man could next to the delighted face of her father. Winifred watched it all with a sense of bittersweet awe.

She was sorry to miss being a part of her sister's planning and shopping for the wedding. The marriage was to take place in the autumn, during the Little Season. Melanie had assured her that she understood her reasons for leaving. In honor of the happy news, the strains of a waltz began and Winifred looked about for Peter. He was behind her.

"Our dance, Athena," he whispered close to her ear.

His hand was warm on her waist as he led her to the floor. All thoughts of her sister and weddings melted away. She could look nowhere but into his eyes, and the admiration she saw there tempted her beyond reason to forget everything she knew about him. For once they had no need for teasing words and Winifred merely gazed deeply into his eyes.

"You are lovely," Peter murmured, and drew her close.

The lilting music filled her mind and heightened her senses. She followed willingly as he pulled her closer than was proper, even for a waltz. The heat from him called to her in ways she began to understand and she trembled with yearning. His thigh brushed hers, and his hand at her waist encouraged her yet nearer, until she felt the hardness of his body.

Melting heat coursed through her veins making her light-headed, and she nearly stumbled. But Peter supported her and they moved as one, whirling around the ballroom. He stared at her, his eyes caressing her face, and Winifred was totally lost. She wanted to feel his kiss, and she wanted it now. Not caring that the music had faded, Winifred focused on Peter's lips, wondering what they would taste like. And then she caught a guest's gaping expression.

Dear Heavens! The dance had ended, and there they stood, practically embracing in full view. She pulled back, but it was already too late. Many of the guests were watching them.

"Peter," she whispered.

"My sweet, sweet Athena." He looked as spellbound as she felt.

But she found her voice and pulled out of his arms. "Excuse me, please." She backed away, none too steady, and dashed from the ballroom. She had to clear her head. What if her father had seen her? What would her aunts do? Oh, what a mull of it she had made. If she was not careful, she would be ruined by the end of the night.

Once inside her aunts' library, she let out the breath she held, but her hands still shook and her insides felt hot and heavy. Even her knees were weak. What had he done to her? Even David Stanton's embrace had never left her this unsettled, this hungry for more.

She stepped over to the table that held a crystal decanter with glasses. She reached for them. Popping the top of the decanter, she poured an inch or so of brandy into a glass and tossed it down with one gulp, forcing herself to swallow. The burning sensation brought tears to her eyes. She fought the urge to cough. At last the fog of her mind felt like it was clearing. She leaned against the bookshelves with a shaky sigh, when the door opened.

Peter!

He closed the door and leaned against it. Except for his eyes, he looked as if he were as calm as could be.

"What do you want?" she asked, suddenly scared to pieces of him.

"Are you all right?"

"No, go away," she choked, close to tears or hysterics, she could not tell which.

"Sweet Winifred, you cannot stay in here, your aunts or your father will be worried."

"But you know what happened out there. How can I possibly return after, after . . ."

"It's nothing, I assure you. We gave only a few people a little shock, but nothing to be ashamed of, my dear. Only our affection for one another, anyone can see that was all it was." His voice was soothing, calming.

He stepped farther into the room. The space suddenly seemed too small to Winifred. She backed up, trying to sink into the bookshelf.

"Come, if you are even slightly as overheated as I, then a walk on the balcony is just the thing." His voice was light and coaxing.

Winifred stared at his face and saw the kindness there, and understanding, but there was a nervousness about him too. She looked around the small library, which was illuminated only by the shine of the new gaslights outside pouring through the windows. The door was closed, and they were completely alone. If her father found her here, like this . . .

"Winifred, please come with me," he said, and stepped closer to her, taking her hand in his.

He was so near that she could smell the spicy cologne he wore. She looked at his lips again, and in a moment of madness she wanted nothing but to feel them on hers. In a state of lunacy, she stepped toward him and put her arms about his neck and settled her mouth upon his.

He jerked back as if burned, but then his hands came up on either side of her face and he kissed her. "My proud Athena," he said.

She had started a fire and it soon began to rage out of control. The more she kissed him, the more Peter responded and deepened the kisses. His hands threaded through her hair, causing her careful upsweep of curls to come undone and pins to scatter. She did not care. She did not care about anything except the attention he paid her mouth as she leaned against the books. She paid no heed to the bindings catching at the spangled gauze of her dress as Peter held her and molded her against him as he trailed hot kisses down her throat.

The brandy that burned in her belly clouded the edges of her vision and fueled the desire crackling within her. She could not get enough of his kisses and returned them with answering need. When he nudged her lips open, she parted them willingly and welcomed his heated exploration of her mouth. Their tongues danced to an intimate rhythm. Winifred moaned when Peter's hands caressed her backside and he pulled her hips bruisingly against his own.

The sensations rippling through her at such intimate contact shocked her. But she had become a complete wanton and she tipped her head back, gasping for air. He continued his delicious assault. He bit and sucked her skin as he had once promised, from below her ear to the curve of her shoulder.

"I want you," he groaned.

Winifred could not answer with anything more than a ragged whimper, when she felt his hand close around the swell of her breast. Her knees finally gave out as did Peter's and they sank down. Winifred's bottom softly bumped every shelf, until they sprawled on the floor.

A warning bell in her mind seemed to be ringing, but she discarded it as only her heated blood pounding in her ears. "Peter." Her voice was ragged and thick.

"Yes, love," he whispered against her chest.

He kissed her flesh just above the low neckline of her bodice. He had trouble pulling it down, so he gave up and kissed her breasts through the thin muslin of her gown. She arched against him, and his arms around her tightened.

"Be my own, Win, now."

Winifred understood the meaning of his words, and finally the warning took hold. She began to fear what was happening.

"Peter, stop, please," she cried.

His head came up and he stared into her eyes, his own dark and molten. "I won't hurt you."

He made no move to get off of her as he caressed her face with his fingertip, letting it tap lightly on her swollen lips. Then she heard the crash of the door slamming behind them.

"For the love of heaven, Winifred!" Her father's voice was low, but the fierce anger in it shook her to the core. Even Peter seemed frozen. In his eyes she saw regret, but then he dipped his head down, his forehead resting upon her chest.

"You will explain yourself!" Her father demanded. "And this time, there will be no escaping the altar, young lady." She had an immense desire to crawl beneath the rug, but could not. Her voice betrayed her when she tried to speak and nothing came out. She pushed at Peter. After what seemed like forever, he pulled himself up and off of her.

He had to pull himself together, he thought as Winifred's father raged, but then something he had said stuck in his mind. *This time?* What the deuce did he mean by that?

"Sir." Peter's voice was low. He stood and faced her father and reached out his hand. "I can explain."

"Well, someone bloody well should!"

He cast a look at Winifred, who continued to sit upon the floor looking dazed and unhappy. That was a mistake. Her hair was tumbled, her skirt rumpled up just above her knees, and she had a red mark upon her neck, and he wanted her desperately. He felt such a longing and tenderness toward her that he could barely drag his gaze and thoughts back to the angry father that stood waiting for some answers.

"Papa, please, do not look at me so," she whispered.

Her father whirled around as the door opened to reveal her aunts' shocked faces. "Shut the door, Augusta, I will handle this. But wait outside." Then to Winifred he said, "Get up off the floor, Winnie." Preston went behind the desk, pulled out the chair, and sat down in it with a weary sigh.

Peter went to Winifred's side and offered to help her get to her feet, but she refused his aid. She would not look at him. He turned to her father. "Sir," he began, only to be silenced by the man's raised hand, gesturing for him to halt.

"Winnie, my lass, you are no green girl to be allowing a man liberties without knowing the consequences."

Peter cleared his throat. "Mr. Preston, I assure you that I will do the honorable thing by your daughter," he interrupted.

"Yes, my boy, you will most certainly make amends, but treating my daughter this way is not at all honorable." Then he turned to Winifred who, standing now, hung her head down in shame. "Didn't you learn your lesson? To let yourself be compromised again, Win, is beyond reason. But this time there's been more witnesses than just me. You'll be wed by tomorrow once we've purchased a special license."

Peter's head was pounding. "This has happened before? Winifred, what is he saying?" The vision that another man had touched her as he had filled him with jealous anger. He squelched it. Now was not the time to accuse her of anything.

She looked at him then, a proud lift to her chin, but tears swam in her eyes. "David Stanton courted me last summer while on leave," she said, sniffing. "He managed to get me alone at a house party last autumn and kissed me. My father found us."

Peter's hands clenched. But she continued. "He was a fortune hunter, Mr. Blessing, much like yourself." She was trying to keep a strong front, but Peter knew that his Athena was crumbling. "Of course he had professed to love me, which turned out to be a bald lie. At least you have been honest in what you were about. Still, I have repeated my foolishness." Tears rolled freely down her cheeks and Peter felt an aching twist in his gut. "Papa, I am so very sorry," she choked out.

Hearing her take the blame upon her shoulders, Peter thought his heart would break. "No, Winifred, the fault must be laid at my feet."

"Go to your room, Win," her father said. "We will talk later."

"Papa, he is only after my inheritance. 'Tis the money he wants, not me. He is a gambler, you see, and he has a large debt . . ." She broke off with a sob.

Peter reached out to her. He wanted to tell her that he did in fact want her, but she ran to the door, threw it open, and dissolved into her aunt's waiting embrace. He felt like he had been whipped.

"How dare you take advantage of my daughter's love for you!" Preston hissed.

"Sir, I never meant for—" he stopped. It was a lie. He had planned to ruin her, force her into marriage. But he had no idea that some cad before him had tried the same thing. And he had never meant to lose control as he had. He had hurt her, deeply. Something he promised her he would not do. The disgust he felt for himself must have been evident as William Preston sat watching him.

"You don't look too happy about what you have done,

son," Preston said. "If you're having second thoughts about marrying her, then think again."

"No, I want to marry Winifred. I never meant to hurt her, or cause her such embarrassment."

Preston quietly let his gaze bore into Peter. "What she has said about your gambling, is it true?"

"Yes, sir. I am sorry to say, it is." Peter looked him straight in the eye. He had no wish to be anything but honest with this man. "I would have thought that John would have told you."

"To his credit, he did not. But we did speak about you and Winifred. He says that you are a good man. Melanie thinks the world of you and she is no fool."

Peter had the good grace to bow, but he felt like the lowest form of life.

"How much do you owe?" Preston motioned for Peter to sit down at the chair across from him.

Peter edged into the seat. "Ten thousand pounds, plus interest due the end of next month. The sooner I can settle the debt, the less it will be overall."

"I see." He did not bother to hide his shock at the large sum. "Tomorrow, I will have my solicitors advance you what you need and the settlements will be drawn up for your review. I shall warn you now that I will not stand by and watch you destroy yourself or my daughter's happiness. Do you understand?" His eyes were hard and his expression, deadly serious.

"Clearly, sir." Peter did not want the wrath of his future father-in-law upon his head nor did he want to destroy anything any more. "I promise I shall not play so in future." He felt an odd release at saying the words. A newly found freedom permeated his being. He did not want to risk the Preston inheritance and it lightened his heart somewhat to have that decided. He was, if nothing else, a man of his word.

"Good." Preston seemed pleased with Peter's answer and a softer expression took over the man's stern face. "I shall have a special license brought around quickly and you shall be wed straightaway."

"If I may suggest . . ." Peter began. Preston nodded

for him to continue. "Perhaps you could still have the banns read. We did not, I mean, that is to say . . ." Peter pulled at his already loosened cravat. "I do not wish to cause you or your family any further shame. There is no reason for us to marry in such haste. For Winifred's sake, please allow her some time."

Preston gave him a hint of a smile. "You truly care for my Winnie, don't you?"

"Yes, sir, I do, very much."

"She could do worse, I suppose." Preston rose and extended his hand. "Very well. We shall have the banns read and you can have a proper wedding at St. George's Church before the end of next month."

Although Peter knew there were more worthy men for Winifred, he was glad for her father's words and ready acceptance of him. He shook his hand and added, "Thank you, sir. I humbly beg your pardon for the grief this has caused you."

But the older man merely dismissed him with a wave of his hand. "I am not the one sobbing upstairs. It is to Winifred that you owe the greatest apology. I'd just as soon see Winifred wed. You appear to genuinely care for her, which is most important to me." Preston paused as if in thought, then added, "Stanton merely embraced her overly warm, Blessing. It was nothing to excuse it and sending him packing without anyone the wiser."

"Thank you, sir, for that," Peter said, glad nonetheless to know that only he had touched her so. "May I speak to her?"

"Nay, I think enough has been done tonight. Come back tomorrow." Preston ran his hand through his hair, then fixed his steely gaze back on Peter. "Make no mistake, you will rue the day you were born should you make my daughter's life an unhappy one. But, I am an excellent judge of character, son. I can read people better than any book. I believe there is more to you than meets the eye."

Peter pondered the man's words, and for a moment he felt as if his own father spoke to him, or John. He hoped that Mr. Preston was correct.

He left the library in search of his brother to tell him that he was leaving. Peter was in no mood for his brother's scorn, so he walked away quickly, before he could receive the much-deserved lecture that looked ready to fall from John's lips. He would explain things to his brother tomorrow.

It appeared that the Fitzhugh ladies had done a good job of smoothing over the sudden disappearance of Winifred. The ball continued with only a few whispers about him. Peter did not know if Melanie knew what had happened, and his conscience suffered another blow at the thought of disappointing his staunch ally. Perhaps she would regret the aid she had given him in pursuing her sister. But he would deal with that later as well, when he had to. He would make it up to them all.

For now, he wanted only to walk in the warm night air and try to forget how he had hurt Winifred. He wished he had dragged her from there and out onto the balcony. Why hadn't he? He had nearly lost control with his sweet Athena. Had her father not walked in at that moment, he would have had her there on the library floor if she'd have let him. Never had he been so filled with aching desire.

He looked up to see a candle burning near a window, and wondered if it was Winifred's room. He longed to comfort her, hold her and tell her he truly desired her. He knew he had lost whatever trust she may have had for him and that caused him far more regret and remorse than he had thought possible. He decided that in the three weeks of their engagement, he would do all he could to make it up to her. And then, when they were married, he would make her his own. Now that everything had been put into motion, he would reach for this chance at happiness with both hands. And he would not let go.

Winifred let the curtains fall back against the window as she saw Peter disappear from sight. She fell onto her bed with a sob. She had brought the worst sentence upon her head. She was to be married to a man who loved her not but for the money she brought him. And she had thought that he truly cared for her!

She had seen his affection, or thought she had seen it, in his eyes all evening. She must have been mistaken. Only a man who cared for nothing but greed would compromise her so disgracefully and bring such mortification upon her head and that of her family.

She buried her face under her pillow as she remembered the look of shock upon her father's face. No doubt Melanie would be ashamed of her as well. Her fall from proper behavior would mar Melanie's good news and take away from the attention and joy that her sister deserved. There would be so much talk and tattle, she would never hold her head high again.

What had she been thinking to kiss him so? She was the biggest sort of fool to think that it would not lead to disaster. Her father was right; she had not learned her lesson. And now she would be punished for it. She had wanted a memory to cherish and instead she had earned herself a husband who could only break her heart. She sobbed anew and did not hear the soft knock upon her door.

"Winnie?" her father's voice penetrated her misery. He stepped into her room, his footsteps light against the thick carpet.

"Yes," she mumbled from beneath the pillow.

"Come now, my girl, it is not the end of the world. You will be marrying a man you love. That is not such a bad thing."

"I do not love him," Winifred lied. Her head was still beneath the pillow.

Her father sat down on the bed and pulled the pillow away. "Now, now. I have two eyes. I can see plainly enough, and Melanie has said . . ."

Winifred sat up and threw herself into her father's arms. "Melanie does not know what she is about, none of you do. Peter Blessing is a terrible man, and I will never forgive him."

"Shh. Hush that kind of talk. That is no way to start a marriage, my dear."

"It does not matter. I will have no wedding, no bride's cake, it will not be a real marriage, only a special license, and 'tis no more than I deserve. 'Tis my own foolish fault." She started crying again, but her father patted her back as he had done many times, having to be both parents since her mother's death.

"You will have your wedding, dear. It may be small, but the banns will be read and you can have your bride's cake."

She pulled away from her father and searched his eyes. "But I thought . . ."

"I know. I was going to have you wed on the morrow, but your Peter would not have it. He assured me that a fast marriage was not required. The announcement will go out tomorrow to the *Morning Post* and the banns will be read on Sunday. Then in three weeks you shall have your wedding."

Winifred sighed with relief. She was sure there would still be gossip, but at least she need not hang her head in complete shame—except around her aunts, of course.

"Get some sleep now, and we will talk more about it in the morning." Her father kissed her forehead.

When the door opened and Melanie stuck her head inside, her father waved for her to go. Again, she was relieved. She did not wish to discuss what had happened.

She rolled over onto her stomach and breathed deeply, but she could not dislodge the ache that had settled in her chest. He had betrayed her, ruined her, forced her into a marriage that he knew she did not want. But it had been her own doing, her own boldness that had landed her in such a coil. She should have known that one kiss from Peter Blessing would not be enough.

She remembered the feel of him holding her, touching her, and her head grew light with the longing she still felt. It was too late for her to escape now. She had blown her chances for that. At least she would have the next couple of weeks to grow accustomed to the idea of marrying him. And she would see if she could not reform the man before they got to the altar. She had to at least try. She feared their very future together depended on it.

Chapter Twelve

Winifred drank her coffee while she read the *Morning Post* when she came upon the bold black letters that announced her engagement to Peter Blessing. It had all seemed like a distant dream, but reading her future's fate in black and white somehow made the thing undoubtably real. With a feeling of dread, she flipped the pages to the gossip column and her shame was made complete as she read the details that had brought about her betrothal.

No one is the least surprised to hear of a certain young lady's betrothal after she was found in a VERY compromising position with Mr. B. at the F. sisters' ball the night before last. Of course, Mr. B. has been seen in Miss P.'s company on a regular basis since the beginning of the Season. One can only guess at the shock of Lord B. and his dear Miss M. P. to have their siblings so engaged.

How dare they! Heat flooded her cheeks in shame and anger. She would not be able to face anyone. It was not fair, not fair at all! Tears of frustration sprang to her eyes, but she dashed them away with the heels of her palms. She would not cry again, she fumed. She had done enough weeping these last two days to last her a lifetime. With a snarl, she threw the paper across the table.

"Good morning, Winnie," Melanie said after entering the breakfast room. She proceeded to the sideboard for a muffin.

Winifred only groaned.

"Ah, so you have read the *Morning Post,* I see." Melanie's smile turned impish when she spotted the discarded papers strewn about.

"Yes, and how shall I ever walk about with a shred of pride now that everyone knows why I must wed?"

" 'Tis not so terribly bad. These things happen and there are always mean-spirited people who revel in it and try to make more of it than they should." Melanie poured herself a cup of coffee and took a sip. "How did you get him to kiss you so?"

"What?" Winifred nearly choked.

"How did you get Peter to kiss you?" Melanie asked more slowly.

"Melanie, please." But Winifred knew that her sister would badger her until she knew the truth of it, so she may as well spill it now. "I kissed him."

"You kissed him?"

Winifred tried to ignore her sister's shock, picking up the closest parts of the *Morning Post* in an attempt to bury her mortified face between its pages.

But Melanie would not be put off and she pushed the papers down with her hands as she looked at Winifred with triumphant glee. "Oh, but that is famous! What a wonderful idea."

"Melanie, what are you talking about? Look at me, I am ruined!"

"Yes, but you will be wed, and that makes a big difference, does it not?"

Winifred was not sure what her sister meant by that, but she was humming and lathering a muffin with marmalade. Nothing seemed to faze Melanie. But Winifred was very much affected and afraid of marriage to Peter. Her dreams of traveling would not come true and her inheritance would be at risk. All because she was a wanton who did not know how to stop.

"Well, I had best go and change. John and Peter will be here directly to take us for a stroll in the park." Her sister took her muffin with her and left.

A knife of dismay cut through her. She did not want to see Peter! Not yet. Had she not made that clear when he had called yesterday and she refused to see him? She stood, wondering what excuse she could give, when the

door opened and her aunts' butler announced the object
of her thoughts. Peter stood in the doorway.

He was as handsome as usual, dressed in a dark blue
coat of superfine. But his eyes looked troubled, unsure.
They stood and stared at one another until the butler
left.

"Where is Lord Blessing?" Winifred heard herself ask.

"He will be here soon. I told him I would meet him.
I was hoping to talk to you alone." Peter closed the door.

"I see no reason why. You have what you want, what
more can be said? You have won our final game, sir."
She was glad to see that her sharp words had effectively
lashed him. She could not help but want to make him
suffer as she was.

"Winifred, please understand that I did not mean for
what happened." He stepped forward.

"Have you seen the paper this morning? The shame
of it all. There is no escaping it, none, not after reading
that gossip column!"

"Win," he said, reaching out his hand toward her.
"Gossip dies down."

"Did you plan to ruin me, Mr. Blessing? Did you plan
for this to happen?" Her voice had grown shrill, but she
had to know. Even though she had been the one to kiss
him, the thought plagued her. He had followed her into
the library, he had shut the door. He had known they
were alone.

His silence betrayed him, and her heart sank.

"I cannot lie to you, Win." He stood so close to her
now. "I wish I had never thought to do such a thing. I
am more than sorry for it now. But yes, I planned to
compromise you." He had grabbed hold of her arms.
"Winifred, look at me."

She did and was sorry for it. She was trapped by his
gaze, his remorse-filled gaze.

"I never intended us to be in such an out-of-the-way
place. I tried to make you come out on the balcony with
me, remember? But then you kissed me and I lost all
control."

She backed away, fearful of letting him touch her

again. Instead, she pulled the hurt, the betrayal that she felt at his admission firmly around her like a shield. "Why?"

"Why did I lose control?" Peter asked as he ran his hand through his hair, making a disordered mess of it. "Because I wanted you, Athena. I want you still."

Winifred's insides turned. She remembered too easily the sensations he had evoked in her when he whispered to her and pulled her close to him. She tried to quell the shiver that raced along her spine and see reason. She could not let him take advantage of her weakness for him yet again. She could not let herself believe he cared for her more than her money. It would be pure folly. The hurt would be all the more painful later on when he became bored with her or came to resent her.

"Why did you think you had to compromise me? You could have asked properly," Winifred found herself saying.

"I have been honest with you, can you not be the same in return? Can you tell me that you would have accepted me, or even considered my suit, had I asked?"

She saw the flicker of frustration in him and thought better of denying what he said was true. "You are right. I would not have accepted you. But you know the reasons why."

"Believe me, my dear, I know them far better than you. I promise I will try my best to make you happy. Give me a chance."

"How can I?"

He was grabbing her hands, touching her again. "Because I am not like this Stanton fellow who lied to you and played you false. I will never, ever lie to you."

She looked at his expression of appeal and was more than tempted to give in and believe him. Her wounded pride held her back.

He caressed her cheek with his hand, pushing a stray tendril of hair behind her ear. "I am not like him, Athena. I care for you."

But he did not love her! Why could he not love her? Maybe they would have a chance if he did. What was she to do? Her fortune always stood in the foreground as the reason for Peter Blessing's attentions and she could not get past the knowledge that he cared more for her inheritance than he did her.

"It is not easy for me to know I am wanted because of my money, Mr. Blessing," Winifred said. She felt too raw right now to look at the thing with any sort of logic. She yearned to throw herself in his arms and hear the words she longed for from his lips. She wanted his love, but he had not offered it. She wondered if he ever would.

"But I want more than that now," he said.

"You have pursued me because of my money and your debt."

"Yes, there is that," he said. "But, there can be more."

"But, there will always be *that,* I am afraid," Winifred said as Melanie peeked her head in to inform them that Lord Blessing had arrived.

The morning stroll had become fraught with tension and Peter knew he was to blame. Melanie had tried valiantly to keep up a bright chatter and carry the conversation, but Winifred was sorely quiet and John kept showering him with scornful looks. He had made a mull of everything and Winifred was still hurting.

He wished he had lied to her, to save himself the pain of seeing her stark hurt and disappointment when he admitted that he planned on compromising her. Blast that man, Stanton! He started her on the road to mistrust! But then he, Peter Blessing, had merely pushed her farther along in her journey.

He had no one to blame but himself for her pain. He wanted more than just her money, but how could he show her that? She did not believe his words; she did not believe that he wanted her for herself. They belonged together, he knew that as surely as his dream had cast her as his wife. Trenton Manor would actually become a home with Winifred Preston as its mistress. How could he make her believe that? How could he make her believe in him?

They walked for what seemed an eternity, but it was

only half of an hour when Winifred finally announced that she was tired. And she looked it. He had not noticed the dark smudges beneath her eyes in the soft light of the breakfast parlor. Not until they were out in the sunshine did he see the evidence of a fitful night's sleep. And all because of him!

If he could feel any lower, he could not imagine it. Winifred had been like a butterfly about to come out of her cocoon and he had squashed her just before she unfurled her beautiful wings.

The first night they had met, she had hung back and taken her place among the wallflowers. But over time, she had become a reigning success and carried herself as if she actually believed in herself. She had danced every dance and chattered amiably with the most sought-after bachelors and maids with ease. She always held her head high.

And he had bruised that confidence with the admission that he needed her money and compromised her for it. He was everything his brother had said to him last night and more. Never before had John been so angry with him.

"You need not end your outing on my account," Winifred said to Melanie. "I can walk back on my own—that is, Mr. Blessing can escort me."

"Nonsense, we shall simply call upon you again. I have business to attend to as it is," John said.

Melanie looked disappointed, but agreed that they should get back.

Peter walked mutely beside his intended bride with his arms clasped firmly behind his back. He had to figure out a way to woo Winifred properly and make things right between them. He longed to see her smile again. Even one of her waspish insults would be better than this downcast demeanor. He wracked his brain, trying to decide what his course of action should be. He looked at John, and realized he would be of no help. He was still angry with him.

Melanie had surprised him. He had expected her to be angry. But yesterday when he had called and Winifred refused him, she had sat with him. She gave him a scold, but never stopped treating him with sisterly fondness. She had encouraged him to give Winifred time. She said that she knew Winifred loved him and would eventually come around.

But he feared that waiting would not do. He needed to make her believe in him and his affection now. If they were to make any sort of go at it, she had to learn to trust him. He had to earn that trust from her.

He needed help. He needed sound advice. There was only one person he knew of who could understand the hurt Winifred must feel and give him instructions accordingly. He needed Lizzie Dunstan's advice.

Melanie watched Peter say his good-byes to Winifred, who looked as if she could barely stand his presence. She hoped they would work things out. They obviously loved one another, they just did not seem to know it. Or at least Peter did not. Poor man. All he need do is let Winnie know that he loved her.

But she could not meddle when she had her own troubles. She looked at John, walking stiff and silent beside her. The man acted as if he could not wait to leave. Ever since they had become engaged, he had been distant and she worried over the reason why.

She hoped that he did not regret his decision to offer for her. Perhaps he thought her too frivolous? She had chattered gaily about her plans for a wedding trousseau yesterday when he called. He had turned positively starch-lipped at the mention of any nightclothes. She had merely tried to tease him out of his quiet demeanor, but her silly comment had not been received with any humor.

She longed for a moment alone to discuss the matter, but John was always dashing off whenever the chance at privacy arose. But maybe she was going about it all wrong.

"John?" She laid her hand upon his sleeve.

"Yes?"

"Do you think you could stay but a moment and take a turn with me in the courtyard?"

She thought she saw him blanch, but he nodded his agreement. She took his hand in her own.

John followed her. His fingers threaded through hers of their own volition. They stepped into the small court-yard and he noticed that it was terribly secluded. That was not at all good. He was trying his level best to not be alone with his bride-to-be, but she was making it dashed hard.

"Melanie, I truly need to get back to my study and the piles of papers there."

"Oh pooh," she pouted. "Sit with me, just for a moment. I would like to ask you something."

He let her lead him along the path flanked on either side with flowers in full bloom. Without thought, he brought her hand, still entwined with his, to his lips. "Very well, but just for a moment, then I must be on my way."

Always, at every gathering since she had accepted his offer, she found a way to get him alone. And it took all of his willpower to keep from pulling her into his arms and kissing her. He wanted to wait until they were safely wed to demonstrate their affection. He wanted to take his time and make sure he did not scare her to pieces with the strength of his desire.

She was young and innocent and the chit had never, ever been kissed. He had planted chaste kisses upon her brow, or cheek, but he hesitated when he contemplated those luscious lips. Blast! He was staring at them again.

"John, is there something wrong?"

"Wrong, no." He let go of her hand.

She stepped closer to him. He backed up, but there was a bench behind his knees and he plopped onto it.

"You seem very distracted of late and I wanted to know if there was anything wrong." Her eyes looked green today. She stood above him, looking down. She was the prettiest sight.

"Nothing."

She took a deep breath and studied her fingers. "Do you regret offering for me?"

Good God, where did she get such an idea? "No, Melanie," he said. "You made me the happiest of men when you accepted me."

"Then why . . ." She stepped closer, her skirts swishing over his boots. "Why are you avoiding my company?"

Why, indeed. He did not answer, he merely stared at her as she inched closer and placed her hands upon his shoulders.

"John?"

"Yes."

"May I kiss you?"

He would never make it to the wedding at this rate, he thought. "Perhaps we should wait," he managed. She stood so close to him, and yet still she stepped closer to stand between his legs.

"Why? I have never been kissed before and I wish to know what it feels like."

She leaned down then, and placed her lips gently upon his. He let her. Her lips were soft and pliant, but they stayed still. She did not move them, only pressed them firmly against his own. Her innocence was more than he could bear. He had to show the poor girl how it was done.

He pulled her into his lap and tilted her head back to better access her mouth, which had fallen slightly open with surprise. Then he gave her what she wanted.

His lips brushed hers and instantly he deepened his kiss. She did not hesitate to follow his lead and she opened to him. Her tongue danced with his own and he shook with longing.

"Oh my," she said when they finally parted.

Her lips were swollen and her cheeks flushed a deep pink. He held her, still on his lap, and knew that if he had any hope of stopping, this was the time. "How do you feel?" he asked with a smile.

She smiled back, her eyes a bit unfocused. "All fluttery inside and a little hot. Can we try that again?"

"No, we shall wait until after we are wed. That way we will not get into trouble." He stood with her in his arms, then he set her on her feet.

She swayed and wrapped her arms firmly about him.

She looked up into his eyes. "John, perhaps we have made our engagement too long."

Yes, he thought as he placed a light kiss upon the end of her nose. "What should we do about it?"

"Let us move up the wedding. Winifred and Peter should be back by the first of August. Let us be married then. Now, will you please kiss me again?"

The next day, Peter decided he would visit Liz. The housekeeper took his hat and walked him along the familiar hallway to the drawing room.

"Peter, what a charming surprise." She stood and held out her hands.

"Liz." He brought both her hands to his lips. "You look well."

"As do you. Come and sit down. You have arrived just in time for tea." She motioned for him to sit across from her and once the housekeeper departed from the room, Lady Dunstan leaned forward and handed him a cup of the steaming liquid. "I read your betrothal announcement. I offer you my congratulations. I had my doubts about Miss Preston, but you have succeeded with nigh three weeks left of the Season. How did you do it?"

Peter smiled sourly. "How do I get anything in life, Liz, but by unsavory means?"

"So it is true. You did compromise the girl."

"I did."

"What a wonderful idea." Her voice did not sound pleased. She sat back and busied herself with her own tea. "And it worked for you."

"It hasn't worked well at all." He sank his teeth into a macaroon.

"Miss Preston must be upset," Lady Dunstan said. "Perhaps just bridal nerves."

"No, I have truly hurt her. She thinks I want only her money."

" 'Tis what you wanted, after all." She had rounded on him and she looked him directly in the eye. He had disappointed Liz as well with his actions.

"Yes, but . . ."

She interrupted him. "I helped you meet eligible young ladies, Peter. But had I known that you would have forced them into a marriage, I would not have been so keen on getting you introductions."

"I'm sorry, Liz, but I had no other choice."

"Peter, this is a woman you are dealing with, not a game of chance. She has a mind of her own. Why did you not simply ask her, and give her a choice in the matter?"

"Because she would not have had me," he said. And I did not want to lose her, he admitted to himself.

"And what of Miss Whent, she would have gladly accepted you. Why did you not pursue her?"

Because I wanted Winifred, he thought, but answered, "Frankly, I could no longer stand the sound of her voice." He had tried to lighten the mood, but Liz did not laugh.

"Surely, a bit of irritation is worth the dowry that she would bring. Her funds nearly match that of the Preston heiresses. Why did you not offer for Miss Whent, Peter, what is the real reason?"

She was studying him intently and he did not like it. "What is it you want, Liz? What do you want me to say?"

"What is it you want, Peter?"

If she would stop scolding him long enough, he could tell her. "I want to make it up to her. What can I do to make this right? Should I buy her gifts? What do you suggest?"

"No," she smiled. "You only wish to stop feeling guilty. Deep down inside of you, Peter, you must have some idea what it is you want for your future—your future with Winifred Preston."

He stopped and thought a minute before responding. Finally he looked at her and said in all honesty, "I would like a chance at true happiness, Liz. I think I could have that with Winifred if only I could be a man worthy of it."

Tears gathered in the corners of her eyes and she reached out and caressed his cheek with her palm. "I want that for you, Peter. And your Winifred, she deserves such a future." Her voice cracked and she stopped and reached for her handkerchief. He gave her a moment to compose herself.

Peter suddenly understood that Liz had no chance at such happiness with Dunstan and his heart went out to her. In all the years he had known her, he had thought her lonely. He never realized how truly unhappy she was.

"Forgive me," she said with a weak smile. "Peter, to make that happen for you both you must simply love her. What a woman truly wants is to be loved."

Something he had never done. He had never let himself love. Could he let go of his feelings and love Winifred? But that opened himself up to such risk. He had seen the grief of a father and a brother, did he want to open his heart to risk that kind of pain?

"Liz, I am so sorry," he found himself saying. He wondered if she had loved him and in his arrogance and selfishness, he had never been sensitive to it.

"For what, Peter? It is not your fault that Dunstan loathes the very sight of me. 'Twas not always this way."

Dunstan! She pined for the love of that pompous fool.

Peter felt a bit lighter at heart knowing that he had not hurt her deeply when he had ended their relationship. They had, evidently, been using one another for their own reasons and had merely forged a good friendship in the process.

"Dunstan is a fool," Peter said with feeling. He cursed her cold-hearted husband for ignoring her.

"Yes, he is. But you are not." She smiled, all trace of sadness gone from his view. "Winifred is no doubt feeling betrayed right now, but do not let her continue to feel that way. You need to be honest with her. Tell her how you feel about her and do not quit until she listens. Of course, it never hurts to shower her with a few presents."

"Thanks, Liz." He took another tea cake, then rose to his feet, anxious to get to the shops for a gift. "I appreciate your words of advice."

"Do heed them." She stood and walked him to the front door where she handed him his hat as he stepped outside.

Still on her top stair, Peter turned and planted a hearty kiss upon her hand.

"Good luck," she called after him as he dashed the rest of the way down the stairs.

"Why Winnie, dearest, what is the matter? You have gone completely white, as if you have just seen a ghost." Melanie grabbed her sister's hands and rubbed furiously.

Winifred sat stunned. She could not tear her gaze away from the window of her aunts' carriage and look at her sister. She had just observed Peter kissing Lady Dunstan outside of her townhouse. She looked about the streets frantically for the sign. Yes, it was Curzon Street. Seven Curzon Street was indeed Lady Dunstan's address.

A searing pain lodged itself inside of her and she breathed deeply in an attempt to calm the shaking that she feared would overtake her. Why had they not gone home the long way?

She turned to Melanie, who remained looking at her, full of concern. " 'Tis nothing," Winifred fibbed. "I have a headache."

"And no wonder, it is rather warm today and you have so many decisions to make regarding the wedding arrangements and your bride's clothes."

"I simply need to lie down and I shall be fine." Another lie. Her heart felt like it had split in two. She did not think she would ever be fine again.

"Of course," Melanie said, and she patted Winifred's hand. "The gentlemen will be joining us for dinner, so you will want to be rested for that."

Winifred groaned inwardly and thought she would be sick. How was she to look at him without killing him? Or without dissolving into a fit of tears? She had forgotten all about tonight's dinner party.

There was no way she would share him with another. It was better that she did not have him at all. She would simply not marry him.

How could he? she thought furiously. She had feared such a thing would happen eventually, but she could not believe he would reinstate his mistress so soon. She had rebuffed his attempts to smooth over what had happened, but surely he could have tried harder. Surely, he could have been a little more patient with her. Winifred looked out of the window as one hot tear after another fell silently down her cheeks.

By the time they reached the Fitzhugh residence, the hurt and betrayal Winifred felt had begun to turn and change. In its place, cold fury and anger rose up from the depth of her soul demanding its due. She knew she could not back out of her betrothal without creating a scandal and causing her family incredible grief. But she could get even! Winifred decided there and then that she would make Peter Blessing rue the day he had been born. And if she was fortunate, perhaps she could cease loving him.

Once inside her bedchamber, Winifred's plan to seek revenge had taken form. She would demurely play the role of a newly betrothed young lady for the next couple of weeks. There was no reason to cause her family any further distress with mean displays of spite. And her already tainted reputation could stand no further mishaps. She would reserve all her fury for Mr. Blessing until after they were wed, and then he would be sorry he had sought her out.

She had just finished putting her new purchases away and thinking of any number of ways to torture a new husband when a knock at the door caught her attention. A servant had a message for her. She flipped open the card and read:

My Dear Winifred,
I look forward to seeing you this evening. I hope you will accept this gift as a token of my affection for you. I do want much more than you believe and I look forward to proving it to you for the rest of our lives together.

Your servant,
Peter

Winifred looked at the footman expecting to see a package delivered. When he merely stood with his hands folded, awaiting his dismissal, she finally asked, "Where is the gift that accompanies this?"

"Outside, miss."

"Outside?" Truly curious, Winifred forgot her anger for the moment. She bounded down the steps to the front door and opened it wide. She walked outside to see a wizened old man standing next to a beautiful mare. "Helen of Troy is my gift?"

The old man nodded. "Aye, she is. Master Pete gave me firm orders to deliver the mare to yer hands, Miss Preston. Ye are Miss Winifred Preston?"

"Yes, I am." She descended the steps slowly. Once in front of the mare, she patted its nose. "Are you the groom?"

"Ye could call me such. My name is Stark, miss, and I am Master Pete's man of many things." The little man bowed.

Winifred could not help but smile at the odd man before her. She stroked Helen of Troy behind the ears and cooed her greetings to the sleek creature.

"Aye, she likes ye, she does," Stark said. "Master Pete said ye was a fine horsewoman. I'm that glad to see her go to such a fine lady with horse sense."

"Thank you, Mr. Stark."

"Just Stark, miss."

"Very well, thank you, then." Winifred turned to lead Helen of Troy to the stables when she noticed that Stark had not left. "Is there something amiss?"

"Do you have a message you wish me to give to Master Pete?"

"No, I do not."

"Then do you mind if I watch her one last time? She is a sweet goer, she is."

"You may come with me to the stables, Stark. You shall see her again. Mr. Blessing and I are . . ." Winifred swallowed the lump that suddenly caught in her throat. "We are to be married, after all."

"So's I heard, and salutations and all to ye. But I won't be seeing her agin."

"Why? Will you not be removing to Trenton Manor?"

"Nay, can't abide the country. Besides, the master will need me here to keep his apartments for his private use when he's up to town for a bit and agin."

His private use? Her mind whirled. "But surely you will be joining us at a London townhouse after we are wed."

"Nay. Master Pete says you have no love of London and that it'd probably only be him coming to town on business. And so's I will keep his flat for him in Belgrave."

"I see. Well thank you for delivering Helen of Troy. I promise she will not lack for anything."

"I see that, miss." He tipped his hat and made his way down the street, whistling.

Winifred stood stroking the mare's nose and staring off into the distance. He had no plans to make Trenton Manor his permanent home. Why did she expect otherwise? He had told her that he did not like living at his manor when they visited there only weeks ago. Did she think that just because he had a wife, he would wish to live with her? Of course he would keep his own quarters in town—how else could he continue his gambling and his arrangement with Lady Dunstan?

What pleasure she had gained from Peter's gift was quickly disappearing under the realization that Peter Blessing could not possibly have any depth of affection for her. He did not even plan to live with her after they were married. But why would he go to the trouble to give her such a glorious gift? And what did he mean about wanting more than she believed?

Perhaps he was simply making sure of his investment. He could not afford for her to balk and back out of their betrothal. This gift and his sweet words were only a manner of trying to win her favor. Did he not know that he had her completely trapped? An ache deep within her chest made her pause and swallow the lump that took hold in her throat.

Could she believe him when he said that he had never lied to her nor would he do so in the future? Was he not lying to her now, with his renewed relationship with

Lady Dunstan? Anger boiled inside of her. Good, she needed to stay angry because then it did not hurt quite so badly.

Raising her head high, Winifred walked Helen of Troy to the stables where she was met by her aunt's head groom. She handed the mare over to capable hands and headed back to the townhouse to wash and change for dinner.

Dressed in a cream muslin gown embroidered with bluebirds along the hem, Winifred entered the drawing room where everyone was gathered. Peter looked up and smiled at her. Her traitorous heart responded with a melting sensation that she still could not overcome. It was horrible to be so affected by him. He appeared perfectly at ease; in fact, his smile was ready when he saw her.

Peter met her in the middle of the room and offered her a small white rosebud that he had been holding. "How are you today?" he whispered.

Winifred accepted the flower and fingered its soft petals. "I am fine." She gazed directly at him, rallying all her strength and fury to keep her from succumbing to his charm. "I must thank you for Helen of Troy."

"I am glad that I have pleased you." He reached out to tug on a loose tendril of her hair, and she nearly jerked her head away from him. "I miss you," he whispered.

She closed her eyes briefly, to keep from breaking down in front of him. How could he whisper such sweetness to her when he had returned to his mistress?

"Win, what is it?" he asked with genuine concern.

" 'Tis nothing, only I shall be very busy with wedding plans and so I doubt we will see each other much."

"Is there something else bothering you?"

"Besides the fact that you have gotten my hand by means most foul?" She had the pleasure of seeing him flinch at her acid words. But he pulled his mask of charm into place and smiled. But not before she had glimpsed the guilt, the shame, and yes, even the anger in his eyes.

And she was almost sorry for her attack, because it had been a long time since she had seen that mask of charm. It made her feel only worse to see its return.

Chapter Thirteen

True to her word, Winifred had kept herself busy with a flurry of activity and planning for her upcoming nuptials. Her initial return to social functions after her disgrace was not nearly the ordeal that she had feared. No one cut her, nor was she treated rudely, with the exception of a snicker or two from Miss Whent, who had recently announced her own engagement to Mr. Oliver, of all people.

The weeks passed and Winifred was relieved that she had seen Peter alone only briefly. But they attended the last of the Season's social functions together along with Melanie and John. As always, he was attentive and charming, but she often glimpsed concern in his eyes when he looked upon her.

His gifts had increased in frequency. They had been small things, really, instead of the token jewels she had expected. His gifts demonstrated much thought and care used in the choosing. He had purchased her a gilt-bound volume of Mr. Shakespeare's plays, a beautifully crafted fishing pole with a box of tied flies, and a set of mother-of-pearl hair combs adorned with carved mermaids. The note with the hair combs explained simply that they reminded him of her. Such thoughtfulness nagged at her belief that he did not care for her. In fact, she knew that he must.

Her heart had been in constant turmoil. When Peter was near her, he displayed utmost respect and restraint. He was not too forward, nor did he press her for kisses. He acted the perfect gentleman toward her. Gone were the heated displays of desire and seductive smiles. This only added to her conviction that he had reinstated his one-time mistress. And that set her blood to boiling with hurt and fury.

She had kept a forced smile upon her face, for her family's sake, even though she felt close to tears at almost every turn. The once-promised-to-be-small ceremony had turned into a grand affair. Aunt Winifred and Aunt Augusta had invited over half of the *ton* to the wedding and the sumptuous breakfast that followed. Word was out that the wedding of Winifred Preston to Peter Blessing was to be the last glittering affair of the Season. One not to be missed.

Peter could not figure out what was eating away at his proud Athena. She refused to open up and share her troubles with him. He hoped her megrims were only due to the hectic pace of an ending season and a huge wedding to be planned. He rarely had a chance to speak to her alone. He continued his assault of gifts but to no avail.

He even visited Liz again, to see what he was doing wrong. She encouraged him to work it out on the bridal trip, once they were alone. The voice of reason assured him that it was just bride's nerves, but he feared he knew better.

Winifred was hurting and trying to bury that hurt in a busy schedule. She had not allowed him to make amends, and that worried him. He hoped that once they were on their honeymoon at John's hunting lodge in Scotland, everything would right itself and he could finally make her his own.

Peter tore off yet another cravat that refused to be tied properly. "Stark!" he yelled.

"Sir?" The old man cocked a quizzical brow.

"I need another one of these blasted things!"

"If ye'd just let me tie it, ye'd be better off."

Peter sighed with resignation as Stark gave a try to a newly starched bit of linen. He would be late to his own wedding if he did not get his cravat tied. He wanted to look his best for his new bride.

He had not expected to be so nervous, but he was.

Everything had been put to order these last two weeks. He had met with Mr. Preston's solicitors and was stunned at the amount of the marriage portion. There had been some funds kept back for Winifred's use alone, but by and large the whole thing was under his control to use as he saw fit. He would lack for nothing. He found the money a pale victory next to knowing how much his actions had destroyed the easy bond between himself and Winifred.

"There ye be, Master Pete, and don't ye look like a prince er some such."

Peter preened a bit further before finally making his way to St. George Church in Hanover Square. The chapel was bedecked with flowers. A heady perfume of roses hit him with full force when he took his place at the altar.

He stood before the parson who was to marry them and patted his pocket where the ring that once belonged to his mother lay. He would soon slip it onto Winifred's finger and they would be husband and wife. As he gazed about the church at all the faces of society, he wondered, not for the first time, if he should not have married Winifred by special license as her father had wanted and spared the fuss of such a grand event.

The church was full when Winifred finally appeared with Melanie, who acted as her bridesmaid. He could barely keep his gaze off of Winifred as she walked toward him. She was radiant, if a little withdrawn. The pale blue silk gown she wore looked cool and perfect for such a warm day. She carried a small bouquet of fragrant blossoms with the same flowers arranged in her hair as a wreath. A veil of lace completed her bride's clothes. Hot desire ripped through him when he thought that tonight, she would at last be his. He wanted to chase the shadows of doubt he saw in her eyes with lovemaking.

Winifred did not mistake the hungry look in Peter's gaze and her body reacted with a shiver, to her utter annoyance. Would she ever not be affected by him? Peter had visited Lady Dunstan again; she had seen him enter her townhouse.

She did not hear the parson's words. She thought only of what she could possibly do this night, her bridal night. She nearly laughed aloud when she bitterly realized that she had been planning ways to punish Peter Blessing since they had first met. Only see what the consequences of such games had delivered. If they were destined to live a marriage of convenience, then she would have her time of reckoning now and be done with it.

She supposed it would not be so very bad, leading a solitary life as mistress of Trenton Manor. She loved the place and it was not so very far from Lord Blessing's estate in Surrey. She would be able to visit Melanie as often as she liked. A sad sigh escaped Winifred's lips as she bent to sign her name on the church's register. Melanie and Lord Blessing were head over heels in love and witnessing them together was rather like having a jagged knife jabbed into her heart. She felt pricked until her heart bled. She could hardly stand being in their presence.

She looked up and glanced at Peter as she handed him the quill. His questioning gaze was full of tenderness. Then his charmingly boyish grin split his face and he leaned toward her and whispered, "Tonight, my sweet."

It was late afternoon by the time they traveled north to start their honeymoon. Peter was more than edgy and the miles seemed to stretch too far and long. He hoped they would arrive at The Rose and Slipper, a pretty inn approximately two and a half hours north of London, in time for dinner. Peter had personally inspected the inn and had reserved a bridal suite for them.

Winifred was little company, as she slept the entire trip. But he watched her nonetheless and his heart felt full. Was this the love that Liz had spoken of? When they pulled into the yard of the inn, Peter leaned over his sleeping bride.

"We are here," he whispered. He watched Winifred's eyelids flutter and open. She yawned and looked straight at him in a dreamy sort of way. Hope soared within him, only to be dashed when she came fully awake and pulled back to withdraw within herself.

"Did you have a nice nap?" he asked.

"Yes, I must have been more tired than I realized."

He escorted her to their suite and soon a fine dinner collation of pheasant and succulent meat pies was set before them. Winifred ate heartily and he was glad that she had rested well on the way as he did not plan to sleep overly much this night.

Although they had spoken little, Peter was heartened considerably when Winifred announced that she must change for bed. Now they would get somewhere, he thought. He needed only the chance to kiss her and let desire take its course and they would be fine.

Finishing his wine, Peter walked to the open windows and looked out over the garden in the inn's courtyard. A soft breeze stirred the curtains about him and he inhaled the scent of roses and summer night.

"I am ready," Winifred said softly.

He whipped around and nearly dropped his glass. She stood in the doorway to the bedchamber dressed in a filmy thing that left little to the imagination. Heat surged through him and settled in his loins. He swallowed hard and realized that he was not quite as sure of himself as he wished. When his legs made no move to take him across the floor to his waiting wife, she came to him.

He stared like an idiot as his Athena, in her nearly naked glory, walked barefooted toward him. She made sure she moved slowly enough that he could take his fill in looking at her. Her legs were long and her hips smooth and the small swell of her breasts enticed him the most. She was lovely.

When she stood directly before him, a hard glint in her eyes, she took the goblet of wine from his hand and brought it to her lips for a seductive sip before setting it down. Her gaze stayed riveted to his own. Finally, he looked at her lips. Her mouth trembled slightly as she smiled, and he wasted no time in kissing it.

Her arms came around his neck and she tipped her head slightly so she could better return and deepen their kiss. His hands grasped her delectably rounded backside and he pulled her against him. "I have waited an eternity for this," he whispered when he broke away from her lips and nuzzled into the soft skin of her neck.

But she pulled away from him. He noticed an odd shimmer in her eyes. Anger and fury poured out of her as she faced him with a look of complete triumph. "You can wait another eternity for all I care," Winifred stated, looking every bit the outraged goddess. "You have married me for my money, sir, and that is all that you shall ever have of me."

"But . . ." Peter sputtered. He could not believe what he was hearing. "What do you think you are doing?" His voice was thick and hoarse.

"Simply giving you a taste of what you shall be missing. But then, you have already sampled such favors from your mistress."

He saw raw pain in her eyes that froze him to the core. Before he could do or say anything in response to such an outlandish statement, she turned and ran to their bedchamber and slammed the door.

"What the devil are you talking about?" he bellowed.

When he heard no response, he charged to the door and rattled the handle, but it would not budge. The minx had locked the bloody door!

"Winifred, what the deuce are you talking about? What bloody mistress? I haven't got a mistress," he roared.

"Lady Dunstan and you deserve one another. Now leave me alone!"

Lady Dunstan? Peter stopped dead. Why on earth would she think he had gone back to Liz? "Win, I broke off my relationship with Liz the night we met. I have done nothing to renew it, I swear to you. I would never do that to you. You are all I want."

A muffled sound came from beyond the door. "Yes, and I am the Queen of Sheba!"

He thought he heard her sob. He rattled the handle again, then pounded on the wood. "Open this door!" he ordered.

"Never."

It was a watery response and now he knew she was crying. He took a deep breath, trying to calm himself, but to no avail. He certainly could not break down the door and ravish his wife in order to prove to her that only she inflamed his blood. That would make matters worse.

With an oath and a curse, he picked up the unfinished wine and threw the glass against the empty hearth. The tinkling sound of breaking glass did little to dampen his frustration. Slamming anything and everything in his path, he pulled open the door to their suite and stomped into the hall.

At the sound of the crash, Winifred sat up. Was he tearing the place apart? She suddenly felt fearful that he would break down the door and beat her. But instead, she heard the parlor door slam, and she knew he had left. She let out a shaky breath and sobbed anew. She felt awful, terrible. Instead of getting revenge solely on her husband, she had punished herself as well. But she could not, would not give herself to him if it meant sharing him with another.

Peter was at a loss to know how to handle his wife. For the remainder of the trip to the Scots border, they had spoken little. She looked like she had spent the night crying. He knew he must have looked like hell as well, since he did not sleep a wink. He had sat in the pub, nursing a pint of ale. He tried to coax her to tell him why she thought he had renewed his relationship with Elizabeth Dunstan, but Winifred kept saying that she had seen them together. That she had seen him kiss her.

He wracked his brains trying to figure out what she was talking about. Out of mere frustration, he let his temper get the better of him. He finally snarled that he did not care what she thought. That had not been the right thing to do at all. But after weeks of her withdrawn demeanor before their wedding and now her outright coldness, he had had all he could take. He wondered for the hundredth time what this marriage that he had won by underhanded means held for him. Perhaps debtor's prison would not have been such a bad place after all.

After they arrived at the hunting lodge, things took a

turn for the worse. They kept separate bedchambers and led entirely separate holidays. She rode daily and fished with a rag-taggle group of youths she had befriended from the village. He spent his time shooting anything that did not move and playing cards with the men in the village pub. All in all it was a prodigiously terrible way to spend one's honeymoon. After three days of barely speaking to one another, Peter decided it was time they aired the subject again.

"I want to talk to you," he said when Winifred entered the lodge with a string of trout slung over her shoulder.

"Yes?" She stood insolently staring at him. Her face and arms were tanned as she refused to wear a bonnet. Her hair was a wild mass of tangles and he wanted her just as desperately as he had on their wedding night.

It must have shown, since she smirked slightly at him. He ignored it and pressed on. "We cannot go on like this, Win. I want to make amends, but you won't let me. You keep punishing me. What do I have to do?"

"I do not know. You are what you are and I am what I am, so there it is."

He listened with bitter irony as she stated what he had so often said to his brother John. He was what he was, a gambler, a fortune hunter, and now a failure as a husband. Had he really thought he could make her happy?

He had taken advantage of her love and betrayed her trust. He had done nothing to show her that he was the least bit worthy of her. He had gambled his nights away in the village. Oh, they were small victories and losses, but it was gambling nonetheless, a thing she abhorred, and he knew it. But what else was he supposed to do?

"You know, I wish you hadn't any money at all. Perhaps if it were all gone and still I came to you, you would finally believe me when I said that I wanted you for you," Peter said in defeat.

When she did not answer, only continued to stare at him, he knew he had lost. "Fine, then. If you love it here so much you can stay, or go, or whatever it is you want. I am leaving. I plan to visit Sheldrake in the Cotswolds. Shelly has a family situation and I can be a source of support for him. Here is his address." He scribbled it on a piece of paper and put it in her hand. "If you need me or wish to try and work this thing out, send word for me there."

Winifred watched as Peter emptied a pile of bank notes for her on a table, then disappeared into his bed-chamber. She looked at the paper with the address of Lord Sheldrake written upon it. He was Peter's dearest friend, the man he admired above all, and after meeting him at the wedding, she understood why. Lord Sheldrake positively oozed respectability and honor. She neatly folded it and placed it in her pocket. He was not leaving her for good, only getting away from her meanness. Perhaps if she tried to talk to him before he left, they could come to terms somehow.

She turned on her heel, ready to follow him, but then hesitated and looked at her string of fish. She had to give the trout to the cook. There were not as many servants as she had at her aunts', though enough to run the place smoothly. When she returned from the kitchens, she sought out Peter but he had already left. She felt so alone and empty. She sat down upon the chair that Peter always sat in while he gazed at the fire and put her head in her hands.

Had she finally given her husband a complete disgust of her? It had been her goal all along and at last she had succeeded. She felt no triumph, only bitter grief. No matter what she did, how hard she tried, she could not drive the love she felt for him out of her heart. It had only grown deeper.

She longed for him, and she knew that he longed for her. She had seen it in his eyes enough times to know. And he had laughed at her, with her hoydenish behavior, and she had felt herself melting all over again. But instead of giving in, she had held fast to her anger, trying to punish Peter because of her wounded pride.

Now, sitting alone on her honeymoon, she no longer knew what to believe. Had he told her the truth when he said that he had no mistress? But she had seen him kiss her hand. Why would he be there, standing upon her step kissing her hand so reverently? What other rea-

son could possibly bring Peter to Lady Dunstan's door?
Peter said that he had never lied to her, was it possible
that still he had not lied?

Winifred looked around at the hunting lodge, a place
that would hold no special memories for them. Guilt for
what she had done to her husband washed over her,
threatening to swamp her with regret. It was time she
stopped acting like an angry child. Like it or not, she
loved him. If there was to be any kind of future for them,
she needed to do something to please him.

She stood up with more resolve than she had felt since
the night she had allowed herself to be compromised.
That was another thing she could not keep holding over
Peter's head. She had been more than a willing partner
in the library at her aunts' ball.

There was much to be done, and with Peter gone, she
could go to Trenton Manor and make it a home for
them. The next morning, she rang for a footman to send
word to her husband of her whereabouts and then she
went to her room to finish packing. She truly hoped that
it was not too late.

Peter again fingered the note that he had received
from his wife days ago. He had been at Sheldrake Hall
only a day when it had arrived, and hope surged in his
heart when he had read it. Flipping it open, he scanned
his wife's femininely neat hand.

Peter,
I regret that our honeymoon was disappointing for both
of us. I am most willing to try and make something of
this marriage and I am ready to hear you out. I will be
removing to Trenton Manor, where I hope I may make
a difference. Please give me a little time before you come
home, as I wish to complete my renovations.

Respectfully,
Winifred

The word *home* echoed through his thoughts with such
warmth. He had had visions of her making Trenton

Manor a home ever since reading her letter. And he had given her as much time as he possibly could. It was difficult not to race away from Sheldrake Hall to his wife regardless of her renovations. But he needed to stay for Shelly, until he was certain that his friend no longer had need of him.

Peter tucked the letter back into his waistcoat pocket. He did not wish to lose it, and would keep it always. Peter wanted to be near Winifred more than he had ever thought possible. Without her, he felt incredibly empty inside, like part of him was missing. He needed her. He loved her.

He had to admit that never before had there been a better time to change his ways. There had to be a way to prove to his Athena that she meant more to him than her money. He feared that even if they talked and came to an understanding, the Preston inheritance would always stand between them.

He lay back upon his bed and stared at the ceiling, his packing forgotten for the moment. He wished that he had known what his feelings were weeks ago when they had married. He loved Winifred Preston with every fiber of his being. He had not fully realized it until he was apart from her. Never before had he been in love, so he was totally unprepared for the depth of feeling he discovered he had. He wondered whether he had told her of his love before they had married, their sham of a honeymoon would have been saved.

He was not about to make the same mistakes again. He would tell her he loved her and he would do his best to prove it. Liz's advice finally made perfect sense to him. Winifred needed to know beyond a shadow of a doubt that he loved her. An idea that had been taking shape in his mind these past days became more clear as he lay there thinking about it. The more he thought, the more excited he became.

Peter jumped up and went to his desk to write a letter to Winifred informing her when to expect him home. He would need some time to perfect his plan of action and therefore he could not be expected at Trenton Manor until after a few days spent in London. After some hesitation, he decided not to inform his wife about the London trip. He promised himself that this would be the only time he would ever again keep something from her.

Whistling, Peter resumed his packing when a knock at his door interrupted him. "Come," he said.

Lord Sheldrake entered his room.

"How is she?" Peter asked about his friend's mother.

"I do not know. She kept staring at Abbott's portrait, but I think she will be fine with time."

"He had it coming, you know," Peter responded. Mr. Abbott had married Sheldrake's mother a couple of years ago. He had made Shelly's life a living hell both before and after his death.

"I know that, I just have to make sure she knows it." Sheldrake flung himself in the chair at the end of the bed. "When do you leave?"

"Tomorrow at dawn. Do you wish me to stay?" Peter prayed that Sheldrake did not need him to remain at the Hall. He paused in his packing and turned to look his friend in the eye.

"No, no. We have been through this already. We will be just fine. Thank you for coming." Sheldrake smiled.

Peter merely bowed in response.

Sheldrake sat forward. "You have been very quiet about this Winifred Preston you have married. Matter of fact, you have hardly spoken of her. Is there something amiss?"

Peter knew it was too good to last. Sheldrake had been so wrapped up with his own world crashing down upon his head, that he had not asked about Peter's shortened honeymoon. "I hope to put things to rights between us."

Sheldrake wore a worried frown. "I do hope that coming here did not cause any grief with your new wife."

"It has not." Peter stuffed a few trinkets into his traveling case. "I caused all her grief, Shel. I compromised her in order to marry her for her money and pay off a gambling debt. She doesn't believe me that I truly want her for herself." Peter did not like having to admit such a thing. Peter admired Sheldrake much the way he did his brother, John. Both men lived by a strict code of honor, but where John judged Peter for what he was, Sheldrake simply accepted him.

"No wonder she looked out of sorts on your wedding day."

"I have hurt her deeply and she has been punishing me for it ever since. But now I think I may have a chance." Peter handed Sheldrake the note he had received from Winifred.

Sheldrake looked up after reading it. "You did not have to stay here this long. You could have gone home straightaway."

"I know, but I wanted to stay. I had to come, especially after we spoke at my wedding and you told me you were worried about your mother. Paying a visit was the least I could do for you. I think Winifred and I needed these few days apart to think more clearly. And Win needed time to clean up the manor."

"You love her," Sheldrake stated, looking amazed. Peter cursed himself for being such a rascal that his own friends were surprised that he could actually love a woman.

"Yes, and it took me all this time to realize that I am in love with my own wife." Peter took the note and tucked it into his coat pocket. "Now all I have to do is prove it to her."

"What are you going to do?"

"I have a plan, but I do not have all the details worked out yet." Peter shut the top of his traveling trunk. "I need to go to London before heading home, but I don't want Winifred to know I am there. I am sending word for her to expect me in a week. That should be enough time, I think."

Sheldrake slapped him on the shoulder. "Do not do anything rash, my friend."

"Rash?" Peter asked in mock innocence. "Now when have I ever been known to be rash?"

"Peter, you are an all-or-nothing kind of man. Be careful."

"You may depend upon it that I will be," Peter said, and meant it.

Chapter Fourteen

Winifred stepped out of the carriage and smiled. The small staff of Trenton Manor had gathered in the drive path to meet their new mistress.

A short, round, elderly woman bustled forward with an extended hand. "Welcome, Mrs. Blessing. It is a pleasure to see you again. You remember my husband, Mr. Toller?" The man bowed.

"Yes, and a pleasure it is to see you both again." Winifred remembered meeting them the day Peter had brought them all here for a picnic. It seemed like ages ago.

"Your things have arrived and have been unpacked and put away in the master chambers, Mrs. Blessing."

"Thank you." She was not yet used to being addressed as Peter's wife, but Winifred gave away no clues to such as she let the woman introduce her to the staff. It was a small gathering and Winifred made a mental note to discuss the matter of hiring more help at a later time. Thankfully, no one seemed surprised at Peter's absence.

"And now you must be tired after traveling all that way, and you will want to rest, I am sure. I shall have tea sent up to you directly."

Winifred agreed and made her way up the stairs, following Mrs. Toller. Sunshine streamed through the windows as they climbed the stairs. The manor was clean but still threadbare with a vacant feeling. That would all change soon, Winifred thought. "Mrs. Toller?"

"Yes, ma'am?"

"I wish to refurbish the manor. I was hoping that you may be able to direct me to some shops in the village where I may make home purchases or possibly place an order."

"Oh yes, there are some very nice shops in Westerham. I will make a list for you," she said.

"Thank you. Perhaps after I have rested, we can discuss the lack of staff and such."

"That will be fine, Mrs. Blessing. I must say how pleased I am that you have come. We are very fond of Master Peter and I am so happy that he has chosen so fine a bride to bring this place into its own. Mr. Toller and I are very happy indeed. Ah, here we are."

Winifred smiled and waited as the caretaker's wife led the way into a large bedchamber that was vaguely familiar from her last visit. But it was not quite so sparse now. A writing desk that had not been there before was placed under the window. Sunlight beamed on the cherry wood polished to a glossy sheen. Several stacks of stationery and inkbottles were neatly placed in various shelves.

Winifred walked over to it and ran a finger across its top.

"Master Peter had that sent down among his other things," Mrs. Toller said. She turned and opened another door. "Here is your dressing room, Mrs. Blessing. Master Peter's is across the room on the other side there. And of course, there is a private sitting room through your dressing area. Master Peter suggested these arrangements rather than two separate bedchambers. I hope they are to your liking."

Winifred barely heard the last portion of Mrs. Toller's statement. Her heart hammered in her chest at the mention of his *other things.* She moved silently across the room to Peter's dressing room and peeked through the opened door. With a gasp she stepped in. Boots were stacked neatly against the wall under hanging rows of male clothes! The room was filled with his things—gloves, hats, and other sundry.

She turned to Mrs. Toller, who was now behind her. "When did his things arrive here?"

"Why, I believe it was over a week ago."

Winifred reached out and touched one of the cravats hanging neatly on hooks. He always tugged on them and some looked decidedly wrinkled. Was it possible that

Peter planned to live here at the manor? Hope swelled within her. "But I thought Mr. Blessing had planned to keep a residence in London," Winifred blurted.

"I would not know about that. Master Peter has given Mr. Toller and myself a pension. We will be leaving soon to live with my sister. He plainly stated that he wished to take over responsibility for Trenton Manor."

"Thank you." Winifred felt like hugging the lady, but knew that would shock the polite woman to pieces. "You may have the tea sent up straightaway."

"Yes, ma'am."

Once Mrs. Toller left, Winifred quickly buried her face in one of Peter's starched linen shirts. Traces of his cologne still lingered upon the fabric. Winifred prayed that Stark was wrong. She hoped that Peter planned to make his permanent residence here, at the manor. And why would he not, after making such arrangements for the Tollers?

It appeared that Peter had been busy making plans before they had married. She had no idea how he had spent his days. She was glad to know that Trenton Manor had been one of his priorities. She looked around and realized that her husband owned a considerably large wardrobe. Surely, there could not be more housed in London.

After her tea and a quick nap, Winifred changed into comfortable clothes and got to work. She found that Mrs. Toller was a list maker and after being invited, she kept record of all of Winifred's plans for each room.

Tomorrow Winifred would go into town to make purchases after interviewing local townspeople for staff positions. She decided that she would not change the walls at this time. That was something she hoped that she could decide with Peter's help. She did not want to leave him completely out of her renovations.

Days passed quickly. Winifred supervised the cleaning and arranging of new furniture and carpets and various household items until Trenton Manor came close to what she had envisioned on her first visit. She was especially fond of the results in the breakfast parlor. She had trans-

.formed the room into the cozy nook she had wanted it to be. She spent every morning there, lingering over her coffee and dreaming of Peter's reaction when he came home.

She clutched his letter in her hand, informing her of his arrival in but a few days. She longed to feel his arms around her again, but before such things could take place, they had to come to terms with each other. She had to know about his relationship with Lady Dunstan. She had to understand what it was that she had seen that day on Curzon Street. He would know that she had no intention of sharing him with anyone else. Ever.

A knock at the door brought her attention away from her thoughts.

"A Lady Dunstan is here to call upon you," Mrs. Toller announced. She had promised to stay on and act as housekeeper until Peter returned home.

Winifred almost choked on her coffee in surprise as the woman of her thoughts materialized before her. She waved a hand for Mrs. Toller to show Lady Dunstan into the room and then stood, still choking. "Lady Dunstan," Winifred managed. "I beg your pardon, what a surprise. Please sit down."

"Thank you. Are you all right?"

Winifred nodded.

"May I call you Winifred?"

"Yes." Winifred sat back down, trying to overcome the coffee that had gone down the wrong way when she swallowed. She attempted to smile, but could barely manage a mere curve of her lips. What on earth was the woman doing here? How dare she pay a visit? It simply was not done!

"I am sorry to intrude upon you, but I felt that I must come," Lady Dunstan explained. Winifred must have looked confused and when she remained quiet, Lady Dunstan hurriedly added, " 'Tis about Peter."

Winifred snapped to attention. "What about him?" She eyed the beautiful woman across from her suspiciously.

"I am afraid he will do something terrible in an attempt to prove his love for you."

"What?" Winifred could hardly believe what she was hearing. Her heart began to pound as a feeling of dread filled her.

"I saw Peter in London yesterday, which was of no concern, but then I overheard some gentlemen discussing Peter's challenge to a game of cards last night at a dinner party. This game is to take place tonight. I am not sure where, but the stakes are quite high. I became worried."

"But Peter is in the Cotswolds. He sent me a letter from there and is not expected home until the end of the week." Winifred could not keep the edge of panic from her voice. Surely, Lady Dunstan was mistaken.

"I tell you I saw Peter walking along Bond Street," she said.

"Why would you come all this way to tell me this?" Winifred felt like she had been in a whirlwind and left to catch her balance.

Lady Dunstan shifted uncomfortably. "Because I care about Peter and I am afraid for him. I have done what I thought I should, and now you may do with the information as you like. I bid you good day."

When she rose to leave, Winifred held out her hand. "Wait," she said. She realized that she had not offered her guest any refreshment. "Please sit down. Would you care for some tea or coffee perhaps? You must have left London very early indeed to arrive here just after breakfast."

"Yes, tea would be most welcome," Lady Dunstan said.

Winifred did not bother to ring for a servant. The kitchen was not far away and she needed a moment to compose herself. "I shall be back directly," she said as she left.

What on earth was she to do? Peter had laid out a challenge at high stakes? It made no sense at all. She gave orders for tea to be brought and weaved her way back to the breakfast parlor, a chill taking hold of her despite the warmth of summer.

"Lady Dunstan," Winifred began when she returned.

She had to get something cleared up once and for all. "May I ask you something?"

"Of course, but you must call me Liz." She looked up with wide dark eyes. She was truly a most beautiful woman and she appeared genuinely concerned.

"I am aware of your relationship with Peter. When did he—that is to say, when did you part company?" Winifred stared directly at her, hoping to detect any falsehoods.

"Peter ended our relationship the eve of the Sefton ball."

"And has he renewed it since?" This time Winifred looked away and took a sip of her now-cold coffee, trying to prepare herself for the answer, should it confirm what she saw that day from her carriage.

"Winifred," Lady Dunstan said urgently, "Peter cares for you very much. He would not betray you."

"But he already has. I saw him at your townhouse on Curzon Street before we were wed," she blurted.

Lady Dunstan smiled, then reached across and patted her hand. "He did visit me, but only to ask for advice."

"Advice?"

"How he could make amends for compromising you into marriage. He is very sorry for having done such a thing. He came a second time for more advice. Evidently you gave him quite a time of it, which he deserved." She smiled.

Winifred winced. She had harbored such anger toward Peter for something he had not even done. She had not believed him and she had made them both miserable because of it. "Liz, do you mind terribly if I return to London with you?"

"I was hoping that you would."

Winifred wasted no time. She ordered her things be packed and in less than an hour they were on their way. Winifred gave Lady Dunstan's coachman directions to leave her off at her aunts' townhouse on Park Lane. She would find out what Peter was up to and prevent him from losing a fortune. A terrible fear that had planted itself long ago took root and began to grow. She would not let Peter lose her inheritance.

As they traveled, Winifred was surprised to find that she liked Lady Dunstan. She spoke so fondly of Peter that Winifred wondered if she was in love with him. Until she spoke of Lord Dunstan. Winifred was sorry to discover that Lady Dunstan was sadly in love with a husband who seemed to care little about his own wife. Winifred promised that she and Peter would not come to such an end. But first she had to stop him.

Once they reached Mayfair, Winifred thanked Lady Dunstan for coming to her. They pulled up before her aunts' townhouse and Winifred jumped down, her bag in hand.

"I promise I shall let you know what happens, Liz. Thank you again," Winifred said.

"You are quite welcome. Peter is a very lucky man."

Winifred smiled and waved as the Dunstan carriage pulled away and around the corner. "So is Dunstan, the fool!" Winifred whispered. She dashed up the steps and opened the door.

"Miss Winifred, we were not expecting you." Her aunts' butler came toward her, looking shocked to see her.

"May I come in?" She hoped he would not keep her standing upon the steps in order to check with her aunts.

"Of course, forgive me."

"I will go on up to Melanie's room. Is she here?" She raced up the stairs without waiting for an answer and burst into her sister's room.

"Winifred!" Melanie squealed when she turned around from the mirror.

"Mel." Winifred dropped her bag and ran into her sister's embrace.

"What are you doing here? Is there something wrong?"

"No, yes. Oh, Mel, I have made such a mull of things!" Winifred fell upon the bed with an anguished groan.

"What is it? Your letter said that you would be at Trenton Manor, have you left Peter there? What is wrong, what has he done, have you two argued?" Melanie finally took a breath.

Winifred sat up to look at her sister. She had her wedding veil upon her head. "That is quite pretty."

"Win, forget about me. What is going on?"

Winifred took a deep breath. "I do not know where to begin, but I need your help and you cannot breathe a word of what I am about to tell you. If Father finds out, I shall be a widow before I shall even have a chance to become a wife. And say nothing to Lord Blessing, or he will have Peter's head after Father has killed him. Now promise me, swear to me, that you will help me and keep completely quiet."

Melanie's eyes were round as saucers, but she nodded her acceptance of the terms.

"We shall say that I am here only to purchase some household items." Winifred stood up and began to pace. She had to stop Peter, but first she had to find him. "Can we pay a visit to Lord Blessing?"

"John? Yes, but do you not think you should say hello to our aunts first? And Father, he is out right now, but . . ."

"I have not the time for idle conversation." Winifred had to find out where the game was to be played, and she hoped Lord Blessing would know. "Come, let us order the carriage and tell Aunt Winifred and Aunt Augusta that we must go to Bond Street before the shops close. Please, Mel."

"Winifred, you are scaring me. What is the matter?"

"I shall explain everything on the way. Now let us go."

They dashed out of the door after a rushed visit with their aunts. Once en route to Lord Blessing's townhouse, they passed the offices of their father's solicitors.

"Stop the carriage!" Winifred bellowed. She turned to Melanie. "I shall be right back."

"Where are you going?"

"I want to check with the solicitors and see what is left of the money."

"But why? If the game is not until tonight, then what is the use?"

"I do not know. I just have this terrible feeling, is all." Winifred dashed into the offices of Smith and Brown and asked to see her father's solicitor, Mr. Brown. She was told to wait and took a seat. After some minutes his door opened.

"Ah, Miss Winifred, or I should say Mrs. Blessing now." Mr. Brown took her hands.

She had known him since she was a child, as he had often visited Hillie Park. "I need to discuss something of importance regarding my accounts. May I have a moment or two?"

"Yes of course, do come in."

Winifred sat down and waited with impatience as Mr. Brown gingerly pulled her account books.

"Miss Winifred, you must know that the bulk of your inheritance has been transferred to your husband's authority. We can speak freely of the portion held for your own personal use, but the rest can only be discussed with Mr. Blessing."

"Mr. Brown, I wish to ask only one question. Are the accounts still intact?"

"I beg your pardon?" The solicitor cleared his throat.

" 'Tis a matter of life and death. Are the accounts still here?" Winifred waited for the answer with held breath.

He looked surprised at her agitation, then answered, "Why no, Miss Winifred. Mr. Blessing came in a few days ago and closed them out."

Winifred felt as though something hard had hit her midsection. She struggled for control. "Did Mr. Blessing say what his plans were?"

"I am not at liberty to discuss it, Miss Winifred. I have given you too much information as it is. Your own accounts are here, if you wish to go over those."

"Mr. Brown, surely you must know that I am worried." She stopped, as she was unsure how to proceed. She looked up pleadingly at the elder gentleman across the desk from her.

"Miss Winifred. Your father entrusted your husband with your inheritance. I am under oath, as a man of my profession, not to discuss the situation and so I cannot give you any further information." He smiled at her as though she should not trouble herself with matters of money.

She almost screamed with frustration. The solicitor acted as if nothing was amiss or out of the ordinary. But Winifred's greatest fear was unfolding before her very eyes. Her father's life-long work to gain her mother's hand was about to be thrown away on some whim of a card game. But this was a planned game of chance, not some whim. What was Peter trying to prove?

"You know, I wish you hadn't any money at all. Perhaps if it were all gone and still I came to you, you would finally believe me when I said that I wanted you for you."

Peter's words on their honeymoon flitted through her mind, haunting her with the reality of what he was doing. She groaned. Did he think that with her money out of the way she would no longer have any leverage to hold against him? How could he be so stupid as to sacrifice her fortune in the name of love? Her father had earned it for his love of her mother, and now Peter was planning to lose it for the same cause. She had to stop him before it was too late.

"Miss Winifred," Mr. Brown shook her arm. "Are you well dear?"

"Yes," she answered distractedly as she stood. "Thank you, and good day." Winifred left her father's solicitor with a burning mission to find her husband before he ruined everything.

"What is it you wish to discuss?" John asked.

Peter sat in a chair in his brother's den. The desk was large and its top shone like glass, it was polished so clean. Although this room was not nearly as big as his brother's study in his Surrey estate, it was big enough to make Peter feel small and uncomfortable.

He was not sure where to begin. He had practiced the speech he wanted to deliver to John the whole way to London. And now, after arriving at his brother's townhouse only last night, he had forgotten everything he wished to say. It did not help matters that his brother was still angry with him regarding his means of winning Winifred's hand in marriage.

Peter took a deep breath and decided the only way to begin was to plunge in fully. "I have a proposition for you."

John turned around from the bookcase. "What kind of proposition?"

"I wish to offer Trenton Manor to you for sale."

John dropped the book he had been holding. "What? Why the devil do you wish to sell it? I thought you had said that you would never part with the place."

"Well, I do not wish to part with it exactly. I'd like to live there with Winifred whether I own it outright or not."

"Then why sell it?" His brother frowned, then a look of complete disbelief took over his face. "Never say that you need the funds. Good God, Peter, you have the Preston fortune at your fingertips."

"I will not take any of it. I need to repay Winifred the original ten thousand pounds that caused me to pursue her. I don't want her money, John. I have to prove that to her. The Preston inheritance will always be between us, and so I must relinquish it all to her. Don't you see?"

John looked confused. "No, I do not believe I do. What has that to do with selling Trenton Manor?"

"I don't have the blunt." Peter took another deep calming breath but it did nothing to ease his discomfort. He needed John's agreement and participation to pull off his plan of action. "I want to sell Trenton Manor to raise the funds. And I want to sell it to you so I can buy it back."

John narrowed his eyes as he looked at Peter. "How do you plan to buy it back?"

"I will put out a challenge for a game of cards in my club. In a couple of days, I will have an opponent, I am sure." He ignored his brother's muttered oath and kept talking. "The way I figure it, if I sell the Manor for twenty thousand pounds, I can pay back Winifred's ten thousand and front the rest in a game of chance. I can double my earnings, then buy the place back from you."

"But what if you fail?" John asked.

"Then I shall be your steward to the place. Winifred need not know that I have sold it to you. And I will work, I mean real work, as long as it takes to buy it back."

"You would have to live there, you know. You could not stay in London."

"Have you not heard me? I plan to live there. I have always wanted to live at Trenton Manor. Whether I own it or not, I want to lend my hand to make something of the place. And I want to make something good of myself in the process."

"I do not like being part of a gambling scheme. I do not care to see Winifred or Melanie hurt by this. Have you even thought about what her father would do if he found out that you planned to play so deep again?"

Peter shifted uncomfortably in his chair. Of course he had thought about it. He had made his father-in-law a promise and now he was breaking it. But he was not using a farthing of Preston money, and for good reason this time.

"John, I have not told Preston about the game, no. But I did meet with him this morning. I explained to him that I did not wish to have control of his daughter's inheritance." At John's look of surprise, Peter continued, "It is true, I do not wish to be tempted to gamble knowing that I have complete financial security. I could not bear it if I lost it all. Preston and I closed out the accounts and have made arrangements for a transfer of the funds to my own solicitors—well, yours really. They have set up a trust that will remain under Winifred's control. I can't touch it now."

At the sheer look of proud approval on his brother's face, Peter felt strengthened and certain that he was on the right path to redeeming himself.

"I say, Peter, I am impressed. But why all this? Why the repayment to your wife? Surely she would understand."

"I love her, John. I have to prove to her once and for all that I do. And I do not want my gambling debt to be between us. I have to make right where I went wrong. I have to honor her with repayment as a gentleman."

"I see."

"Will you help then?" Peter stood, his hand extended.

"Yes." John reached out and grabbed Peter's hand for a firm shake as agreement to his proposition. "I cannot like it that you are gambling, but I will just have to trust that you know what you are about. Demme, if only Father were here to witness this turnaround. He would be proud."

"No doubt he is rolling in his grave," Peter said with a lopsided grin.

"With pride."

Peter felt like his chance at happiness was finally near enough to reach out and grasp. His innermost desire of becoming a worthy man seemed possible to him now. He had Winifred to thank for finally getting through to his thick, stubborn heart. He knew that he would never have to face his wife with complete ruin as he had done in his dream. He would not let her down this time.

The carriage pulled up to Lord Blessing's townhouse and Winifred prayed earnestly that she would find Peter. She barely waited for the coachman to open the door, before she was hopping out of the vehicle and dashing up the steps of her brother-in-law's residence.

"Winifred," Melanie called. "Wait for me!"

She tried, but her impatience got the better of her and she pulled on the door knocker and let it go with a resounding bang.

"Yes?" A pinched-faced butler opened the door.

Melanie had bounded up the stairs and stepped in front of Winifred. "We would like to see Lord Blessing, please. Tell him his betrothed and his sister-in-law are here," Melanie said in a rush.

"Do come in." The butler bowed, then asked that they follow him. "You may wait here in the den while I let his lordship know that you are here."

"Thank you," both sisters answered in unison.

"It is not the thing at all to be here, in a gentleman's home," Melanie whispered.

"But this is urgent. Lord Blessing will understand. Besides, there are two of us."

"What on earth are the two of you doing here?" John burst out as he entered the den.

"Well . . ." Melanie stood.

"Is Peter here?" Winifred asked.

"No, and I thought you were in Kent," John said.

"Yes, but I came here today." She gulped for air. "I must speak with Peter. Where is he? Is he staying here with you or at his flat?"

"Winifred, you must calm down. Come into the drawing room," John said. He exchanged a look with Melanie, then ordered tea before escorting the ladies across the hall. "Peter is staying with me since he has given up his flat."

Winifred paused only briefly to let the glorious confirmation that Peter had no intentions of living in London without her sink in. "John, I haven't much time. Peter has planned to gamble tonight and I must stop him before he loses."

"How do you know about it?" he asked, surprised.

"Lady Dunstan heard of it and came to see me." Winifred waved her hand with impatience. "Wait a moment, you know about this as well?"

"Yes, and I can assure you that Peter knows what he is doing."

"John," Melanie protested, "you have never approved of Peter's card playing before."

"This is different. Now, why do you not both go home and we shall drop by once Peter returns."

What on earth had taken hold of Lord Blessing? Had he lost all the sense he had been born with? "Where has he gone?"

"I do not know. He arranged it through his club. Winifred, you could not follow him even if I was of a mind to let you. Ladies cannot enter a gaming establishment. Now, just leave it alone and wait for Peter."

Winifred looked at John. She could tell by the stubborn tilt of his chin that he would brook no argument. Tea was served and her mind raced furiously. She had to find Peter before it was too late and, for some reason, John did not seem to understand the severity of the situation. She was not about to sit and argue with him when he obviously did not know where Peter had gone.

"Perhaps you are right, John. I shall return with Melanie and wait for word from Peter when he returns."

"But . . ." Melanie started, then turned quiet.

"If you would please excuse me," Winifred said as she stood. At her brother-in-law's questioning gaze, she added, "I have need of the necessary."

Melanie nodded and Winifred nearly laughed aloud at Lord Blessing's embarrassment.

"Of course," he finally said.

Winifred made her escape and asked the housekeeper the directions to the water closet. She made her way up the stairs and with a quick look about, she dashed into a room she was certain belonged to Lord Blessing. Once inside, she walked straight to the dressing room. She perused the breeches, lawn shirts, waistcoats, cravats, and jackets that hung along the walls. She had to admit that Peter owned twice as many clothes as his brother.

Hurriedly, she snatched an outfit and dashed out into the hallway. She made her way to the water closet, where she put the extra clothes on as best she could under her own dress and pelisse. Fortunately, she had never taken off her pelisse. Those items she could not put on without notice, she tied to her waist under her skirts with the strings from her reticule. Winifred had a plan, but she needed to dress as a man in order to carry it out.

She returned to John's drawing room and as demurely as possible she resumed her seat. She waited as Melanie finished her tea, but it took all her might to keep from tapping her foot impatiently.

When Melanie finally set down her cup, Winifred jumped to her feet and said, "Thank you, John. Please send word for me as soon as Peter returns."

"I will, and Winifred, do not worry. He knows what he is about."

She nodded and the sisters departed, Winifred walking somewhat awkwardly to accommodate the bulk of her brother-in-law's clothing she had taken. Once inside their carriage, Melanie gently lifted Winifred's skirt and frowned at the hem of a pair of gentleman's breeches that greeted her curiosity.

"I knew it! I knew you were up to something. Winifred, whatever are you thinking?"

"I cannot enter a gaming establishment dressed as a woman. You heard him. So, I will go dressed as a man."

"But what if you are found out? You shall be scandalous and worse yet, what if you come into trouble?"

"No one shall realize I am female. I am as tall as both Peter and John. John is more slender of build than Peter, so his things will fit me well enough to disguise my sex. That is the only way I shall be able to reach Peter in time."

Melanie looked doubtful, then finally she said, "What about shoes?"

Winifred reached inside of her crocheted reticule and pulled out a pair of Lord Blessing's black evening pumps. "You see, I have thought of everything."

"Have you thought about what Peter will do when you find him?"

Winifred chewed her bottom lip. She had not given any thought to what she would say to Peter, nor what she would do if she was too late. She could not think about any of that right now. The important thing was to find him. The rest she would deal with as it came to her.

Chapter Fifteen

Winifred turned in front of Melanie's mirror. She was satisfied with her reflected image and pulled the short beaver low on her head. She would not be able to take the thing off or her hair would be revealed.

"What do you think? Will I pass as a young man?" Winifred asked.

Melanie sat on her bed. "Actually, you look surprisingly well. John's clothes are a little big on you, but I suppose that will only help you to look like a young unlicked cub."

"Exactly. I am Peter's cousin, Freddie, up from the country with an important message to give him." Winifred disguised her voice as best she could. "Did I sound like a young man?"

"Try not to speak so deeply. It sounds too false and may give you away."

"Very well." Winifred walked back and forth across her sister's bedchamber in an attempt to practice a swagger.

Melanie started to giggle. "Are you not glad that we are women and that we do not have to worry about such silliness as walking like a gruff and tumble type?"

"I suppose, but I must say there is wonderful freedom in breeches. I could easily get used to wearing them." She continued to pace.

"Oh! Please say you are only jesting. That would be absurd."

Winifred merely smiled at her sister, then checked the pocket watch that they had taken from their father's room. It was half past eight o'clock. She needed to head for Brooks's to try and find out Peter's whereabouts. "Mel, I had better leave. Please, wish me luck."

Melanie ran to her sister and gave her a hug. "Do be careful, Winnie. If I did not love you and Peter so much, I would never let you do this."

"Thank you. Thank you for everything." Winifred squeezed tighter, then let her sister go. Fortunately, their aunts had left for a dinner party and neither cared that the two sisters had stayed behind to "catch up." Their father had also gone out to join a friend for dinner. She would not be missed.

She peered into the hall and eased her way out. She took the servants' back stairs and in no time she was stepping out of doors onto Park Lane. She had a good walk before her, but if needed she could always hire a hack. She had all her pin money in her pockets and jingling it as she walked served to calm her nerves.

For once in her life, she was grateful for her height. No one seemed to notice her as she walked by. She was careful to keep her head cocked slightly down and she made sure that she did not meet anyone's eyes. She would be thoroughly sunk if someone should recognize her.

She dashed up the steps to Brooks's and hesitated. What if the men inside could tell that she was a lady? Or worse, what if they found out who she was? Winifred forced her fear down to a manageable level. She had to do this. Squaring her shoulders, she opened the door and walked in. She was taken aback by the quiet elegance of the place. Candles burned brightly and gentlemen seated in various chairs smoked cheroots and conversed in hushed tones. She did not know where to start.

"Lost, young man?"

Goodness, it was Lord Stanley!

"That I am, sir." Winifred tried not to speak so deeply and her voice cracked. "I am looking for my cousin."

"Ah, I remember the days when my voice began to change. Dreadful nuisance, eh?" Lord Stanley slapped her on the back and she nearly choked. "Who is your cousin, cub?" Lord Stanley asked.

"Peter Blessing, sir."

"Is he now? I am Lord Stanley, a friend of his."

"I am honored, my lord." Winifred did her best imitation of a bow. "My name is Freddie Trenton, my lord, and I have an urgent message to give to my cousin. Do you know where I can find him?"

"Urgent, you say. Well then, I shall give you the address where he is. 'Tis one of the gaming hells on Jermyn Street, but I cannot remember which one. Perhaps 'tis better if I take you there myself. The hells are dangerous, my young Mr. Trenton. I would not want to hear that you have been set upon by ruffians or worse."

Winifred nodded but did not welcome the idea of being in Lord Stanley's presence. If he should recognize her, it would be her undoing. She kept quiet and meekly followed the lord out of Brooks's and along the few blocks to Jermyn Street. She was mindful to keep the beaver's rim low.

"So, what do you think of London, Mr. Trenton?"

Winifred thought quickly. "Fabulous place, my lord." She kept up the inane chatter as best as she could with her insides twisted into a ball of tension. What if she were too late? What if Peter had already lost? What would she do when she found him?

The walk to Jermyn Street was almost too short, Winifred thought. Panic rose to her throat threatening to choke her when her escort stopped and looked around.

"He's in that one there with the red sign. That is where you will find Peter Blessing. Would you like me to wait until you have delivered your message? Gambling can go on into the wee hours of the morning."

"No, I thank you, Lord Stanley. You have been most kind." Winifred truly meant it. "I will stay here with my cousin."

"Happy to help. You seem very familiar to me, lad. Have we met before?"

She ducked her head down lower. "No, my lord. This is my first visit to London."

"Very well. Have a care, and try to keep Peter out of the River Tick. Although now that he's wed, I am sure his pockets are indeed plump."

Winifred nodded and ducked into the gaming hell called Beaux Rouge. Inside, the air was stale and the smoke thick. Heavy wooden tables that were covered with red wool stood scattered about. The place was filled with men. Some appeared to be gentlemen and some were clearly from other walks of life.

There was not a single woman to be found. Winifred wondered if they were considered too distracting a presence. For all the laughter that occasionally erupted, she expected that this was serious business not to be taken lightly. She looked around but could not find her husband.

She inched further into the place and padded quietly

across the plush carpet. A soft din of gambling terms and various conversations tickled her hearing. Try as she might, she could not distinguish a single voice. So, this was the gambling world, she thought. The faces of the men surrounding her were tight with excitement or forced into a show of indifference.

This had been Peter's world for a long time. The undercurrent of bravado and male camaraderie was so thick it was heady, almost intoxicating. She wondered at such a world where a lady would never be welcomed but instead considered a threat to its very existence.

She searched the tables, but Peter was not to be seen. Panic swelled in her chest. Perhaps Lord Stanley was incorrect in his directions. She frantically peered through the smoky haze, checking every corner, when finally she spotted a golden head of hair. Relief washed over her only to be replaced by fear. It had to be him at the far table and it was time to make her move.

She weaved her way quietly through the tables of men, all the while keeping her gaze firmly fixed upon Peter. Astonished, she thought he looked like a king holding court with his subjects. But it was not a castle or a kingdom where Peter ruled. Instead, 'twas a strange land where men worshiped each other for their bold reckless abandon with wagers.

As she inched closer, she noticed that a small group of men had formed around her husband's table to watch. Peter played against another man who was not much older than he. His opponent appeared to be in funds, if his jewels and excellent tailoring were any indication. They played picquet and Peter looked like he was enjoying himself immensely.

Winifred leaned against the gray silk brocade-covered wall and worried. She had never seen her husband exhibit such sheer delight. His eyes were alight with a feverish excitement that she had never before witnessed, and her heart sank. How was she ever to compete with the thrill of gambling? How could they possibly forge a future together if this dark, enticing world continued to seduce him? Winifred refused to share her husband with any mistress, including the sultry world of gambling.

After Peter took another trick, he raised the stakes and Winifred's stomach turned over. A sick feeling settled in her soul, but she was at a complete loss to know what to do. She feared that all her hopes for saving her marriage were for nothing. She was not in the least prepared for the fight of a lifetime that coming to the Beaux Rouge had revealed. Whether he won or lost, Winifred did not believe Peter would ever be satisfied with a quiet life in Kent.

Peter held his cards and tried to reign in the anxiety that had taken hold of him. Sweat trickled down his forehead, but he paid it no heed. Never had he played so well, but never had he been more afraid. So much was riding on the outcome of this game, and his opponent, Hodge, knew it. They had been playing for hours and it was as yet still early. Peter was exhausted, but he hoped it would soon be done and over.

"I was surprised to hear about your challenge, Blessing," Hodge said.

"Yes, well . . ." Peter tried to concentrate on his cards. What had been the last point Hodge announced?

"And now you have a fortune to play with, I hear. Married very well, have you? And does your wife know you are here?"

Peter tried to ignore the taunts, but the mention of Winifred on the man's lips was nearly more than he could stand. "I will not have my wife discussed in such a place. I thank you."

"Oh my. Respect her, do you? Well, that is wonderful news. I thought you had married the giantess only to pay off what you owed to me the last time. I guess you had not gotten enough, eh?" Hodge winked, then began to chuckle.

Peter could have easily put his fist between the man's eyes and been happy to do it. The cards had gone Peter's way all night and Hodge was doing his best in trying to throw off his concentration. He once used to think Hodge a clever fellow, but now he despised the sight of him. A heavyset man, he was arrogant, rude, and disrespectful. Peter exchanged two cards of his hand from the remaining pack. The ones he received were good cards.

It was ironic to Peter that Hodge, the same man he had lost ten thousand pounds to months ago, was about to lose double that to him. He only need take a couple more tricks and his gambling days would be done.

Never before had he had a reason to walk away. Gambling had been his excuse, his reason not to try and make something of himself. He had to admit that he felt a twinge of anxiety at what his future held. But he no longer feared failure. Winifred had become his reason to walk away and she would, no doubt, help him to find his purpose. He had only to turn his talent for cards into something good this last time.

"Are you not going to answer me?" Hodge pestered. "What, your wife's charms got your head muddled?"

"Say another word about my wife and I swear it will be your last," Peter said with deadly calm.

He was glad the man shut his trap. Peter traced back the cards already played in his mind before discarding. It was now or never, he thought as he lay down his cards ready to take the win. An already sweaty Hodge dripped with new nervousness. Peter watched with amusement as his opponent wiped his brow. Hodge hesitated, scratched his arm, and exchanged a card.

Peter leaned back against his chair waiting for Hodge's move. The minutes seemed to tick by like hours and a hush had settled upon the group of men around them. Peter closed his eyes, trying to calm his nerves. Lay down your blasted cards! he screamed silently in his head.

"I believe I have taken your hand and the winnings, Blessing, old boy."

Peter opened his eyes and looked at the man's hand. It made no sense, Peter thought. He had memorized every card discarded, every point announced by Hodge, and he did not think the man had kings. How did Hodge get the four kings that he had?

"Double or nothing, that was the bid. I did not lose so I cannot double, while you shall lose what you have fronted, I believe." Hodge grinned and hurriedly scooped up his cards.

Peter thought he would be sick. His heart pounded so hard that he thought in any moment it would come out of his mouth and bounce onto the table to die there. He heard a decidedly feminine gasp that jerked his attention to the small crowd that had gathered around them. A pair of watery blue eyes trapped his gaze. His own wife had witnessed his loss.

He stared at her and she at him as if they were frozen in time. Peter cursed his existence. He had never deserved her and in front of her very eyes he had proved it to her. Unable to look away from her, Peter watched the array of expressions change and form on Winifred's face. It killed him to see her disappointment. He had lost when he so wanted to win.

Winifred choked with the knowledge that Peter had lost. She had no idea how much, but if the look in his eyes was any indication, he had lost all of it. She did not know what she was supposed to feel—in fact, she could not feel a thing at the moment. She stood there, completely numb. At one time she had wanted her husband humbled, but she had never wanted it to be like this. She had never wanted Peter to be so terribly destroyed. She had never wanted to see this bleak look of utter failure carved across his face.

She had to rally. Her insides in turmoil, Winifred continued to stare at Peter. As much as it hurt to think that he had lost her inheritance, Winifred realized that she had to let it go. If they were to have any future together she had to forgive him. She could not keep the money between them as she had done since they became engaged. She could no longer hold it over his head in punishment. If she had not done that, then perhaps Peter would not have felt the need to sacrifice her fortune to prove that he wanted her, that he cared for her.

She swallowed hard and tried to stop the tears from falling. As much as she wanted to rant and rave at him, she could not bring herself to do it. Not with the dejected expression on his face. She had to let him know that she loved him and forgave him. She had to put this behind her and show Peter that they could get through this.

She tried to speak, but her voice was hoarse and only a whisper. Peter cocked his head, trying to hear her words. She smiled at him then and mouthed the words that she knew he needed to understand and she needed to believe.

"I am sorry. I do not care about this. I love you."

What did she say? What on earth was Winifred trying to say to him? Peter felt his chest swell with hope when he saw his wife's encouraging smile. His heart had not died on the table; it was beating so hard with new life that he did not hear the raised voices behind him. But then Winifred looked away and Peter turned to see what had captured her attention.

A scuffle broke out between Hodge and two of the onlookers.

"Ye stinking cheat!" A large man was shaking Hodge. Cards fell from Hodge's coat sleeve.

"What the . . ." Peter stepped closer and bent to retrieve the fallen cards. They were all kings, printed with the same pattern as the cards they had been using. Hodge had in fact cheated. "Is this how it was the last time we played?" The anger inside him rose.

"No, I beat you squarely that time," Hodge said.

"Then why the kings? Why today?" Peter stood an inch away from the man's nose.

"They are my safety net, my security. Damn your eyes, you wanted this too much. I have never seen you play so well or so seriously."

The two onlookers grabbed Hodge's arms on either side to hold him steady. "You have the right, sir." The second man, a military gentleman, took off his glove and handed it to Peter.

Peter accepted the leather glove and reared back, ready to strike Hodge across the face. Anger seared his veins to think that he had not lost. The scum in front of him had almost cheated him out of buying back Trenton Manor!

"Peter," Winifred yelled.

He turned and looked into her fear-filled eyes. It was too much to risk. The idea of a duel frightened his wife and he had to admit that Hodge was more than likely a better shot than he. Pistols had never been his forte. He did not wish to leave Winifred a widow just yet.

"Thank you but no, not this time," Peter said as he handed the glove back to the young man dressed in uniform. "But let us see what my next card would have been had I exchanged them, shall we, Hodge? Let us see just what my hand would have been."

Peter stepped back to the table and drew his next card. An ace brought his total to four which would have beat four kings. "My trick, I believe. I shall lighten your purse, Hodge, and you can count yourself lucky, as I am in no mood to lighten the life from your body just now. Ten thousand pounds was the bid, double or nothing, and you shall have to double it."

Peter enjoyed watching his two champions throw Hodge into the streets after he collected his winnings. The man's name and reputation would be mud by morning. That was punishment enough for Peter. Twenty thousand pounds rested snugly in his pocket next to the ten thousand that he owed Winifred. She was making her way toward him, a smile of satisfaction on her lips and a look of mischief in her eyes. She gave a whoop of glee just before launching herself onto his back.

"You did it!" she yelled.

"Win . . ."

"Cousin Freddie," she whispered in his ear.

"My young cousin Freddie," Peter explained to the curious stares he received from the group of men that had watched the game. "He's up from the country and doesn't know the first thing about getting along." Peter felt his ear being nipped. He quickly dropped Winifred before he did something disastrous to them both, like pulling her into his arms. With a playful shove he ordered, "Have my carriage brought around, will you, bantling?"

Winifred gave him a saucy smirk and a vulgar flip of her coattails when she turned to do his bidding. He suddenly noticed for the first time what she was wearing. The breeches stretched too nicely across her rounded behind. He wanted that behind, he thought, and desire shot through him. It was about time that he made Winifred completely and irrevocably his wife.

Peter quickly bade his gambling cronies good evening and, without a backward glance, left his favorite gaming hell knowing that never again would he return to it. His carriage had been brought around with his wife inside, waiting.

"Lord Blessing's townhouse on Oxford Street," Peter said to his brother's coachman. "But first take us through Hyde Park, and do not hurry." He needed some time to explain what he had done for her. He doubted she would remain happy about his gambling win for long and she needed to know why he had planned this night's challenge.

He climbed in and sat across from her.

"Never have I been so worried. Peter, whatever do you think you were doing?" she gushed. "I thought you had gambled away my entire inheritance."

He held up a hand. "Let me explain. First of all, what were you doing in a place like the Beaux Rouge and whose clothes are those?"

She had the decency to blush, but he had to admit he rather liked seeing his wife in men's breeches. "I borrowed them from John."

"He told you where I was? He let you go into a place like that? I'll have his hide." Peter's voice rose.

"No, he told me nothing. Actually, he told me to go to my aunts' and wait for you like a dutiful wife. But how could I do that when I thought you were sacrificing the Preston fortune to prove something stupid!" Winifred thrust her finger into his chest and poked him repeatedly to emphasize her frustration. "Just what were you trying to prove?"

"Wait a moment, how did you even know I was in London? I sent word that I would not arrive at Trenton Manor until the end of this week."

Winifred looked away.

"Win . . ." He leaned forward and grabbed her hands

in his. "Who told you where I was? Was it Sheldrake? John?"

She shook her head. "You must promise me not to be angry with her. She was only doing what she thought was right." Then her voice rose. "And shame on you for fibbing to me regarding your whereabouts. You said that you would never lie to me!"

"Yes, and I am humbly sorry, but I had to . . . Wait. She?"

"Lady Dunstan."

"Lizzie? How the devil did she know I was in town?" Peter sat back against the seat with a groan and let go of Winifred's hands.

"She saw you and she overheard someone talking about your challenge. She rode all the way to the manor to warn me. And she was right to do so. I am sorry that I did not believe you when you said that you had ended your relationship with her." Winifred looked down at her hands, now clasped in her lap. "She told me that the only reason you came to her after we were betrothed was because you wanted advice about how to make amends. I am sorry that I did not give you that chance, Peter."

He caressed her cheek. "I am sorry too, for everything."

"You said that you wished I had no money to hold over your head. You said that with all of it gone then I would know that you wanted only me," she said softly.

Her eyes were so blue and her freckles so endearing that Peter had to wait a moment before he could speak. He had given her no reason to think anything other than that he had planned to lose her inheritance. It hurt that she would consider him that low, but then he had threatened such a thing before he had left her. That was a mistake he would never repeat. He would never leave her like that again.

He reached out and pulled off the beaver hat that she wore. "Where did you get this, from John also?"

"No, Melanie found it in the attics. I had no place to hide a hat on my person, else I would have taken John's. I wore what I could under my pelisse."

He chuckled at the thought of Winifred hiding his brother's clothes under her own. He reached out and carefully unwound the braided hair that was stacked atop Winifred's head. He threaded his fingers through the reddish-gold strands until they hung in luxurious waves past her shoulders. Twirling a stray curl between his fingers he looked at her. Her lips parted and Peter knew that she wanted him as much as he wanted her. But he had to wait until he had explained.

"I do not know where to begin," he whispered. She nodded but did not speak, so Peter reached into his pocket and pulled out ten thousand-pound notes. He took his wife's hand and counted them out to her. "That is my repayment of the debt I owe you."

"Debt? I do not understand."

"I do not want my gambling debt to ever come between us again. I give you back the amount I received from your inheritance when we became betrothed. Think of it as a debt settled."

Winifred looked down at the notes, then back into his eyes. Confusion clouded her gaze.

"I did not use any of the Preston inheritance to front the money for tonight's card game, Win."

"Then where did it go? I met with my father's solicitor and he said that you had closed the accounts."

Peter shook his head. "He was not supposed to say a blasted thing! He shall hear about this. No wonder you have been so worried. No wonder you thought I had all of it riding on a bet."

"Yes, I thought you were trying to lose it."

Peter took both of her hands back into his own and brought them to his lips for a solemn kiss. "I, with your father's help, have transferred all the accounts into one trust to be managed by Blessing solicitors who will act only on your command. I can't touch it and I don't want to."

Her eyes widened into large pools of surprise. "But . . ." She took a breath, looked at him as if she were afraid to believe what he was saying. "You do not want my money? You are relinquishing your control? What is it you want then?"

"You," he whispered. "Only you."

"But I am not even beautiful, how can you want only me after all you have had—the gambling, Lady Dunstan?"

Peter placed his finger on her lips to quiet her. "In your eyes I see what I can be, what I have dreamed of being. Give me a chance, Athena, to be the man I want to be—a man worthy of your love."

There were tears brimming along her eyelids again, but this time her face was full of joy. She reached out both her hands and pulled his face closer to hers. "Oh, Peter, I love you so very much. I have never stopped loving you, no matter how hard I tried to make you hate me. There is no man worthier than you. 'Tis I, I am unworthy. I was so ready to believe the very worst of you. Can you ever forgive me?"

"Sweet Athena, there is nothing to forgive." Peter's voice became thick but he had to continue, he had to tell her. "I love you more than life itself, Win. Without you, there would be nothing for me. I do not want anything of my old life. I do not even wish to be tempted to gamble. I want only you."

Winifred kissed him, hard. It reminded him so much of the night in her aunts' study that Peter chuckled under his breath.

"What is so funny?" she murmured against his mouth.

"I was only thinking what happened the first time you kissed me like this." Peter stopped talking long enough to trail kisses down her throat.

"You ruined me," she whispered.

"Yes, but not completely." He pulled at the starched linen of her cravat until it came undone so he could better access the bare skin of her neck.

"Then I think you should finish my ruination, Mr. Blessing." Winifred reached to pull down the window's shade.

"Saucy wench," he whispered. "But not here, not

now." He lifted the shade before he was tempted further. "You deserve a proper wedding night."

"Mr. Blessing, have I not proven time and again that I am not a proper young miss?"

"You have. Perhaps I shall simply have to reform you as you have reformed me." Peter's grin disappeared as he gazed into his wife's eyes. With reverence, he cupped her chin with his hand. "You have reformed me, Win. For that, I am forever grateful."

Tears pooled in her eyes again. She took his hand and brought it to her lips and whispered, "I love you Peter."

His chance at happiness had finally become a reality that promised to last a lifetime.

Epilogue

October, 1821

Peter scratched his head and looked through his papers again. Then he checked the figures he had received from the 'Change. It couldn't be. A smile split his face and he feared that there was no removing it. His investment had paid off. No, it had done better than that, it had nearly doubled.

"Win!" he yelled. When there was no answer, he left his study and entered the hall. "Win!"

Still, no answer.

Where had the confounded woman gotten herself to?

He ignored the housekeeper, who looked ready to come to his aid, and bounded out of the back door. Autumn leaves the colors of rust and yellow fell freely now. The day was surprisingly mild and the sun shone brightly. He checked the orchard. No wife.

Then he knew. Rushing along the bank of the brook, he headed up stream and there he found her. "Win!"

She turned and looked at him then, a welcoming smile

to her lips. Again, he noticed how she belonged out of doors. No bonnet graced her head and her nose looked decidedly pink, but she obviously did not care.

"Try again, William. This time, keep the tip of your pole up." She leaned over to help their son, William Jonathan, cast his line.

"What about me, Mama?" Their daughter, Emily Marie, looked with adoration at Winifred.

"You are doing very well, indeed."

He stood and continued to stare at his family, soon to grow when Winifred delivered their third child near Christmas. He had everything a man could possibly want. It should not matter what his investments had done. All that truly mattered was standing before him. And he felt humbled.

He walked up silently behind his wife and kissed her neck. She leaned into him and he counted himself the most blessed of men. He had been given a whole new life and it had proved to be more than thrilling.

ONYX

MAY McGOLDRICK

The acclaimed author of THE THISTLE AND THE ROSE *presents an exciting new trilogy. Three sisters each hold a clue to their family's treasure—and the key to the hearts of three Highland warriors....*

THE DREAMER
❑ 0-451-19718-6/$5.99

THE ENCHANTRESS
❑ 0-451-19719-4/$5.99

THE FIREBRAND
❑ 0-451-40942-6/$5.99

"May McGoldrick brings history to life."
—Patricia Gaffney

"Richly romantic." —Nora Roberts